BH 6/80

w w w

P9-CDU-525

The Best of the West

also by Joe R. Lansdale

THE MAGIC WAGON

The Best of the West
Edited by

JOE R. LANSDALE

DOUBLEDAY & COMPANY, INC.

GARDEN CITY, NEW YORK

1986

HBDB 2

"At Yuma Crossing" copyright © 1986 by Brian Garfield

Library of Congress Cataloging-in-Publication Data

Best of the West.

1. American literature—West (U.S.) 2. West (U.S.)—
Literary collections. 3. Western stories.
4. American literature—20th century. I. Landsdale,
Joe R., 1951–
PS561.B47 1986   810'.9'3278   86-13475
ISBN 0-385-23256-X
Copyright © 1986 by Western Writers of America
All Rights Reserved
Printed in the United States of America
First Edition

This anthology is dedicated to Dorothy Johnson, Rex Bundy, and Omar S. Barker. Three good people who did much to further Western literature.

Contents

Introduction

WESTERN.

When you read or hear that word, what comes to mind?

Cactus?

Blue Sky?

A little town with a loud saloon, a dusty street?

Maybe you think of tall men in tall hats with big guns on their hips. Men who on the spur of the moment wade into violent situations hell-bent for leather and, by pure force of will, courage and expertise with firearms, solve their problems and before the tale is over, still have time to kiss the school marm and buy the ranch.

If that's what you were expecting when you picked up this anthology, well pardner, all I can tell you is, you may have the wrong book.

Certainly there are stories here that contain the aforementioned components. The traditional has not been dismissed, not by any means. But I like to think it is presented here with fresher rhythms than one usually encounters; that you will not find among these stories what my dad used to call "the same ole, same ole," meaning, of course, retreads.

Horizons, friends. Horizons. That's what Doubleday is allowing us to do here. Expand our horizons. Look beyond the usual Western clichés, reach out and slap the blurry-eyed readers and writers into thinking in new and exciting directions. Make the term "Western" mean more than dusty streets and smoking revolvers.

Confession is good for the soul, right?

Here's mine.

When I first advertised for this anthology, I said I wanted—insisted on—unusual stories of the West, or traditional ones that pulled me in like quicksand.

You know what I got?

Got your answer written down?

If you wrote something akin to my dad's "same ole, same ole," you hit the nail on the head.

I asked specifically not to see reprints, not to see "classic" gun-duel stories unless the author had a new and interesting twist on it, and what did I get?

Yep. I got reprints. Lots of them. Sometimes packets of ten. Many of them were from the pulps and *Zane Grey's Western Magazine*. In other words, I got a lot of stories about two men walking down dusty streets, hands cocked above their revolvers, one of them a good guy, the other a bad guy, and suddenly, they would draw, and—yawn, heart be still—the good guy would blow the bad guy's brains over the poorly visualized scenery like so much confetti, then turn and walk back up the street, now able to hang up his guns.

Least until the next story, where suddenly, zombielike, the bad guy, not having learned his lesson from previous stories, would reappear in all his stupid glory, walk down the same dusty street toward the same good guy, and . . . well, reread the paragraph before this one, then this one over and over and over until you're so bored you pass out, and you'll have some idea what I was up against.

This is not to say I didn't get some good stories. Of course I did. They're in this book. And I got some good stories I couldn't use. Sometimes the problem was length or repetition of story lines (this was the year for panther stories—I got six of them), or it was some quirky idiosyncrasy on my part that kept them out.

But the overall crop of good stories, fresh stories, was, to put it kindly, dismal.

I had to go out shopping for most of the fiction I wanted, asking specific writers to write it. That worked. I got some fine stories that way. But I came to a rather sad understanding as to why the Western story is in trouble.

The pulps didn't burn it out. Neither did television in its most hectic and copycat Western heyday. Changing times are not even the culprit.

Sure, these things wounded the Western, but they were not responsible for putting it on the critical list. The lack of originality in the fiction itself was its greatest assailant.

It made me realize that, like science fiction in the sixties, we need to grow, expand our horizons. It's time for us to experience our *new wave*.

I'm not saying writers should abandon all semblance of story, as was the case of many works of science fiction during its *new wave*, nor am I saying the stories should be arty, academic and inaccessible. Certainly the stories in this anthology are not that way. Some are blatantly traditional, and proud of it.

What I am suggesting is that they approach the old themes with new enthusiasm, style and characterization. Let's use different methods of attack, not be afraid to break a few taboos. Experiment a little.

Okay, you say, sounds good. But does this anthology do that?

I think so. Each story is honestly written, and even the least ambitious among them has tried for a personal voice, a tremor of vitality. An effort has been made to amuse, surprise and kindle some spark in the reader. Each story, in its own way, is good. And some of them are very, very good.

Enough. Maybe this is not *The Dangerous Visions* of Westerns—certainly in style and content it was never meant to be. But it has much of the gusto of that famous volume. It wants the reader to expect more of the Western story than "the same ole, same ole"; wants him or her to encourage its existence; help push complacent writers to new heights; help make this book the starting shot for a series of fine anthologies to follow, all of them stampeding madly toward bigger and better horizons.

The Best of the West

At Yuma Crossing

BY BRIAN GARFIELD

Brian Garfield has been an innovator in the Western field almost from the start. Long before the rash of "adult" Westerns, he had incorporated sex scenes into his novels, most notably Sliphammer, *and they were done with considerably more intelligence than the current crop of sex-and-pistol epics being written. His work has always been strong on character, and he has the best kind of style a writer can have. One that goes away as you read. Suddenly you're no longer reading a story, you're living it.*

Among Garfield's many fine Western novels are The Last Hard Men, Sweeny's Honor, Tripwire, Relentless *(a modern Western) and a classic in the field,* Wild Times. *He is also the author of many non-Westerns,* Death Wish *being the best known among them. Others include* Hopscotch, Deep Cover, *and* Kolchack's Gold.

He is the recipient of an Edgar Award, is a past President and Vice President of the Western Writers of America.

The following story shows Garfield's sure hand with character and dialogue, as well as his feel for the past. It's the perfect tale to kick off this anthology.

The Southwest Passage route explored by Cooke's Mormon Battalion crossed into California at the junction of the Gila and the Colorado rivers. Here on the river at the Yuma Crossing was a ferryboat, built by Indians and run by Dr. Able Lincoln until, in 1850, a band of cutthroats led by John Glanton overpowered Lincoln's crew and set out to make their fortunes by exploiting the ferry monopoly. Glanton, a Texan, was wanted for murder and other crimes in Texas and Mexico. At the Yuma ferry he treated the Indians badly and, in reply, on the twenty-first of April, the Indians fell upon Glanton and his crew of toughs with clubs and arrows, and thereafter for a time the ferry was without an owner.

Whoever made the southwest crossing—up from Mexico on the des-

ert Camino del Diablo, or down the Gila River from central Arizona—
had to pay the toll at the Yuma ferry.

The Gringo came out of the desert on foot, carrying a dragoon pistol at one
hip and a Texas knife at the other. A Colt rifle dangled in his right hand, a
canteen in his left by the strap: by the way the wind moved it back and
forth it was evident the canteen was empty.

From a hilltop he had his first view of the groined rivers flowing together;
he paused there, half a mile above the rivers, for breath. The tongue came
out of his mouth and scraped across dry-split lips.

The sun had both feet on his shoulders. Behind him the desert winked
and glittered with particles of mica and pyrites; heat haze undulated in
torpor above the withered land. His own tracks went back into it along an
unsteady line. In front of him the long slope went down to dust-dry reed
bottoms and the river, a shining muddy flow rushing through the sands. A
single wagon stood sagging on the near bank of the Colorado just below the
junction of rivers.

The Gringo started forward. He put each foot down with the flat-footed
carelessness of exhaustion. Half a mile was, just then, a formidable distance
to him. His boots stirred little clouds of powder dust. It took him a quarter
of an hour to reach the fringe of the reed bottoms, and here he had to push
his way through the dry stalks like a man walking through a crowded cornfield. The effort of it sapped him halfway to the river and he had to stop to
gather energy; and that was when he heard a rustle of movement.

With the unthinking speed of practiced habit the rifle came up and lay
across his left hand; his thumb curled over the hammer and drew it back.
He went down on one knee and swept the dry undergrowth in a steady arc
with his eyes.

A flutter of brown movement drew his attention to the left. His hand
whitened on the rifle.

A ragged small figure emerged from the reeds, staring at him with large
grave eyes: a dark little girl in a filthy sack of clothes.

She spoke to the Gringo in Spanish, in a piping high voice: "Who are
you?" And she came toward him without fear.

The Gringo lowered the hammer of the rifle. His voice was hoarse with
the desert-thickness of tongue. "You come from that wagon. How many of
you are there?" His Spanish came without hesitation.

"There is just me," the little girl said. "And then there are the Mexicans."

"How many?"

"Who are you?" she said again.

"*Corazón,*" he said very dryly, "I do not have time to fool with you. How many are the Mexicans?"

"The old man and the woman, that's all." She stood back some paces away, held there by a stiff reserve; her eyes were big and bottomless and held distrust, perhaps contempt, but not fear. Her skin was the color of old copper. She had a narrow triangular face and black hair tangled with burrs that fell below her shoulders. She seemed very thin. She might have been anywhere from nine to thirteen. The Gringo said, "You're Indian."

"I am Yaqui."

"All right." He had a stubble of beard and a cruel mouth; his face was like a mountain crag—rocky, broken, ungiving: it appeared as though it needed sorting out.

"You are a *ladrón,*" she told him. "You look like a *ladrón.* Like the man Glanton."

"Who?"

"The Mojaves killed him."

"John Glanton?"

"I do not know—what are names? You are a *ladrón,* a thief, an outlaw— is it not so?" For the first time she grinned.

"Get out of my way," the Gringo said. He tramped toward the river.

The little girl buzzed around him like a horsefly. The Gringo knelt by the bank and put his rifle down on the earth beside him; then his flat gray eyes touched on the girl, and he put his hand on the rifle and held it there while he crouched over the river and drank. He put one foot on the rifle and used both hands to scoop water, splashing it into his face. With his hat off he displayed a head of dark, filthy straw-colored hair, bleached yellow about the edges where the sun had reached it below his hat brim.

He stood up gaunt and tall, hefting the rifle in the circle of his fist. He said, "You look like a stinking Gypsy to me."

"I am Yaqui," she said angrily. "Who are you to say I lie? Ask the Mexicans. They know what I am."

"Get away from me," he told her. But she kept worrying about his heels while he walked along the bank toward the wagon. Once he stopped short and wheeled; he put his hand on her bony shoulder and pushed her away. "Don't dog me," he said in grating English, and went on. Behind him the little girl's voice piped defiantly:

"I do not speak that tongue. You must speak to me in Spanish."

"*Ve,*" he snapped, and gestured with the rifle.

The little girl shrugged. She did not move. "I do not belong to you. Why should I obey a *ladrón?* Have you killed many men?"

The Gringo walked to the wagon. The old man and the woman sat in its narrow band of shade and the old man had a Spanish percussion rifle aimed at the Gringo. The Gringo walked up within two paces and stopped, and spat. "Put your rifle down, old man."

"You do not address me in that way, Gringo. Put your own weapons down and then I shall do the same."

The woman was dried up and fat; the old man looked sick, his cheeks were hollow, his eyes had an unnatural shine. He was lying still but his chest heaved up and down with his breathing. His face was lined as though he had slept with it pressed against a rabbit-wire screen.

The Gringo looked at both of them and then he kicked the rifle out of the old man's hand. It had not been cocked and it did not go off. The Gringo pushed it away with his foot. "I want food, old man."

The woman kept staring, saying nothing. The Gringo reached down and picked up the old man's rifle, and said, "This is not loaded."

"We have no ammunition left," said the old man. "There is little food but I suppose you must eat. Lupe."

The old woman stirred. She sat up and brushed strings of hair away from her eyes; her face was round and pouched. *"Nina,"* she said to the little girl, "build up the fire. Bring wood."

"For him?" the little girl demanded.

"You will obey or go without supper," said the fat woman.

"On the run," the Gringo said, and met the little girl's angry glance. The little girl screwed up her lip and then went away to gather reeds for the fire.

The old man had not moved; he lay with his head on a bundle of cloth. Soon the sun would reach its midpoint and either the old man would have to suffer its rays or move underneath the wagon. Now and then the Gringo saw the old man droop. His eyes closed slowly and popped open again. He wore dust-coated remnants of expensive clothing, the ornate costume of a don, but old, now: worn thin and patched.

The Gringo squatted in the shade with his back against the front wheel. Its iron rim was hot. "What happened to your mules?"

"Two Mojaves came here the night before last night. They ate our meal with us and then stole our mules and our cow."

"No mules," the Gringo said, and cursed in English, and said, "How do you expect to get anywhere without mules, you old fool?" The old man's eyelids had sagged. The Gringo wiped a forearm across his face and looked at the river. The ferry landing was there, empty; the ferry was tied up on the far side of the Colorado. It all looked deserted. The little Indian girl brought an armload of reeds and banked the fire against the wind that came damp and sultry off the river. The fat woman sighed and heaved to her feet; she brought a slab of smoked meat out of the wagon and put it on the fire. The Gringo watched it hungrily.

The old woman said, "The Indians cut the rope for the ferry when they killed the boatmen. There is no way to bring the ferry here except to swim across with a rope. The old man is sick and I cannot swim."

The Gringo didn't seem to pay any attention to her. After a while, with the smell of singeing meat in his nostrils, he said, "The Mojaves killed Glanton?"

"And all his friends. That is what the two Mojaves told us before they stole our animals. They were very pleased but I think it was not the Mojaves but the Yumas who did the killing. It does not matter, of course. Glanton is dead and his men are dead and the rope is cut, and the ferry is over there. That is what matters. Can you swim, Gringo?"

"I can swim." Unable to restrain himself, the Gringo turned to the fire and took the meat and gnawed at it half-raw. The old woman, having got started, seemed unable to stop talking.

"We had a servant, the Yaqui girl's mother, but she died on the desert and we buried her. We have seen much misfortune. The revolution has robbed my husband of his properties that were granted to his ancestors by the king two hundred years ago and now we are poor, and my husband, as you see, is ill. We must go to my uncle in California, in the county of Tuolumne."

The Gringo spoke around a mouthful of meat. "That's where they've found gold."

"Yes, I suppose it would be so. My husband is very ill and we must get him across the river, for he wishes to die in a house with a roof over him and a family around him. This desert is not a good place for a proud man to die. You see that, do you not?"

The Gringo made no answer of any kind. He finished eating and scraped a palm across his mouth; he took his rifle and walked down to the ferryboat landing and stared across the river. It was wide and there was a powerful rush to the current, swollen by melting snows in the faraway mountains. The little girl darted down to the dock and said, "How many men have you killed?" And he ignored her, finally turning to go back up to the wagon. Its stripe of shade was very thin now. The fat woman said, "Will you help me get him under the wagon?"

"To hell with him," said the Gringo, and sat down frowning at the river crossing. The old woman struggled with the old man's weight, pulling him under the wagon. The old man tried to help but he seemed weak to the point of helplessness. It was curious he had been able to hold a rifle.

The little girl stared down at the Gringo and said, "You were a friend of the *ladrón* Glanton."

"*Ve, ve,*" he told her irritably.

The old woman crawled out from beneath the wagon and spoke sharply to the little girl. "Get away from him, little savage."

"I am better than you," the little girl shouted. "My father was a warrior."

"Your father is dead a long time," the old woman said wearily. "And now your mother too. You are an Indian and you had better learn what that means. Go away and leave the Gringo. He does not want you troubling him."

The little girl spat dry. "He is a *ladrón*. He takes your food and does nothing for you, but you take his side against me because I am Indian."

"Go," the old woman said. The little girl wheeled and darted into the reeds. There was a great crashing around which presently subsided.

The old woman sat down by the Gringo. "The *ladrón* Glanton and his friends stole the ferry from another Gringo. They charged much money for ferry passage and then they robbed many passengers afterward. No one is sorry the Indians have killed them. It was Glanton who sold Mexican scalps as Apache, for the bounty in Sonora. If he had stayed we would have killed him there. And you—you are a friend of Glanton?"

"I am a friend of no one," said the Gringo.

"Then you are a fool."

"You talk a lot, old woman."

"You came here because you heard that your *amigo* Glanton was making much money by robbing travelers—and all travelers must come by here. You expected to join the *ladrones*. But now Glanton is dead and there are no *ladrones* except yourself, and no one to rob except ourselves, and we are poor; it would not be worth your trouble. You must either go back or swim across to California. But you cannot go back, for you have no horse. What happened to your horse?"

"Broke a leg. You will hurt yourself talking so much."

"I have nothing to do but talk," she said, "and you have little else to do but listen. You cannot return across the desert without a horse because by yourself you cannot carry enough water. You must swim across. You will rest today, and tomorrow you will swim across."

"There's gold in California," he said.

"And rich men for you to rob."

"You have a loose tongue. What if I am not a robber?"

"Do you deny you are a robber?"

The Gringo said, *"Señora,* I would deny anything if the denial served me. The last time I told the truth when I knew it might hurt me was when I was the *niña's* age. They sent me to the county farm."

"It was not the truth that hurt you."

"Be quiet, old woman."

"You must swim across tomorrow," she said. "I only ask that you carry the end of the rope and tie it at the ferry landing. When the rope is up we can pull the ferry across by its pulley."

The Gringo brooded upon the river. "Old woman, a rope is a heavy thing and when it is soaked with water it is heavier still. To build the ferry they used oxen to swim across with the rope."

"A strong man can do it."

"Old woman, you can die without my help." The Gringo got up and went down to the dock and sat there, taking off his boots and soaking his feet in the river. Today he was too tired; tomorrow he would take their food, as much of it as he could carry, and he would cross the river and leave them. All of them knew that much.

In time, travelers would come to the crossing. If they were soon enough, they would help the old man dying and the fat woman and the Indian girl; if they were not soon enough, they would bury the three.

The Gringo studied the brown flow with hooded eyes. After a while in the sun he climbed down underneath the dock, took off his clothes and buried himself in the shallow eddies under the dock. The flies were numerous but he paid them no mind.

When the little girl came down to the dock he reached out his hand and laid it upon his rifle and locked glances with her, and said, "You're a witch. Get away."

The little girl said, "The old man does not notice me. The woman keeps me because I can do work, but they hate me because I am Yaqui and they know the Yaqui is better than they are. You are a *ladrón,* you can understand. My father was a warrior and he killed many of them."

"And they killed him, didn't they."

It was sudden: she turned her head away from him, she put her back to him; her shoulders lifted. The Gringo said, "Yaquis are not supposed to cry. You are no Yaqui."

The little girl ran away.

After the Gringo dressed he picked up his rifle and went back to the wagon; he was hungry again and he took the last biscuit from the box. The old woman stared at him without expression. The old man was awake, breathing heavily beneath the wagon, a flush of heat on his cheeks. The little girl sat across the camp, staring with hate at all of them; presently she went into the reeds, and when she was gone the fat woman said, "The truth is that the *niña's* mother was not a Yaqui and that the *niña* never met her father. He was a mountain thief." The woman shrugged her fat shoulders. "You know the Yaqui, how they are. *Ladrones.* The little girl is arrogant and thinks herself better than the rest of us because she believes her father died gallantly."

"Your mouth flaps," the Gringo told her.

The old woman grinned at him. Her teeth were gapped and yellow. She said, "Would you shoot me for that, tough one?"

"Aagh," the Gringo said in disgust.

"You will not shoot, but you will leave us to die. Is there a difference? It would be kinder to shoot us all."

"Old woman, I have trouble enough of my own."

In the late afternoon the Gringo was lying on his back in the shade of a reed clump; he had one knee bent and his rifle across his stomach, and the hat tipped forward over his face. The little girl came forward in her bare feet and kicked at the sole of his boot and laughed at him. The Gringo said, "Maybe I ought to shoot you."

"Your talk is very tough, *ladrón.*"

"*Ve.*"

The old woman was calling for the girl; it was time to build the fire. The girl squatted by the Gringo and said, "If we go to California the old man will die and the woman will have her family. They will have no use for me."

"Then you will have to learn to make your own way."

"I am a clumsy thief. What else can I do?"

"Work," said the Gringo, with a brief smile that fled quickly.

"What would you know of work? Who would give work to an Indian girl?"

He sat up angrily. "Why do you bring your problems to me? *Ve—ve!*"

Her eyes were moist. The old woman was calling in a strident voice. Her heavy footfalls sounded and she came to stand ponderously above the little girl. "The fire is waiting."

"Make your own fire," the girl said.

"Then you will have no supper."

"I will steal food when you are asleep."

"Urchin! Build the fire or I'll whip you."

"You cannot run fast enough," the little girl said, taking a step backward.

The old woman said, "You will not build a fire—why? Because you are too good for it? Because you are the daughter of a Yaqui? Let me tell you, little *ladrón*, your father was an ordinary thief—he died with his hands in another Yaqui's pocket. He was killed by his own people. That is your proud *padre*. Now build the fire."

"You are a liar!" the little girl screamed, and ran off into the bottoms.

The old woman sighed. "I hope she does not come back. She is an unpleasant mouth to feed. But now I must build my own fire. Will you break wood for it?"

"I'm hungry," the Gringo said. "I'll bring the wood."

The old woman propped the old man against the wagon wheel. When they were half through their meal the little girl came reluctantly out of the dusk and stood across the fire staring; and the old woman said, "All right, eat—but if you eat our food, you must do our work."

"You lied about my father."

"No," said the old woman, "I did not lie. It is time you know."

"I will eat."

The little girl sat a little distance away from them and ate her supper. The food was meager.

After dark the Gringo picked a spot away from the wagon and lay down with his hand on the warm metal of the rifle cylinder. The little girl came up and the Gringo looked at her out of one eye. "Go away—go to sleep."

"I will sleep here," she said, and dropped prone with a blanket which she wrapped around herself.

"Am I to feel honored?"

"I have no father," the little girl said. "I am the child of a thief. I will sleep with a thief."

"I'm not a thief."

"I don't believe you."

"Believe what you want," said the Gringo, and closed his eye.

The little girl said, "How can you swim across the river with the big pistol and the rifle?"

"I'll manage it."

"Your powder will all get wet. I have been thinking about it. If you swim across with the rope you can bring the ferry back and take your rifle and pistol over on the ferry. It will keep them dry."

"You think too much for a little girl," he said. "Go to sleep."

"You could also take the old man and the woman on the ferry."

He opened his eye. "Why should you care what happens to them?"

The little girl was watching him; she did not speak.

The Gringo said irritably, "The old man is too weak to travel. What purpose would it serve to get him across the river? That side is no better than this side."

"But the old woman would be alone on this side."

"Alone?"

"I will follow you," said the little girl. "I will not stay with them."

"Go away and sleep by yourself."

"I can swim," she said.

"The current is swift. You would drown."

"I will try," said the little girl. "It will make no difference to you if I drown."

"That's right."

In the morning the Gringo awoke and stretched. The little girl had a fire going and the old woman was grinding knuckles into her eye sockets. The old man lay under the wagon breathing shallowly, his mouth open and slack; his eyes were half-lidded but did not appear to see. The Gringo took his breakfast and then went down to consider the river. The flow was steady and strong.

He heard the old woman yelling at the girl, and in a moment the girl came running down the slope to him. The Gringo said, "You run away too much. If you want her food, stay and fight her."

The little girl said nothing; the Gringo said, "Why do you come to me?"

"I will swim across with you."

"The devil you will," he said in English.

"What is that?"

"Stay here," he told her, but he made no motion toward the water, and in a moment the girl said,

"You are afraid of the river."

"Why not?"

"I am not afraid of it."

"Then you're stupid."

"I know how to swim," she said proudly.

The old woman came down to the dock and said, "The rope is here," and pointed to where the hemp line lay coiled.

"Forget that," said the Gringo.

"The old man will die."

"He will die anyway, old woman." The Gringo kept frowning at the river, looking at neither the woman nor the rope.

The woman said, "Perhaps we could bring help for him. Warner's Ranch is not too far. But it is on the other side."

"Two days' walk, maybe more. The old man would be dead before you got back. Leave me alone, old woman."

The woman barked at the little girl and turned slowly to plod uphill. The little girl said to the Gringo, "If you are still tired today, you can wait and swim across tomorrow."

When there was no answer she moved closer to him and threw her head back to look at his face. "If I swim across with you and I do not drown, will you take me with you?"

"Where?"

"Where you go."

"*Ve,*" he told her. "*Ve allí.*" He waved an arm toward the reed bottoms. "Leave me alone."

"Do you hate everyone?" Her head was cocked to one side.

The Gringo looked at her with his eyebrows drawn together. When he drew the back of his hand across his face it scraped on the abrasiveness of his jaw. The girl said, "Will you stay today?"

"Why should I?"

"If you are tired," she said. "Will you stay and talk to me? You are a thief and—"

"Damn, I am not a thief."

"And I am a thief and we should talk together." She brought a strip of dried beef out from beneath her clothes. "You see? I have stolen this today from the old woman. We are thieves together." She regarded him gravely and began to chew on the string of meat.

The Gringo sat down on the riverbank and toyed with the frayed end of the rope coil. The sun, climbing notch by notch, blasted his back.

The little girl moved around him, stood beside him and said, "I have no father and no mother." The Gringo looked at her. She said, "I must go with my own kind. We are both thieves. You see, I have stolen the meat. I am a thief. You can trust me."

For a moment the Gringo appeared on the verge of laughter; but his face turned sour. Heat glistened on the muddy surface of the Colorado and the water made a steady slap-slap against the banks.

The old woman came down the hill and said, "He is dead."

The Gringo looked up at her. As if he had been released, he stood up and said, "I'll bury him."

"There is no shovel."

"I'll scoop a grave with sticks."

"It is kind."

The Gringo shook his head and went up toward the wagon. He scratched a shallow grave and they wrapped the old man in a blanket and buried him; the old woman mumbled words and the Gringo filled in the hole and tamped it down with his boots. The old woman said, "That has given you something to do for an hour or two, but now you are not better off than you were. There are still the three of us."

"No," said the Gringo. "There are two of you and then there is me."

"And we are not three? You have no arithmetic?"

"I have no ties," the Gringo said.

He went back to the dock and stood on the end of it where the water was deep; he looked across toward the ferry, tied up and swaying slightly with the ebb and flow of the current.

He protested, "The rope will be too heavy."

The old woman's slow smile crawled across her face but then the Gringo said, "No, I'm a goddamn fool. You can get across the river by yourself; the old man did."

"And now you are a philosopher?"

"I have wasted too much time here," said the Gringo.

The little girl said, "If there are two and one, it is not as you have divided it."

"Then we are one and one and one," said the Gringo. "You are not mine, *niña*."

"Nor mine," said the old woman coolly; she went back toward the shade of the wagon with a slow stride of resignation. The little girl said, "She will sit in the shade and die. Don't you care?"

The Gringo said, "She doesn't care about you. Why think about her?"

"She does. She is only gruff."

"I thought you hated her."

"I do," said the little girl. "Maybe she does not care about me. Maybe I do not care about her."

"Make up your mind."

"What are you going to do?"

The Gringo said, "I will swim across the river." He stripped off his hat and boots and after a moment's consideration his gunbelt; together with his rifle he laid them in a neat pile on the dock and took off his shirt as well, and his trousers; he stood pale in his faded red trapdoors and put his troubled gaze on the river. Then he reached down and tied his shirt and pants into a bundle, which he wrapped around his waist and knotted by the shirt-arms. The boots he laced together and hung around his neck. He considered the gunbelt and rifle, and sat down to stuff the rolled gunbelt and pistol into his hat, which he then grasped in one hand.

The little girl said, "You cannot take the rifle."

"I'll have to do without it. If you have a use for it, you can have it."

"It is not a gift if you abandon it."

"Who said it was a gift?" Balancing the hat, he walked back to the bank and turned toward the river so that he could walk into it.

The little girl followed him and stood in water up to her knees. Up above, the old woman was sitting in the shade of the wagon fanning herself with the dead man's hat. The Gringo stopped and turned his head and looked at her over his shoulder, and then at the little girl who had no father and no mother and who was a thief.

The Gringo felt water lapping around his calves and felt the suck of the mud bottom. He turned and faced the little girl. She lifted her hand toward him.

The sun was very hot on his bare flesh. He wiped his mouth and turned to the dock beside him, and put his hat on the dock with the gunbelt and pistol; he untied the shirt-sleeves and laid that bundle and his boots with the hat.

The girl had taken a step closer to him, and when he turned again, her hand was still lifted, and he reached out to grasp it and walked with her toward the coil of rope.

The old woman waddled down and said, "If you walk upstream to the limit of the rope, it will be easier to swim across in an arc. The current will help you."

The little girl clung to the Gringo's hand and the Gringo said, "Let go of me, damn it." He picked up the rope and tied a small loop in the end of it, and inspected the dock cleat to make certain the rope was secured.

When he dragged the rope out to its full length, moving upstream along the bank, the little girl walked with him. He pulled the rope taut and stepped into the river, and found it warm and rushing. The little girl said, "I am a Yaqui and you are a Yaqui too."

"I guess maybe I am," the Gringo said in English, and struck out with the rope into the current.

Take a Left at Bertram

BY CHAD OLIVER

Chad Oliver is a novelist, short-story writer and anthropologist from Austin, Texas. He is also a teller of preposterous fish stories. His fine novel The Wolf Is My Brother, *which is long overdue for reprint, won the Spur Award for the Best Western Historical in 1967. Of the following story Chad said, ". . . it's got all the ingredients: Texans and Indians, and even a Ranger and outlaws. And, I pray, some feel for the land and a few other things. It's a story I wanted to write."*

What he doesn't say is, the Ranger is a Ford Ranger, and the Indians . . . well, read and find out.

Going northwest from Austin to the ranch, the Ford Ranger pickup moved visibly from one world into another. Starting in the hot bedlam of US 183 — PRAY FOR ME, the bumper stickers read, I DRIVE 183—the truck buzzed past 3M and the sprawling computer complex of Texas Instruments, weaved around squadrons of cars and vans, and ran the familiar maze: Kentucky Fried Chicken, Catfish Parlour, Southwestern Bar-B-Q, Pizza Hut, Burger King, McDonald's.

The developments, first the plush condos and then the scorched trailer "estates," blotched the land as far as Cedar Park. The tentacles of growth snaked all the way to Leander: banks and malls and real estate offices, chiropractic clinics and Whataburger boxes.

More than twenty miles from Austin, the country began to open up. A man could sense the blue vault of the sky and there was room for white clouds. The land was cleared and parklike, with only the scrub oaks and pecan trees still standing. There were bluestem grasses and sunflower stalks and old fences.

Russell Bremner switched off the air conditioner in the cab and cranked the window down. The October air was warm but it did not stink of the city. He glanced at Fred Hall as they took the Burnet fork at Seward

Junction. Some of the tension went out of his leathery hands that gripped the wheel.

"Hang on," Russ said. "We may make Bertram yet."

"Hell, Pops," Fred said. "We've waited damned near a year. What's another half hour?"

The highway was narrower now. There were a few ranches, ranging from last-gasp to Big Money. The earth was dry and battered from the blasts of summer, but at least it was rural rather than urban.

They hit the metropolis of Bertram. Population: 824. Old churches and white frame houses that needed paint. Town buildings of stone, half of them abandoned. Bertram was poor but not unpleasant. It had a few years to wait before Progress roared down the road from Austin.

Russ made the well-remembered right turn, then took a left at the long-empty Gulf station. They were on 1174, which wasn't much of a road.

The transition was so sudden that it was almost a shock. This was a different Texas, an older Texas. Windmills and tin-roofed houses. Cattle. Dirt driveways with sagging gates. Gray wooden barns and precious pools of stagnant water.

They crossed the San Gabriel River, or what was left of it at this time of the year, and the parched land was open and rolling. You could see a long way: brown grass and tangled vines, scattered stands of oaks, clumps of faded green cedars that had dodged the axes. There wasn't much mesquite left and the wildflowers were long gone with the summer heat.

They passed the lonely metal marker that had been stuck in the weeds by the State Historical Survey Committee in 1970. Russ Bremner and Fred Hall did not need to read it; they knew it by heart. It proclaimed to the dusty wind and the silence that this was the site of the town of Strickling. It was in the big fat middle of nothing. Strickling had been founded in 1853, when Mrs. Martha Webster Strickling had settled there with her husband, a man with the unlikely name of Marmaduke. Martha had survived an Indian raid near Leander that had killed thirty settlers. Strickling had prospered for a time, hauling lumber and buffalo hides by wagon. When the railroad bypassed Strickling in 1882, the town folded. Only the cemetery remained.

Like a good horse, the green pickup with the rattling camper top knew the way. It turned off to the right along a cracked one-lane asphalt road. The little graveyard was there, screened by weeds and baking in the sun. Russ and Fred had explored it many times. Some of the stones were too faded to read. Others were legible: PALEN, 1854–1893, PATRICK, 1823–1899, HUTTON, 1823–1882, a child, ELLA OLIVER, 1870–1878. A section of the old cemetery had been used fairly recently. There were shallow graves with gravel mounds and artificial flowers. All of the names were Spanish.

Russ and Fred did not stop. It was time to go fishing.

They drove past another marker, this one for Black's Fort. The legend said: BUILT AS A DEFENSE AGAINST THE INDIANS IN 1855 BY WILLIAM BLACK, 1815–1907. No tourists ever came there, and in truth it hadn't been much of a fort. There had been a stockade and a stone building where guns and ammunition were kept. Sentries had been posted on nights when the moon was full—the Comanche moon had been very real then—and Black's Fort had been a place to make a stand. Black's Fort was unrestored. The cedar logs that had formed the stockade were gone. There was part of a stone wall still standing, an old wooden cabin, and a view that stretched for long empty miles beneath the sky. . . .

The pickup bounced along for half a mile more, and then Russ and Fred were at the ranch gate.

Fred climbed out and worked the combination on the padlock that fastened the heavy chain that was looped around the galvanized steel gate. He slid the gate open and Russ eased the pickup through. Fred closed the gate, leaving the lock unsnapped, and piled back in the truck.

The place that Jim had called El Rancho Diablo wasn't really a ranch, but the name had stuck after Jim's death. It was just a little old hundred acres of plains country rolling down to the San Gabriel River. It had a few cows wandering around on a cattle lease, but they were there for tax purposes. Then again, Russ figured, any chunk of land in Texas that was bigger than an acre or two was usually called a ranch. Why not?

El Rancho Diablo was a place to hunt and fish and drink and restore the soul. That was how Jim had used it, and that was how his friends continued to use it.

They jolted down the dirt trail and through the gap in the unmortared limestone wall that may or may not have predated the introduction of barbed wire. It was too hot and too bright to see any game, but Russ could remember the time when he had counted over forty whitetail deer filing along that wall. They topped the rocky ridge and passed the stilt-crumpled windmill. They entered the timber that lined the river: live oaks and elms, sycamores and cottonwoods, a few hackberries and buckeyes.

They reached the clearing where the cabin was and stopped. The cabin wouldn't win any awards from *House Beautiful* and it had no plumbing or electricity. But Jim had built it, board by board and tar-paper shingle by tar-paper shingle, and that shack had some good memories.

Russ and Fred had been around the barn a few times, and they sprayed themselves from green cans of Deep Woods Off before they got out of the truck. The chiggers were fierce here, and there were enough ticks to bleed a hog.

They pulled on their fishing boots, opening up the camper on the back of the pickup. It wasn't that the water was cold or even unpleasant on a warm day, but it was impossible to fish the San Gabriel without climbing in and out of the stream. Boots were good insurance against snakes and even better protection against poison ivy.

Russ assembled his Cortland graphite fly rod and Fred checked his spinning rig. The two men split a Dr. Pepper from the ice chest, clamped on their hats and Polaroid glasses, and were ready.

"Made it, by God," Russ said.

"About time," Fred agreed.

Russ and Fred were no longer young and they thought their more adventuresome fishing trips were behind them. The San Gabriel was about their speed now. They were both big men with the look of the outdoors stamped on their lined faces. In fact, Russ was a retired petroleum geologist and Fred was still plugging away at his insurance agency. None of that mattered when they fished or hunted together.

There was no need to discuss plans. The afternoon was wearing on, and Russ went upstream and Fred went down. There was not a lot of water in the San Gabriel, but it was flowing with a detectable current and it pooled up in spots.

The fish were there. Torpid, maybe, but not spooky. Nobody else ever fished this place.

Time stopped and the warm air was still. Buzzards soared on the thermals in the sky and squirrels chattered in the dusty oaks. There were coon tracks on the riverbank.

Russ knew that a fly rod was less than ideal on the San Gabriel. He didn't give a damn. He lost himself playing with his Rio Grande King, casting sidearm to avoid the brush. He caught a pile of potbellies and popped the warm fish into his creel: bluegills and sunfish and crappies. He even fooled a nice catfish on a hare's-ear nymph, and *that* was a triumph. Fred, of course, did better with his spinning rod. He worked the shaded pools next to the banks and hauled out bass that looked too big for the river.

At first, neither man noticed it when the weather changed. They were totally absorbed in what they were doing. That was the great thing about fishing a stream, any stream that had no people on it: you were sealed in a universe of your own, a world where nothing mattered except the next pool, the next riffle, the next bend of the river. . . .

But something was happening, something that could not be ignored.

A wind stirred through the dead leaves of the trees. At first, it was just a nuisance: it interfered with casting and the drifting leaves put the fish down. Then Russ lost his hat. The wind grew stronger. Somewhere, a branch cracked and crashed to the ground. Quite suddenly, the temperature dropped about twenty degrees. Russ had been sweating; now he was chilly. The October sun disappeared. Heavy black clouds raced through the sky. The light changed from a sleepy brightness to a subdued glow that was almost violet—

You couldn't call it a blue norther. Not in October. But you could call it ominous. Russ was reminded of the old saying about Texas weather: if you don't like it, wait a minute.

The two men made it back to the truck at the same time. The wind was blowing so hard it nearly knocked them down. They pitched their fish into the ice chest without cleaning them. The camper was carpeted with dead leaves. Russ didn't bother to break his rod down. He tossed it in and slammed the tailgate.

They had to clear the leaves out of the cab with their hands before they could climb in. There was no rain yet, but Russ knew that the caliche trail could get slippery in a hurry.

He hit the starter. It engaged—the battery was strong—but the engine did not catch. He tried again. Old Reliable, the Ford Ranger, would not start.

"Crap," said Fred.

The howling wind buffeted the truck, rocking it on its springs. Russ saw no lightning, but there was electricity in the air. It was damned near dark, and then the violet light intensified.

The wind stopped. Just ceased in an instant, the way a high wind never did. There was a dead-still calm. The violet light glowed.

The edges of Jim's cabin began to blur and waver—

"Jesus H. Christ," Russ said.

They both saw them coming. Steadily, out of the brush into the clearing. Right smack toward the truck.

Fred twisted awkwardly in the seat and yanked the rifle out of the gun rack. It was a heavy Mossberg .22 automatic and it was not designed for a quick draw. A varmint gun, but it was all they had. He pulled the safety back.

"Tell you what, Pops," Fred breathed. "You call the signals."

There were five of them. Small lean brown men with eyes hard as stones. They were nearly naked and their tough-muscled bodies were scarred. They carried short spears with flint tips.

They were hunters and they were Indians. That was that.

Not Comanches, no. And not Apaches or Tonkawas. No, they were older than Black's Fort, older than Strickling, older than history. No horses, no bows and arrows, no beads or feathers or metal knives.

Nameless Ones. Walking in a violet glow. One of them limped. All of them were displaced in time.

They were the hardest men Russ had ever seen. There was no fat, no flab, and no wavering. They had two things on their minds: meat and survival.

They kept coming.

Neither Russ nor Fred questioned what they were seeing. The gut accepts what it cannot deny.

"Maybe they've come to give us a lecture about pollution and the unity of life," Russ said.

"Sure," Fred replied, his finger curling on the trigger.

The five Indians must have been disoriented. The fluid blurred outlines of Jim's cabin marked whose world this was. Certainly, they had never seen a pickup truck before. Still, they were unafraid and unrattled. They said nothing. They seemed to blend into the earth.

Abruptly, with a whoosh and a rattle and a startling force of impact, a stubby wooden spear sailed in through the open window on the driver's side, slammed across the dashboard, and spider-webbed the glass of the slanted vent window next to Fred's .22. There was no malice in the throw. That was just what you did when you encountered something strange.

Russ cranked up the window, fast. "Close yours, Fred."

"Can't shoot through it—"

"Got an idea."

Russ waited until he saw one, short and real and implacable in the electric violet glow. He hit the horn, loud and long.

The cry of a beast unknown?

The Indian was profoundly unimpressed. Hell, this man had heard the trumpeting of a mammoth. The horn of a Ford pickup didn't worry him. He cocked his arm—no atlatl, Russ noted wildly—and let fly his lance. It banged into the radiator grille.

Fred laughed despite himself. "The horn was a great idea. What do we do next—strike a match?"

Russ tried the starter again. Close, but no cigar. He could still see Jim's cabin. It was unsteady in the ethereal light, but it was there. Thank God it hadn't turned into a tipi or a wickiup or a rock shelter or whatever those jokers lived in—

The Indians did not attack again. They did not retreat. They just waited.

Sizing up the green monster? Low on ammo? What if they could not leave? What if they could not get back to their world?

What if the truck slipped back through the millennia?

Russ snapped his fingers. "The fish," he yelled. "God damn it, *the fish!*"

There was no convenient sliding panel between the cab and the camper. Russ did not wait to think. He could still move when he had to.

He jerked open the door, ducked around the truck, dropped the tailgate, and threw the ice chest out. He scooped up the pile of fish. He shoveled them out into the clearing. He ran back to the cab, hurled himself in, and locked the door.

His heart was hammering. His hands were slimy. There had been no more spears. His actions must have seemed weird, to say the least.

For an eternity, nothing happened. There was only the violet glow, the wind beginning to moan again through the tree branches, the electric air. . . .

"What time is it?" Fred asked.

"Very funny."

When it happened, it happened fast. The five hard little men flowed into the clearing. They examined the fish and picked them up. The Indian with the limp bit into a bass, raw. He smiled. His teeth were rotten.

Without so much as a gesture, the Nameless Ones faded into the brush. They all had fish. For a moment, they were frozen shadows in the strange light. Then they were gone.

"Thank the Lord we weren't skunked today," Russ said.

"Try that damned starter again," Fred muttered. He still had a death grip on the .22.

Russ smiled. "It'll go now," he said.

It did.

Russ gunned the pickup out of the clearing, out of the violet glow, out of the eerie electric wind. He could see the dirt trail, the stone wall, the galvanized gate.

It was their world.

Fred relocked the gate and closed up the back of the camper. He wasted no time.

Russ switched on the lights. It was full dark now and lightning forked the sky. Big fat drops hit the windshield and then sheets of rain came.

He didn't floor it but he drove as if the devil were on his tail. Maybe he was. Somehow, he was afraid to go back the way they had come. He took the old side road and rammed the pickup through the thunder and rain. He roared past the lost little villages with names like Joppa and Mohamet. He barely paused at Seward Junction and then, incredibly, the pickup was on 183 again.

Research Boulevard.

Lights, cars, buildings.

The tires squished on the rain-swept pavement.

Through the splashing arcs of the laboring windshield wipers he could see the familiar signs: Texaco, Safeway, Captain Boomer's, Angus Plaza.

Russ did not know what he felt. Relief, yes. Wonder, awe. A sense that the universe had tilted. Some sadness. It would take time to sort his emotions out.

He slowed down a little. He was regaining control.

Fred sat as still as it was possible to sit in a fast-moving pickup that had a tendency to skid on a wet road. Pickups had lousy traction. He had two weapons on his lap. One was the .22 automatic rifle. He had slipped the safety back on. The other was a short wooden spear with a fluted flint point. The point was broken where it had hit the glass. The shaft was polished and smooth with the sweat from a human hand.

"I forgot to fasten my safety belt," Fred muttered. It was something to say. Something to break the tension of silence.

"The rifle is loaded and it's not in the gun rack," Russ said. "You know what that means."

Fred managed a parody of a laugh. "We're outlaws, by God."

"Anyhow, the insurance is your department. You'd better be creative when you explain about the window and the radiator."

"Explain," Fred snorted. "That'll be the day."

The words faded and died. All the words they knew were empty.

Even the smells were different now. The sweet scent of the cedar in the clearing by Jim's cabin was replaced by the wet-sand odor of rain-washed concrete. The world was not the same.

The two men could not talk directly about what had happened to them. They could accept it, with the wisdom that sometimes comes with age, but they could not zero in on it. They had to talk around it.

Absurdly, Russ wondered whether the ice chest would still be out there if he ever went back.

"You know," Fred said, "I hope they made it too."

Russ nodded. He felt no kinship with those five lost hunters, but he felt a deep continuity. There were times when a man had to go a long, long distance to find his way home.

The silence threatened them again. After all their years together, Russ and Fred had hit something that choked off words. They knew that they would never be able to discuss it with anyone else.

The night pressed in on them. The hard rain drummed on the metal roof of the cab. There were lights everywhere, but there were shadows too. Shadows—

Shadows of generations beyond number that had walked this land. Shadows of human beings born and unborn, living and dead. Shadows of the past and present and future. . . .

Shadows.

Fred looked down at the .22 rifle. "What do you think would have happened if I had fired?"

Russ made a joke of it. He didn't know what else to do. "You'd have missed," he said. "As usual."

But he gripped the wheel very tightly and he rejoiced in the steady hum of the engine.

That damned starter.

He'd have to get that thing checked, one day.

The Second Kit Carson

BY GARY PAULSEN

Gary Paulsen is most noted for his Young Adult novels, which are as fine as books written anywhere for any age. Simply put, the man is a master. He is the author of such amazing novels as Sentries, Dogsong, Tracker, Popcorn Days and Buttermilk Nights *and* Dancing Carl, *which he set to dance to be produced and aired on Minnesota Public Television. He has taught at the University of Colorado, Bemidji State College, won various awards, done some acting, some living, but mostly writing. He is married to a lady named Ruth. They have one son named James, and Gary's hobby is dogsledding. "I run races, five hundred to a thousand miles. Have twice run in the famous Iditarod trans-Alaska race from Anchorage to Nome."*

He is currently working on a series of short stories called The Madonna, *a study of the relationship between men and their mothers. The following is one of them. It is Western by the thinnest definition, and I'll not spoil it for you by explaining that.*

A strange story. A fine story. Eat your heart out, Hemingway. I give you Gary Paulsen.

In that time when there was only the insanity of the incoming shells, day after day, hour after hour in that time when they came in while he sat in the bunkers and smelled the damp mud-sand in the bags around him, felt the tight jolts as they hit—in that time was when he started to drink.

He knew that.

In that time when he was beyond life into death he started to drink and drink more to make it end but of course it didn't end. Not until they finally tore him enough so that he was sent back to the world, the World, and by then he was too good at drinking to stop.

He knew that. Knew when he started to drink. It was in that time and then they sent him back and let him go to California, let him go back into the World and he was not one of those who could kill himself so he kept to the drinking and left California and went to the small town in New Mexico.

He could live cheaply there, he had heard, and it wasn't too bad. At first there had been some fighting because they thought he was a hippie, but when he didn't fight back and only wanted to drink, when he didn't talk back but only wanted to drink, when he did nothing back but only wanted to drink they at first laughed and then took pity and left him alone. Or maybe it wasn't pity, but he felt it to be that, and in any event they left him alone and that was all that counted. To be left alone to drink in Taos, New Mexico, was all that counted for him and he thought all that counted for everyone until it was given to him to deliver the second Kit Carson.

When he could think clearly, or more clearly than at other times, that was how he thought of it—deliver Kit Carson—and often when he awakened in the mornings, or came up to find the bottle next to the bed he would fight to remember just how it had happened. It wasn't much of a fight, the fight to remember, but he stayed with it until he got a headache and the feeling from the bottle would come in and for just the briefest time he would see it all as it happened.

Or as he thought it happened.

The nights had started as they almost always started when he got the check they sent him for breaking him—he called it his repair check. They sent him the check each month and when he got it he went to the plaza and to the Cantina and he tried to shoot pool and he would buy drinks for everyone until the check was gone. Then they would buy drinks for him until he was too finished to drink more and he would leave. Out, across the plaza, he walked until he found the small street that led back to the room he rented where he would fall into the damp nest of his bed and end that day.

And this night was much of that except that he tried to get Sally to dance with him before he left. Sally painted signs and was fun to watch when she danced but she said he was too drunk. Yet she said it in a way that made him happy, a smiling way, and so he left to cross the plaza that night in a happy mood and because of that he decided to stop by Kit's grave and think about being happy. Kit Carson was buried in a small grave in back of the hotel near where he walked to go home and because he was happy and decided to stop and think at Kit's grave he was the one who got to deliver the second Kit Carson.

Or that's how he remembered it.

It was the scream that stopped him and made him crouch down until he fell. He was in the alley near the back of the hotel, not too far from the grave when he heard the scream.

It started high, a pain scream—he had heard many of those and knew them well—and faded off into chunks of sound mixed with breath and spit that he also knew well. At first he thought something had happened and he was back in the country and fell to the ground for that, but he knew that wasn't true and he stood again. There was only silence for a time and he began to think he had dreamed the whole thing—he had many dreams while walking—but another sound followed the scream and he knew it was a woman and that she needed help. He had also heard that sound before but did not like to think about it.

In a few steps he realized that the sound was coming from Kit Carson's grave, or near it, and he moved that way. He thought perhaps it was a woman being raped, but when he got to the grave he saw a young woman alone, lying near the grave on her back, her hands pulling at the small fence surrounding the grave itself.

"Help me," she said, or he thought she said. She might have thought it and he got it from the bend in her body. "Help me now."

She was pregnant, huge with it, and he still did not understand. "I don't know what to do," he answered. "What is the matter?" His words rolled on him in his mind with the drink so everything echoed.

"It's time. Help me."

So, he thought. She means the baby. "There is nothing I can do." He meant it literally. There was nothing he could do. He would have stopped it for her but he could not do it. He could do nothing.

"Please," she said, a tiny sound. "Please."

And there it was. As they always said it when there was nothing you could do. They always said "please" in the small sound and he kneeled next to her and put his hands in his lap and waited. He had done that before. Sat next to them and waited when they made the small sounds, waited for them to die and he thought that was coming now. He knew of that.

But instead of dying she screamed and heaved, great doublings of her stomach, great heaves, and they were of pain but they were more, too. The heaves came from inside her, from the earth beneath her, from something he did not understand or know and the heaves took him back farther. Back to when he kneeled next to another person who heaved.

She screamed again and the scream went into his thoughts and mixed with the memory and he was not there, not at Kit Carson's grave watching the hippie girl have a baby but back more, back where he started to drink, back where Wendell was leaning against the tree holding his stomach in with the heaves coming. Wendell who was dying and who said "please" in the small voice but he could not stop it. He went back to that and the girl heaved again, tightened and heaved and her dress rode up and the head came but he did not see it as a head. He saw instead Wendell's coil and thought that was it, thought it was the same and he reached to push it back in, as he had done with Wendell, but she heaved again and the baby slid out on the ground, slid out between her legs in blood and placenta, slid out before he could push it back and it all mixed in his mind, Wendell and the gray coil and the short pain sounds and the head of the baby and he reached down and picked the baby up as tenderly as he'd picked up Wendell's coil and put it on the girl's stomach as he had placed Wendell's on his stomach and that's when she looked at him and smiled and said, "Ki——Ki——"

And he thought, of course, it's Kit, Kit Carson, and that was how he came to meet the Little Mother and deliver Kit Carson and he left her there, left her and went home and nights later he went to the Cantina and tried to tell a man at the bar that he had delivered the second Kit Carson but the man moved away. That was the way of it, he thought. When he talked of the incoming insanity they thought much of it and bought drinks to hear of that time, but when something important like Kit Carson came along they moved away.

He knew it would never happen again and many nights after drinking in the Cantina he would go out across the plaza through the drunk Indians in their blankets and sit near the fountain and cry because he had met the Little Mother, had met her and delivered the second Kit Carson and it had changed nothing for him. When the crying finished he would sit and try to think about it, but all that would come would be the memory of it and a nudge of wonder about what she was doing now, the mother, and the little Kit Carson. Then he would go back into the Cantina if they would let him and drink some more and watch the artists shoot pool in the back room and tell the stories about the incoming explosions for the drinks they would buy him

Night of the Cougar

BY ARDATH MAYHAR

Ardath Mayhar is a full-time novelist, award-winning poet and short-story writer. Her most recent novel, The World Ends at Hickory Hollow, *takes place in a near futuristic version of her native East Texas. Though labeled science fiction, it's something of a postholocaust Western. It's also very good.*

The following story also takes place in East Texas, and is part of the verbal folklore handed down to her from her family.

She watched Jody as long as she could see the glint of his red shirt through the leaves along the brushy trail. The dim thuds of old Sam's hooves came to her ears for a little while longer. Then they were both gone, and the birdcalls in the woods around the cabin didn't seem to interrupt the silence at all.

Julie sighed as she turned toward her garden plot. With Little Jody and the baby both napping, her house was quiet, too. She had always liked the woodsy spot they'd picked to homestead . . . East Texas was much like her southern Mississippi birthplace . . . but when Jody went off to work with the loggers it got mighty lonesome.

Her sunbonnet was hot against her neck, and its curving brim cut off her view of anything around her when she stooped over the rows, her hoe busy among the tender sprouts of cabbage and turnip greens and onions. She didn't really like sunbonnets . . . never had. It had taken the full weight of her father's authority to make her toe the line and wear one to keep the sun from browning her fair skin.

" 'Tain't ladylike!" had been his most devastating indictment of any female. But she had never liked the girls he pointed out as ideals of feminine behavior. It was just as well that Jody had come along and carried her away from Laurel and its cadre of ladylike prototypes.

There was motion . . . she turned her head to watch a coachwhip snake go slipping along the fenceline by the cowshed. No danger there, she knew. But she kept a wary eye on any serpent about the house. Little Jody was at an age when anything new got chased and usually caught. She had no intention of letting him get bit by a copperhead or a moccasin.

The late spring sun was warm on her back. Sweat began sliding down her beneath her wool serge clothing. It was time to get out the summer-weight stuff, to cut Jody out of his winter underwear. She'd shed her own three weeks ago, amid her husband's dire warnings about late cold snaps and pneumonia.

Then the sweat all but congealed on her skin. A long wail cut across the morning woods-noises. A cougar, hunting late maybe. She hated the sound of them, the long lonesome cry like a woman in pain. And once she'd been warned about the beast she had hated it even more. A critter that craved human babies was something downright evil.

There were tales among the old women she saw occasionally at camp meetings of the church in the summertime; they could tell you tales that would curl your hair and kink your bones. One of those women had lost her own babe, some forty years gone, when a cougar had come right into the yard and taken it out of the basket where it was sleeping while she washed. Julie shivered, remembering.

Though she knew better, she put away her hoe and went into the house to check on the children. Little Jody slept in total relaxation, boneless, his small mouth open, his eyes partway open, too. Lissa was beginning to squirm in her hickory-splint basket, the way she always did when she was getting ready to wake up. It was just as well she'd quit in the garden. The baby would be ready to nurse any minute now. And Jody would wake up hungry. He always did.

The infant whimpered. Julie bent over the crib, felt the dampish forehead. Lissa hadn't been feeling too peart for some time now. Likely some spring ailment . . . she'd make up some herb tea and spoon it down the child. Everybody needed a tonic in the spring, seemed like.

She lifted the plump baby and sat in the small rocker she'd brought from Mississippi in the wagon with the rest of their few bits of furniture and Jody's plow-tools. Unbuttoning her bodice let in a grateful bit of cool air as the baby suckled. Before they were done, Jody began to grunt and thrash, the way he did sometimes. Seemed as if a body needed to be twins, when you had so much to do.

She didn't put the children in the little pen their daddy had built in the front yard, when both were fed. She'd heard that cougar, and she was no fool. She kept them in sight all afternoon, though it meant taking off her ladylike sunbonnet and putting on her husband's old straw hat while she finished up in the garden.

Jody was fine, just playing with pine cones and marking in the dust with sticks and watching Coaly, the fiery black horse, pace round and round the lot where he was penned. But Lissa wasn't herself. She whimpered a lot, gave little bubbling cries from time to time. Julie began to feel uneasy about her. Something was amiss, and Jody had always been so healthy that she hadn't learned much about baby sicknesses in dealing with him.

There was a quiver of uneasiness inside her at the thought. With her husband gone and the nearest neighbor twelve miles east, through woods so thick you couldn't see ten feet in any direction, it was scary to contemplate what she'd do if one of the children got really badly sick. She had tackled a lot of hard things since leaving home and her mother. She shook herself, took a deep breath.

Nobody had ever promised her it'd be easy, Jody least of all. In fact, he'd stressed everything he could think of that might have made her change her mind. He'd wanted her to marry him, no doubt of that, but he'd had no intention of taking her off to something that wasn't what she thought it'd be. She couldn't fault him for the fact that there'd been things that neither of them had been able to guess at.

Like the lack of doctors. There wasn't one nearer than Nicholson, twenty-five miles to the west. It was pure luck that had put them as near as they were to Gramma Dooley, though twelve miles was a long way and took a half day to cover, with the road nothing more than a rough track through the woods. On horseback it was quicker, but if she were forced to make it there on her own she'd have to take the buckboard. You just couldn't manage a baby and a three-year-old on horseback. Particularly when the horse was Coaly.

She finished in the garden and took the children inside. It was midafternoon, already hot and steamy, though it was only April. She took the cotton clothing out of the long chest and shook it out, then hung it on the clothesline to air. The heavier woolens they'd worn all winter had already been washed or aired and gone into storage. By the time she finished it was twilight.

When she was fixing Jody's supper, nibbling along as she did it, as she usually did for her own meals, she heard a sound from the sleeping room where she'd put Lissa back into her basket. A choking sound.

Her heart thumping in her throat, Julie ran across the dog-run hall and caught up the baby. The child's face was scarlet, and she was struggling for breath. As she lifted her, Lissa began coughing harshly, wheezing for breath between spasms. A dose of honey and vinegar didn't relieve the baby's coughing. The struggles to breathe made the baby try to cry, and that made everything even worse. The herb tea didn't seem to help at all, nor did goose grease rubbed onto her chest. By full dark, Julie knew that she needed help.

She hitched Coaly by lantern light. Crickets were chittering all around in the grass. Frogs of all sizes were chorusing down at the creek. A screech owl's shivering cry punctuated the rest, making her shiver. But she didn't hear the cougar. That was something she was thankful for.

She put blankets in the wagon bed for Little Jody. He was almost asleep when she laid him on them, and by the time she came back with Lissa in her basket he was sound asleep. The baby was still making those strange barking sounds. She seemed to have a fever, too, though Julie was so hot with haste and work that it was hard to tell.

She hung the lantern on the hook let into the pole at the front of the wagon, led Coaly out into the track that went roughly eastward past their front porch, and climbed into the buckboard.

"Hup! Coaly, giddap!" she said, and the horse snorted, tried to dance sideways between the shafts, then reluctantly moved forward. The night air was so much cooler than the afternoon had been that it felt almost cold to her hands. She tugged the spare quilt she'd brought for Jody about her shoulders and smacked the horse's rump with the end of a rein.

The forest was in darkness . . . deeper than the moonless sky. Leaves shone fitfully as the lantern passed, but the feeble gleam couldn't penetrate far into the dense wood on either side of the track. And the track itself took much of her attention. Coaly's neat hooves could pass easily over ruts and roots that jounced the wagon so hard it endangered its wheels.

Her eyes soon ached with the effort to see ahead, to guide the horse around the worst of the bad spots in the road. She was tired to the bone, too, for her day had been work from beginning to end. But she wasn't sleepy, no matter how her eyes protested or her body ached. She heard every effortful breath her baby drew, flinched at every wheeze or coughing spasm.

The night seemed to pass as slowly as the miles. She had no clock, but the stars moved in a narrow ribbon above the cut where the track ran, and she could tell, when she looked, that the constellations were progressing westward. But so slowly!

She figured that she was somewhere about halfway to her destination when she heard the cry again. Like a woman, screaming. The cougar! Had the beast been following her all that distance? Silently, creeping behind the slow-paced wagon, drawn by the scent of her child?

Coaly was tired now, though she had stopped twice to let him drink at creeks they'd crossed and once to let him rest a bit. But she sat straighter and flicked him with the reins. He snorted with irritation, but he picked up his hooves a bit faster.

Julie felt beneath the rough plank-board seat and found the handle of the bullwhip Jody kept for running the stock out of her garden. Coaly had never in his life felt the weight of that four-ply lash . . . but she knew that the time might well be coming when he would.

Behind them there was another sound . . . not the scream, now, but a rough, coughing growl. As if in answer, the baby went into a fit of coughing that seemed as if it would tear out her tender lungs. She found no relief until Julie reached down, one-handed, and lifted Lissa into her lap. Lying on her stomach, head down, the child gave a last choking wheeze and got a lungful of air.

Having to secure Lissa on her knees added one more burden to Julie's load. Coaly was moving faster, bouncing the wagon over obstacles she hadn't the time to pick out and steer around. Behind her in the wagon bed Jody was whimpering, still half-asleep but disturbed by the rough jolting of the wagon.

"Go back to sleep, baby," she said, over her shoulder. "We'll be there soon."

The little boy reached up to catch a handful of her skirt that hung over the back of the seat-board. "I don't like it, Mama," he said. "Don't like to sleep in the wagon. Don't like goin' in the dark. Less go home. Please?"

"We'll be at Gramma Dooley's in a little while. You like Gramma . . . remember when we went to the revival and she gave you the horehound candy? She'll likely have some more for you. And sugar cookies. You know how you like her cookies!"

The wagon lurched over part of a stump left in the track, and Jody forgot about cookies and began to howl in earnest. As Julie spared a glance back, she thought she saw something in the track. It was too dark to tell what, and it was a long way back, but there was a deeper darkness there. Moving.

"Jody!" she grated, her voice harsher than he had ever heard it. "Shut your mouth! Lie down and roll up in the blanket! And be still. I'm not playing any game! There's a cougar back there, I'm pretty sure. We've got to move fast, and it's going to be mighty rough. Now you do like I tell you!"

When he had rolled into a dark lump, she reached down and lifted the lantern from its hook. Then, holding the baby against her with both knees, keeping the reins in her left hand, she turned, holding the light high, and looked fully backward.

Two reddish sparks glinted with reflected light. Then they blinked once and were gone. So was the shadow, but she knew that the animal had taken to the trees. It could travel as quickly through that tangle as Coaly could along the roadway. There was no way a horse could outrun a cougar while pulling a buckboard, even if it had a good surface to run on. But she had to try to make Coaly do the impossible.

She put the lantern back in its place. One-handed, jouncing and bumping as she worked, she put the baby into the basket on the seat beside her and tied that securely to the braces holding the seat in place. Then she swung the bullwhip in a long arc overhead and cracked its wicked tip just above the black horse's nervous ears.

"Go, Coaly! Whup!"

Coaly went. Faster than she'd have thought he could, burdened as he was. The wagon seemed to leap into the air as it cleared a big bump, and it hit with a tooth-rattling jar. Jody cried out, and she heard him scrambling for a handhold.

Around blind curves, through masses of foliage that had leaned forward into the track the horse flew, and the wagon bounced along behind as best it could. Julie had her feet hooked into the seat-brace beneath her, reins clenched uselessly in her left hand, while her right steadied the basket and the baby.

When the scream sounded again it was entirely too close. Behind the wagon . . . but not by much. She risked a glimpse back, and a shadow was flowing along with the wild shapes cast by the swinging lantern. When the wagon-shade bounced and jumped, that other moved smoothly and steadily. Not ten feet from the tailboard!

Julie was thinking faster than ever before. The creature wanted Lissa. That was what all the folktales suggested . . . unless it wanted Coaly. They liked horsemeat, too. But she felt sure it would prefer something tender . . . and human. What if she could distract it? Throw something out that it could smell baby-scent on?

She took the reins in her teeth and dug into the basket, pulled out a soiled diaper, and flung it over the side of the careening buckboard. Then she cracked the whip again.

But by now Coaly had caught scent of the big cat, and the horse's instinct told him what words could not. The stocky black had leaned his chest into his work and was making his former pace look slow. It was all Julie could do to keep from being flung out into the darkness, and nothing but the basket-straps had kept Lissa from being dislodged from her place. Jody was rolling around in the wagon bed, too frightened to whimper.

They flew along the track for a half-mile before Julie pulled Coaly down a bit . . . enough so that she could risk another look to their rear. The other shadow was gone. For now. She had no illusion that the cat would waste much time on the diaper, once it was sure it was empty.

With the horse under some control, she tore through the woods. And now she was able to see some landmarks that told her she was getting nearer her goal. The immense oak tree that leaned over the track—that was less than three miles from the Dooleys' house. With any luck at all, they just might make it. She cracked the whip again, but not quite so close to Coaly's sensitive ears. He kept moving, but he wasn't bolting now.

"Jody . . . how are you making it, son?" she asked.

"M . . . M . . . Mama . . . there was a great big *something* back there!"

She made her voice matter-of-fact. "Yes. That was the cougar. Remember . . . I told you, just before we went so fast."

"Oh. I didn't know they were so *big*. It was like Aunt Tilly's tomcat, but lots and lots bigger. It was scary, Mama."

"Well, it didn't get us . . . yet. And it won't, I think. I believe I've figured out the combination, Jody. You just get a good grip on the seat-braces, and you watch for it for me. Its eyes will shine in the light that gets back there from the lantern. You sing out if you see it coming after us again."

"Yes'm." His voice sounded as frightened as Julie felt.

The wagon went swaying and jangling and creaking around more bends in the track, and Julie had begun to hope they'd left the beast far behind when Jody's warning came.

"It's there, Mama!" he shouted.

Once more the thing neared the tailboard, its shadow mingling with those of the wagon and its passengers. Again she picked a bit of cloth from the basket and pitched it into the road. And they gained another half-mile or so.

There was the skillet nailed to the ash tree, set there as a marker of the trail by some long-dead explorer of the region. It gleamed rust-red in the lantern light for an instant. Only a mile left to go. And then the wagon hit something with an ominous *c-r-a-a-ck!* The right front wheel went, and the bed pitched forward at an angle.

Even as Julie went over the side, she was trying to see behind . . . to see if the cougar was there again. She was up almost before she hit the ground, rescuing the lantern from its hook, unhooking Coaly from the harness.

"Jody! Climb down, son. That's right . . . come here to me. You're going to ride Coaly, you know that? Do you think you can ride him?"

"But Daddy said he's too uppity for me!"

"Ordinarily, that's true. But this is something out of the ordinary. You're not only going to ride him, you're going to see to Lissa, too. See? I'm tying her basket right here onto his back with the harness straps. You can hook your legs right into here . . . that's right. Whoa, Coaly. Easy, boy." She settled the two children into her makeshift rig of hamestrings and bits of harness, checked it out for security, then stepped back.

"You head right up the track, Jody. You can see where it is by the stars, and Coaly isn't going out into the brush, and he certainly isn't coming back here where the cat is. I'll be right behind you with the lantern. But you make him *run*, you hear me? Kick him with your heels. Slap him with the reins. Go, now!" and she struck the horse sharply with the stock of the whip she had taken from the wreck of the wagon.

As the hoofbeats rattled away up the red-dirt track, she turned where she stood and held the lantern high. No eyes sparked at her . . . yet. She backed slowly up the way, watching sharply. Then she turned and ran as hard as she could for a couple of hundred yards. When she turned again there were red points of light there in the road.

Julie's heart thumped high in her throat. Beads of sweat sprang out along her hairline, as she watched the tawny shape that she saw clearly now for the first time.

The cat was cautious. An adult human being wasn't its usual prey, and the fire in the lantern filled its eyes disturbingly. But its gut growled with hunger. Julie could see the creature weighing its hunger against the unknown threat she might pose.

Before it could make up its mind, she was upon it, the whip swinging down in a wicked arc, the metal tip cracking viciously as it drew blood that showed bright against the tan coat. The cougar crouched, snarling, its ears flat against its head, its eyes glaring. But Julie was past caution. To buy time for her children she was prepared to risk everything. She danced to one side and cracked the whip again. Another trickle of blood gleamed against the creature's neck.

The lantern that she had hung on a stub of branch beside the track gave her enough light for maneuvering, and she struck again as the beast backed away, keeping its head toward her, its eyes focused on her as the pressing danger it knew it faced.

Then a rain of whipstrokes drove the creature backward into the edge of the wood . . . deeper. And then it was gone, a frustrated cough of anger coming back to Julie's ears as the last twitch of brush marked its passage.

Julie listened hard. The only sounds were treefrogs, a whip-poor-will in the distance, a hoot owl somewhere nearby, and the many small noises of a wood at night. There was no scream to be heard, nor any other sound that might mark the hunt of a big cat.

She turned in her track, the lash of the whip marking the red dust of the road. She took the lantern from the stub.

Now she could hear sounds from the road ahead. Men's voices, calling . . . but she was suddenly too exhausted to make a sound. The children were safe . . . that was all that mattered. If they hadn't reached Dooleys', nobody would be calling in the forest in the early morning hours.

Letting the lantern dangle wearily from her hand, dragging the whip, she started up the trail toward the east. The early morning constellations hung above the cut. A mockingbird was tuning up his song in the woods.

Jaspar Lemon's Ba Cab Ya Larry

BY LEE SCHULTZ

*Lee Schultz is a professor of English (one of the good ones), a horse
fanatic and a writer. His poetry and stories have appeared in a number of
literary magazines and journals. Though the following poem is in a different
style and mode than the poetry of the late Omar Barker, I think he would
have enjoyed it.*

> *where seldom is heard*
> *a discouraging word . . .*
> Traditional

The worn and wrinkled slate-haired woman
slid the story into their saddlebags
just before the posse left for the hills:

That morning Jas had fed the roaring deep-hole stove
the family Bible, chapter by chapter, book by book.
Chipper as December northers slowed his eighty years
he rustled the dally-rigged saddle
from the rec room,
whistled the double-decade roan
up from the mesquites,
"wrapped a round of cheese and some sugar-cured
into that holy slicker the cat's been beddin' on,
poured a quart o' pure dandelion
in the banged-up canteen he hangs in the hall
'n' took that bottle-kneed brute over the ridge
into Aztec Canyon."

The crow's-feet squeezed the hazel eyes
to thoughts behind such loathful times.

"He said somethin' to Baxter's kid
before the big boy helped him saddle."

While Jaspar's weary wife awaits the words—
the only ones her leathered companion
has brought to life these last three weeks—
Baxter blows his smoke rings over corncob,
shoos his sulking two-hundred-pound towhead
toward the importance of the horsebackers.
"Tell 'em, Jim Bob, 'bout ba cab ya larry."

The bronze-faced boy, he turns to face the sun
that melts the head of horseback deputy
while the overweight buckskin stirs cold clouds
of caliche with newly nailed forefoot.

The boy, he reckons, long remembers
of Jaspar Lemon's ways;
nineteen years he's known the ranchman's life
that links the cows and horses, dust and time
to growing dreams and fading cowboy's trails—
the dreams, the boy's, the trails of aging Jaspar Lemon.
"Jas said that words don't work no more.
He's lost his damn vocabulary."

They listened long, again . . . again . . .
The boy returned to feeding hogs
or other chores so seldom done by ranchmen.
He knew the high hill pass where Jas had gone.

Six miles were all the aging pair had made that day.
They found him where the roan had slipped from rocks
and failed to gather for his spring across the draw.
The roan lived on, his limp and all, for nine more years.
Could be—they never proved it so—a diamondback
had brought things to an end the older faster way
where horses rear and riders fall to desert deaths.

His lips squeezed tight on shattered tooth and tongue,
a boulder's touch had gathered him for dreams.
The rocks were harder than the words he'd lost.

Stoned on Yellow

BY LOLO WESTRICH

The following story blends the modern West with the mystical with great skill and finesse. When I first conceived of this anthology, it was exactly the sort of story I had in mind.

This is the first fiction I've read by LoLo Westrich, but it certainly won't be the last. Her byline is one I'll watch for henceforth. She has a special touch.

Westrich lives and works in Santa Rosa, California, and is both a writer and illustrator. Her writing has appeared in numerous magazines, among them the now defunct Western pulps Farm Wife News, The Redwood Rancher, The Christian Science Monitor *and* Country Gentleman. *Her illustrations have appeared in such periodicals as* The National Humane Review *and* Modern People.

I had just walked onto a street called La Roca, in the little California town of Spanish Needle, when I saw a red-tailed hawk perched on a high snag overlooking a sandy vacant lot where desert holly grew in wild profusion. That creature seemed to me to be as stamped upon the face of the wide beige sky as an eagle on a quarter—stamped and fixed forever, along with all it scanned with its hungry eye.

I pictured myself as brother to the rodents who would hide from that eye. A dissimilar brother, to be sure—prime specimen of the species Homo sapiens—but brother nonetheless and ferreted away in a hole that would secrete me forever not only from the hawk, but from the adobe house and the woman behind its door.

Not that it made any sense to stall off an inevitable encounter—especially one that could get me back home to New York and fatten my wallet so roundly. But such was my fancy even so—a hawk on a coin I could not flip.

In the world of fact I walked on down La Roca Street inwardly murmuring, "C'mon, Thornton, get moving!" but dragging my feet.

The adobe house, when at last I stood before it, seemed as uncomplicated as burrobrush, creosote, or the afternoon siesta. The walls were sun-baked as summer mud pies. And the big clay pots that flanked a yellow door on either side looked like great-bellied old men who'd fallen off to sleep. I could almost hear them snoring.

Still, I couldn't bring myself to knock immediately. I had first to call to mind Radley's catechizing on what he called "picking the human brain," then rehearse the borrowed spiel on how just a few more sales of certain magazine subscriptions could win for me none other than—by God!—a college education. Considering that even my barber knows my degrees, the latter marked an irony I found hard to stomach.

When at last I did knock, my rap was answered almost immediately with a cry that began like that of a hungry infant, continued like the yipping of a number of terriers, but drifted enigmatically at last into a clear, single wail, at once chilling and melancholy.

This was the only time in my life I ever experienced the phenomenon known as colored hearing, common, I've read, to mystics as well as to habitual hallucinatory drug users, of which, notably, I am neither. I didn't just hear the infant-terrier emission; it was as if I saw it too—as pure yellow velvet stretched across a sort of wire-frame tube that moved like an endless caterpillar through the air about me and somehow through me, through my chest.

Even before this experience, which I chalked up to the effects of the heat, the day had been one I would have described as yellow. In point of fact, I already had. I'd composed a descriptive paragraph in my mind, as was my wont on these days of dedication to one cause only. "The cotton-wood trees," it went, "had shed yellow leaves that lay now in circles around their trunks, so that it was as if, instead of affording shade, those branches marked the only place where the sun came shining through. The world then was all awry. Only open space gave shade."

At precisely the moment that the sound of the keening died away, the door opened and there stood before me a woman whose hair was as rumpled as the work shirt she wore, on which—oh yes!—a garden of embroidered sunflowers grew all down its front, just next to its buttons, yellow as butter. Her face was rumpled too, wrinkled, bagged, weathered, parched, the irreparable face of a desert woman aging before her time.

"Ah, you've been startled," she said, with the air of one adept at reading faces. And she spoke placatingly, as one might speak to a troubled child—with that same kind of undue familiarity. For a moment I thought she might reach forward and pat me on the shoulder.

I nodded dumbly.

"It happens all the time," she said good-humoredly, raising her arms from her sides and letting them drop again. "I'm sorry. You see, I have this pet coyote who thinks he's a watchdog. He thinks—"

"A coyote!" I cried. And at once I was in awe of myself—that my feigned surprise should ring so genuine.

In truth I knew the howl's origin before she told me. And, in the light of what I'd seen on a motel TV the night before, I might have guessed if I hadn't known. According to the newscaster, sales of the best-selling book, J. C. Day's *Ah Lonesome,* a tear-jerking tale of a poor old bony coyote, were still rising, and the nation was afflicted with a rash of coyote-inspired gim-crack ranging from stuffed coyotes for toddlers to mail-order chrome-plated coyote hood ornaments. It was predictable, really, that the popular predator should begin to be kept as a household pet.

"Boy oh boy, ma'm," I said with guile, "if you'd let me—I mean if you wouldn't think it out of place for me to ask—it sure would be a treat for me if I could have a look at a coyote."

"Well, I can't really think of any reason why I shouldn't let you," she said. But she frowned critically over her own words; she had the air of someone accustomed to arguing with herself, "except I suppose you really ought to say who you are and why you're here."

"Oh yeah, sure," I hastened, "sorry about that, ma'm. You see, this company I work for—we're having this contest, highly competitive, you understand, and it sure would be a help to me if you'd vote for me. I only need six more points, and then, you see—"

"Oh no!" she cried, casting eyes and arms heavenward in exaggerated woe. "Don't tell me! Let me guess! If I'll only subscribe to some of the magazines you're selling—which I can naturally get from you much cheaper than I can anywere else—why, then you have a chance to win a scholarship to college. Is that it? Am I right?"

"Well . . ." I said, putting on my sheepish face, glancing down at the sand-dulled shine on my shoes.

"If you people could only come to the door and tell it like it is, explain that you're selling magazines, that you . . ."

"I have to do what I have to do, ma'm. It's a job."

"Well, it's a shame," she said. "And you know, you don't really look the part either. You look so honest, and—well—frankly a bit older than most of the young fellows I've seen with this sort of job."

"Pardon me, ma'm, but if you don't mind me saying it, there's no age limit on needing money."

"Yes, I guess that's so," she said ruefully.

"Would you like to see a list of the magazines I'm selling?" I asked, looking down at the packet of subscription blanks and forms I clutched in my sweating hands. "I mean, since you've already brought it up yourself and all."

"Okay, okay," she said, smiling suddenly, the palms of her hands turned outward and patting the air, "but you might as well come on back to the patio first and have that look at Lonesome."

"Hey now, that's really something—you naming him after the coyote in the book!"

She didn't answer but gazed at me squarely with an expression I couldn't read. Quizzical? Guarded? I gulped. She turned then and led me through the house, and I was so caught up in analysis of her back (which appeared younger by far than her face) and my own behavior, that the decor and floor plan escaped me completely. I was left only with a vague impression of cool tile and potted cacti.

It was only after I was standing on the patio looking down upon the coyote that I began taking mental notes again, and then I was so totally enthralled by that animal as he played about our feet—while she chattered on about how she got him from a trapper, nursed him from a bottle, tamed him like a dog—that the only observations I made were of him. Nothing else about the patio lingers in my mind.

Even in the coyote's case, however, where my mental notes were copious, I don't fall back on them now to describe how I saw him, but rather borrow J. C. Day's words straight from Chapter 6 of *Lonesome*. They speak for me quite well.

I saw that his eyes were a yellowish beige, the color of sand, [it reads]. "So too was all the rest of him, or at least the overall effect of him, for I could see when I studied him closely that fur of the softest tan overlay fur of a more or less rusty hue, and that in the places where the wind had rumpled the pale hair, the rustier parts shone through in specks that by contrast, seemed orange as tangerines. On his body his coat was thick and heavy, lending a plump look to his midsection, but his legs were slender and called to mind a blown-glass figurine—delicate, elegant, the work of a master glassblower.*

In some ways—like in the way he wagged his big plume of a tail —he seemed much like a domestic dog. But in other ways he was completely undoglike; he was a wild creature or a blown-glass figu-

rine; he was an old hungry-looking ventriloquist with blown-glass muzzle pointed toward the sky.

And when he howled, I was so close I not only heard the howl but saw it too. He seemed to brace his front paws against the patio where he stood, and he threw his head back until his nose pointed, not at the sky before him, not even at the sky above him, but at the sky behind him! "MaaaaAhhhhAhhhh," he howled, and his lower jaw vibrated like the strings of a harp.

When he was done my ears and chest were full of his cry. He looked straight in my direction, as if he'd known all along who I was.

Exactly! And I didn't mind. I thought, that's okay. That's as it should be. Let all know me, as I know all. I was like Aldous Huxley eyeing the creases of his trousers after taking mescaline and opening up to everything—only in my case no creases—except those on the woman's face. And it didn't matter. Or it did matter.

At any rate, everything was perfectly all right. I saw myself at least momentarily as a most honest man. After all, I asked myself, where have I lied? Where have I stooped so low? Isn't all fair in love and business? And am I not doing this well—carrying it all off as coolly as if I were not stoned from yellowness?

"Now, how about the magazines?" I asked, blinking my eyes and turning to face J. C. Day.

She smiled at me warmly. She's seen how enthralled I am with her animal, I thought joyously, watching with wonder the pocketing and creasing of that sand-colored face.

"I've been thinking," she said, tapping the fingers of one hand against lips creased with whistle marks, "I have a grandson—he's a teenager now—a little sport if there ever was one. I'm thinking he might enjoy a subscription to *National Ball Player.*"

"I'm sure he would, ma'm," I said, reaching for pen and appropriate subscription blank. "I'll just put you down for that right now. You can't go wrong there. And now how about you? You need something too, don't you? I mean, every lady's got a right to some time for sitting back, taking it easy, feet propped up and all, reading her favorite magazine."

"By all means," she said, and she chuckled. Did she find me disarming that she chuckled so? I chuckled too. I grew quite giddy. I thought that it would be nice to give myself something to laugh about later—and Radley too. My God, how he'd guffaw!

"How about a subscription to *See*, ma'm? You sure couldn't do better than that."

"I couldn't do worse!" she cried with a shudder.

"Honest? You mean that? Now I'll have to say that's something I never heard before. Not ever! All I've ever heard is good reports like, you know, how *See* always gets the scoop on what's going on in the world, how—"

"Oh, it gets the scoop all right!" she said with vehemence, closing her eyes. "It goes to *any* lengths to get its scoops."

"Well, what's wrong with that, ma'm?" I asked, putting on a mask of innocence. "Isn't that the way it's supposed to be with a news magazine?"

"Oh, forget it!" she said, throwing up her arms, tapping her foot, turning her back.

"I don't understand," I said.

"Then I'll tell you," she cried suddenly, spinning about to face me again. "Why not? You're just a salesman passing through, for heaven's sake! I couldn't find a more likely listener, could I? And who knows? I just might feel better if I talk to someone."

"I'm all ears, ma'm."

"Well, the thing is, I'm a writer, you see—and—"

"A writer?" I cried, letting my jaw hang lax, my eyes widen.

"Yes—yes, and a successful one, by God!"

"Hey, you wrote *Lonesome!*" I cried suddenly, pointing a finger in her direction in a gesture meant to convey detection, discovery, surprise. "I bet you did. Yeah, you wrote *Lonesome*, and you've got a coyote of your own, and . . . well, I'll be doggone now, how about that?"

"I worked hard to get where I am," she said, her face livid in the wake of my exclamations. "I'm proud—but I'm proud before myself, if you understand what I mean. I detest publicity; it's purdah I prefer. Anyway, I've made it my practice not to talk about my writing to anyone but other writers; they're the only ones who understand."

"I know," I said, nodding.

"But privacy doesn't come easy after you write a best-seller; I'll tell you that. You need a fort and a moat."

"It's that bad?"

"Let me tell you how bad it is!" she cried. And she told me. She sat me down upon a bench that, woefully, I cannot describe. She sat herself down beside me and told me, in a tone of the utmost confidence, how the editor of *See* had the temerity to send some goofy young writer to plague her for an interview. It was ironic, really, she said, for she used to write for *See* herself, and although she'd never met the editor in person, she'd assumed that after all her dealings with him, he was her friend. But now this dreadful young man he'd hired had put an end to her assumption, calling her so often she'd had her phone number changed, sending her letters and telegrams begging for an interview, staking photographers all up and down La Roca Street. Because of him, *See* now had shots of the exterior of her beloved adobe house plastered from cover to cover. A cheap display at best. This was *her* place, she avowed, *her* private property; they had no right!

And she continued in the same confidential tone that left me feeling at once guilty and giddy, leaning so close to me I could smell the clean soapy scent of her suntanned skin. And so it went right up until the moment that she and Lonesome ushered me through the patio gate and walked me out in front of the house that *See* had desecrated, where the cottonwood leaves still shone at the foot of trees in mimicry of shade.

She's made of me her friend, I told myself—because I love her yellow coyote. In all sincerity I love her yellow coyote, and that cancels out my trickery, cloaks all my guile, and makes it all quite beautiful.

"Well, so long now," she said, her voice airy as a girl's. "Thanks for being such a good listener. I think you're just what I needed."

"Glad to oblige," I said, taking the hand she extended and wringing it, pumping it, feeling like patting it, reluctant to let it go. At that moment it was as if she were a girl instead of a crinkle-faced woman, a girl as young and lovely, in fact, as her back looked and her voice sounded. It was as if I had been courting her, a patient suitor, ardent but unhurried, in her sagey patio where the ventriloquistic coyote had served only as a door to conversation that would suit us until we moved on to other ways of touching.

"Thanks yourself," I murmured. "It's been fun seeing Lonesome and all . . ."

I rearranged the subscription blanks under my arm and walked away. When I reached the curb I turned back. I wanted to see her again. The courtship feeling still lingered; there hadn't been time enough to shake it off. But I found both woman and coyote almost indiscernible in the yellow blur of blinding sun.

It was then she called to me. "Oh, by the way," as if she'd had an afterthought, "tell that boss of yours I said hello."

"Boss?" I could feel my eyebrows lifting upward as if by their own accord, causing the whole of my scalp to crawl and prickle. *"My* boss?"

"Yes! *Your* boss—good old Gus Radley, you know the one. I'm telling you to give him my regards."

From her place in the yellow blur she began to laugh uproariously—as I had planned to laugh with Radley. I squinted my eyes until I'd filtered out the glare and blur and could see her face quite clearly, how it took a new form, how it rearranged itself even as I watched it, like a design in a kaleidoscope, and how once the changeling processes were done with, the new face was etched on the day like a work in intaglio. I gasped and ran stumbling from the boundaries of her yard.

For a while I tried to fool myself. It was the sun playing tricks with my eyes, I told myself. Or it was the shock of such blatant perfidy. That, together with the desert heat, had me pixilated. And when the fooling wouldn't work, I diverted myself with questions. God knows they were disconcerting enough!

When had she found me out? I asked myself all the way to the bar. At what juncture? Due to which blunder? Was it when I mentioned *See* so soon after she said she'd subscribe to a magazine for her grandson? Was it when I answered "I know" to her statement that no one understands a writer but another writer? Was that the giveaway? Or could it be that she had known all along and played cat and mouse with me as I had with her?

The latter I discounted quickly. For after all, she'd given me her time, hadn't she? Surely I'd had her fooled for a while or I couldn't have gained entry, could I? Hadn't she leaned so close to me that the scent of her soapy skin still clung in my nostrils, so close I could see the outline of her nipples like small button mushrooms beneath her wrinkled shirt? Hadn't she confided in me, told me things she'd told to no one else?

How many drinks had I downed when words of Radley's began to move through my mind like words on ticker tape? How many drinks from the pale, unsunned hands of a bartender who pulled at his bar towel as if it were taffy—in an ugly little bar, far too brightly lit? Four? Five?

At any rate, I fancied ticker tape falling out my ears and down onto the floor to curl at the foot of my barstool, pretty as confetti, and it read: "Now this time I want a story, Thornton. Her house, how she lives, the rooms where she writes. Remember we've got a pack of photos of the outside; it's the inside I want. An inside story in every sense of the word. Describe everything you can lay your hands on. Furnishings, wall hangings, whatever. How she keeps house, all the little details of her daily living. And check for signs of a man around the house. People want to know about her love life. I warn you now, Thornton, don't come back and throw me a crock of bullshit everyone knows already—like the kooky way she dresses or how she loves her goddamm coyote!"

"Or how pissed she is at *See*, huh?" I murmured drunkenly. For it struck me then that this was all I really knew about J. C. Day that hadn't been told before. Except, of course, what had happened to her face, how it had loomed up out of the blur of blinding sunlight, the face of a wrinkled woman melting grotesquely, unmistakably, into the face of a hawk whose eyes were hard yellow marble and hungry. And Radley wouldn't buy that.

Making Money in Western Banking

BY JEFF BANKS

Jeff Banks grew up loving Westerns, and the bloom is still on the romance. He picked up a lot of Western lore from a granduncle "who had met many of the Western gunfighters (he didn't call them shootists), the most notable being Pat Garrett." His favorite Western hero is still the Lone Ranger, the radio version. He is the author of Railroaded, *written under the name Rufe Jefferson and printed by Leisure Books in 1981. His biggest ambition right now is to sell enough Westerns to qualify for active membership in WWA. Nice goal.*

The following O'Henryish story points up Jeff's strengths. Conciseness. Cleverness. A sense of humor.

Enjoy.

Wes Gurton was no master of timely decisions, but maybe his luck was about to change. He had delayed carving the popular "G.T.T." in the door of his farm shack until the Crawford County sheriff was breathing down his neck, then felt like the fugitive he was his first few years in Texas. It took another failure at hardscrabble farming in the red-dirt country near Lufkin to send him farther west, where he learned to handle the feisty cattle with the long horns that had made his adopted state famous.

He would always carry the scars of the hard, slow learning to be a cowboy. Seemed he always learned hard and too slow, up to now. Why, he hadn't gone north with a trail herd until that way of life was dying. Wound up stranded in Abilene, his pay squandered and no job and no prospects. Foundered (like a cow critter with a bellyfull of bad greens), Billy Bob had called it.

They might still have been there, or in Dodge or some other dying terminus of a dying trade, in jail or the county workhouse, had not Billy Bob struck up a friendship with the right bunch of played-out cowpokes.

Crow Martin had known just what to do. Take their living from these furriners up here that had shut it off, what with their quarantines and tolls and fees.

Take it right out of their banks.

Stealing from thieves was the way the whole bunch saw it.

Wes had gone along, not knowing anything else he might do at that point. Only he had the good sense to see from the first that bank robbing was no way to live out his life—not for anybody that wanted a long one.

He saved his split, anyway most of it, right from day one. While Handsome Harry womanized, Crow drank and Billy Bob and the rest gambled. With each other whenever they couldn't find a game in a town where they weren't known yet.

So it had gone for almost a year as they worked the little towns (safer that way, less law to look out for) across Kansas, with side trips into Missouri once and Nebraska twice. More than a dozen banks, and now the names of all of them and bad line-drawing likenesses of most were likely posted in any town they would come to.

Wes had decided, and announced last night, he had had enough. More than one man in these troubled times had made his stake with a gun and then settled down respectable. He kept those thoughts to himself. It was enough to tell Crow and the boys he was through riding with them. Would have been foolhardy to tell them about what he had laid by.

His $4,000—and yes! he had almost that much—would buy him a new start back in Georgia. They knew he had saved, but to a man would have underguessed the amount. Most, he guessed, didn't even have a clear idea of how much gold had slipped (easy come, easy go) through their hands while they had been desperadoes.

They had drunk to him and wished him well, and then settled down to a low-stakes card game. Uncharacteristically, he'd sat in. "For old times' sakes," he said, but with careful reservations about the amount he would lose before dropping out. He meant to plead the long ride ahead of him if anybody objected.

Instead, he won. The rest had jeered about beginner's luck, and he had kept the jeering friendly by taking care not to win too much when he saw how strong his luck was running. He took that as a good omen.

Come morning he did up his little bit of packing, mainly moving gold-hardened saddlebags from under his head to the back of his pony. "Reckoned you'd light out early," Billy Bob told him with his infectious grin as he rolled out of his own sugans.

Wes answered with something more pointless than it sounded about the early bird. Then listened patiently to his old pard's sad-luck story.

"Yep. I could see you was big loser last night." He reached for the pocket with his poker winnings. The loan he thought he was about to be asked for would be more of a gift, but his savings would more than do for him in his new life.

"No. No, Wes!" Billy Bob was offended. "I don' want no handout."

"Then . . . ?" It was unnecessary to complete the question: why tell me your sad story?

The answer was all about the next bank Crow had marked down for the gang's attention. And that, with two of the boys shot up, they just wouldn't have enough men to handle the job.

Crow himself, nor either of the walking wounded, could have persuaded him to go along. He was getting out while the getting was good. He had a feeling it was time to quit. More importantly, he had saved the amount self-set as a goal when the idea of mending his ways had first taken shape.

But *dammit*, this was Billy Bob.

And the bank was "flourishin', flourishin'!"

If Crow was right about its ripeness, there could be maybe a thousand dollars for every man that rode into town.

Wisdom, Kansas, was east of where they had camped. The planned escape route was easterly too. It was right on his way home.

Didn't $5,000 have a better ring to it than $4,000?

Well then, one more venture in Western banking before heading back East.

George W.—not for Washington, but he had never told anyone that and never meant to—Mitas was an old hand at making money in Western banking. A second-generation Greek-American, he had been successful enough to stop resenting the humor that led people to call him "Midas" since years back. After coming West, George really did seem to have a golden touch.

His little bank here in Wisdom had grown up with the town. Faster than the town, in fact.

He had reached the point of seriously planning to branch out into other towns. Already he had heavy deposits in some of them. The only thing he was waiting for was finding somebody both shrewd and honest enough to trust with managing the Wisdom bank while he took his own shrewdness to work elsewhere.

Sadly, he had not found the man. He was still having to watch the every move of his two tellers himself. Was looking over their shoulders when the cowboy-dressed strangers appeared across the counter just at closing time.

They answered the polite "What can the bank do for you?" by pointing handguns.

No chance telling them he was only the manager, that he couldn't open the safe, or any other money-saving lie. The dark and deadly circles of those mouths to tunnels leading straight to Hell had a way of bringing out the truth.

Moments later the bandits were outside getting mounted for a fast get-away. George fired the first shot at them himself.

The banker's bullet swept the hat from Crow's head as he was about to vault into the saddle. It also burned across his horse's back and set the animal to pitching. That caused Wes and Harry to return the fire, fanning the hammers of their colts while Billy Bob helped the boss fight that wild pony.

If the tellers had thought to join old Mitas' shooting party, they changed their minds right straight, and hunkered down out of sight (and harm's way) during the next critical two minutes while the Martin gang fled. Which is not to say they went unmolested.

Wisdom was no Northfield, and there had been no advance warning of the raid. Still the natives were at least as fierce as they were wise. They drove a hailstorm of hot lead across the bandits' route out of town.

Fearing just that reaction, Wes emptied his spare six-gun behind him, then lifted the heavy saddlebags from the horse's rump and swung them from his own neck before lying almost flat along the horse's neck as he spurred for speed.

He heard the thunder of guns from behind, the hissing whistle of shots that missed and the more scary *crack* of several nearer misses. Two slugs *thunked* into his friends' mounts but none of them were hit solidly enough to bring them down. Once as he looked back, he heard and felt one *spang* into a saddlebag.

Not only did the gold save his life then. As he was carrying coin, not dust, there was no danger of it leaking out through the bullet hole.

They all felt rather than heard the pounding of the hooves that were carrying them toward safety. There was just too much noise and confusion.

It was always like that. Another good reason he was glad this would be his last bank.

Past the last houses was the dangerous illusion of safety. The road's sharp turn shielded them momentarily from the withering fire. But an instant posse was forming to give chase. The gang had been at this work plenty long enough to be sure of that.

"Anybody hit?" Crow's question dimly penetrated their ringing ears. He was still being boss.

They chorused their "no!" and pounded on. It was two or three miles to where the wounded men waited with spare horses.

The town marshal and several others came in hot pursuit. Mitas led an even bigger force in another direction. Here the Wisdom-dwellers' supposed quality came into play. Or maybe it was just a knowledge of the local terrain.

A creekbed circled the town from its western limit, then led east far straighter than the meandering road. Mitas and his group took the shortcut.

Just as the marshal's men were falling back and the bandits were remounting, this second force from town caught up with them. They had the further advantage of surprise and laid down as withering a fire as that which had ushered the robbers out of town only moments before.

There was the same confusion of sight and sound, the same desperation. Wes felt one bullet tug at his hatbrim, another came so near his ear that he actually flinched for the first time since becoming a bandit. Whether it was that shot or another that cut the saddlebags loose from him, he was never to know.

Somehow they all got away to live to rob another day. It was a while after realizing they were safe that Wes noticed his savings were gone.

Even as Mitas was thanking his lucky stars that little of his own money was kept in his bank, the marshal rode up to hand him the severed saddlebags. "Here's the loot, sir. Er anyways some of it."

The banker waited to count the money after sending both posses over to the saloon for drinks on him. That was when he got an even bigger surprise, and one that his shrewdness prevented his ever telling anyone else about. The bandits had taken something very near to $3,000 from the bank. What had been recovered was closer to $4,000.

Whoever heard of a bank making a profit on being robbed? Nobody was ever going to hear it from him. Greeks know better than to look gift horses in the mouth.

Cutliffe Starkvogel and the Bears Who Liked TV

BY JOHN KEEFAUVER

John Keefauver is a highly original author of wacky stories. Fantasy. Horror. Mystery. Mainstream. You name it, he can write it. He's one of those rare things—a professional short-story writer, a species that is rapidly going the route of the passenger pigeon and the dodo.

Keefauver is perhaps the only author I know (maybe Philip Jose Farmer or Neal Barrett) who could mix an old rancher who sings to bears, television, a mysterious elixir, as well as a number of other unlikely elements and make them jell. A mad jell, mind you, but a jell, nonetheless.

Keefauver lives and works in Carmel, California. His work has appeared in many prestigious markets, among them Omni, Playboy, Alfred Hitchcock Presents *(several volumes in this series),* Cold Sweat: New Masters of Horror, National Review *(satire and humor),* The Sewanee Review, Texas Quarterly, Twilight Zone; *the list goes on into infinity.*

I didn't think it was out of the ordinary when Cutliffe told me that black bears had taken to watching television through his ranch-house window. After all, he was a bear lover as well as an all-around rancher (retired), outdoorsman, and free-lance carrot-cake consultant—and a bit odd generally, anyway. Like his idea, for example, that there were ony fifty-nine people left living in the world, and saying it without a bit of a smile.

He didn't smile, either, when he told me about the bears looking at TV through his window. They were very particular black bears, it seemed; he could get only two channels, and if they didn't like either program they'd rip shingles off the top of his place. Not that he was worried about his ranch house. What worried him was that the TV habit would ruin the bears' social structure.

"It purely ain't normal for a fine, clean-living California bear to stay up all hours watching the 'Late, Late Show,' " he told me not long after somebody gave him a television set. "Next thing you know, them bears will be riding a horse, wearing a vest, driving a pickup to town, and honky-tonking on Saturday night and bowling Monday."

Then he gave me a fierce scowl.

"Why, already there just ain't no satisfying them. They don't like 'Beverly Hillbillies,' 'Star Trek,' or 'Tic Tac Dough.' Ain't much left except 'Bear World,' which, of course, we all enjoy."

" 'Bear World'? I've never heard of that one."

"If you like bears the way I think you do, you will."

Cutliffe and I lived way back in Carmel Valley, a good hour's drive or more inland through fine ranchland from the Monterey Peninsula. His place was farther in than mine, and although I wasn't required by the post office to deliver him his mail all the way up to his ranch house, I took it to him rather than put it in a mailbox at the entrance to his property because I liked the old codger. I had to walk the last few hundred yards to his house; that will show you how he'd let the road (and about everything else) go to seed; seems like he was more interested in bears than what was left of his cattle, sheep, and horses. But he hardly ever got any mail until he started getting the weekly packages from Hair Growers, Inc., which surprised me, because even if he was bald, he wasn't the sort to worry about it, especially at his age.

"Cutliffe," I said, handing him that first package, "don't tell me you're trying to grow something on that lunar rock of yours."

He never answered me. He just stood there looking down at the package, his old leathery face wrinkled up in pure joy, acorn eyes shining. "Well, what do you know, it's finally come."

"You been waiting long?"

"All my life."

"All your life? When did you order it?"

"I never ordered it. It just came by itself."

"You mean this is junk mail?"

"Junk! The fifty-nine people left say it ain't junk, and I'm one of 'em."

And that's all he would say about that, except to add that I could sure use some of the stuff myself, which is true, since I'm as bald as he is even if I'm younger—and generally more presentable, too, I might say. Cutliffe ain't one to dress up for nobody. Only thing he ever wore were old overalls, and they were always too big for his skin, bones, and orneriness.

It was plain he wanted to get in his house with his hair grower, by himself, so I left—wanted to get inside so bad that he didn't even mention bears while I was there, which was unusual for him. Bears are his favorite subject. He talks to them, which isn't unusual if you get back in the valley far enough. Not that he talks to them much. "You got to realize," he told me once, "that there ain't one bear in ten that's really got a helluva lot to say."

I've always agreed with him on that. Not that I've ever talked to bears— or sung to them. Cutliffe tried once. I came up to his place, and there he was on one of his horses singing away as if he thought he was an old Gene Autry. Oh, it was horrible! He told me he was singing to the bears.

"What bears?" I asked him.

"Those behind that clump of bushes yonder."

I didn't see any bears, and I told him so.

"You will," he said. "You will."

He quit the singing, thank God, after a few tries. He told me it was driving them away when his whole idea was to get them to come closer and sing along with him.

Me, now, I haven't even talked to 'em, like I say. I haven't lived around them enough, I guess, like Cutliffe and some of the others back in the valley have. I've got me a little spread (I used to cowpoke until I got thrown and broke a hip and had to do some other kind of work, like deliver mail), but I've never seen bears on my place. Cutliffe says I'll be seeing 'em and talking to 'em in time because I'm basically a bear lover, too—and he's right about that—and that's what it takes, according to him. Maybe that's what he really means when he says there're only fifty-nine people left living in the world. They're all bear lovers and they're the only ones who count. After all, he sees more than fifty-nine in one week of watching TV, even if he can't get more than two channels. That's two more than I can get. I don't own a set.

So, even with the extra work they cost him nailing shingles back on his ranch house, Cutliffe, being a bear lover, was awful worried about their TV habits—except for their watching "Bear World," which he thought was healthy.

Anyway, old Cutliffe Starkvogel and I were friends, and so I was a bit put out when he wouldn't even open the door when I made a special trip in my pickup to deliver him his second package from Hair Growers a week later, on a Friday. He just yelled from inside, "Leave it by the door, I'm busy." He didn't sound busy; he sounded impatient for me to leave so that he could get the stuff.

The same thing happened the following Friday. He wanted me to leave it outside. "Are you all right, Cutliffe?"

"Sure I'm all right, damn it! I've always been all right, and I always will!"

The fourth Friday, when he yelled from inside for me to put the package by the door, I asked him how his hair was coming along.

"Fine."

"Well, aren't you gonna give me a look?"

"Not until it's finished. Nobody sees it until it's finished. I don't want to be the laughing stock of the neighborhood."

Which wasn't like Cutliffe at all. Like I say, ordinarily he didn't give a good damn how he looked to anybody, hair or no hair, clothes or no clothes.

The next Friday I admit I walked up to his house quieter than usual and stood real close to his door for a moment before I knocked. I heard him talking to somebody. Or at least somebody was talking, or it might have been his TV going. I couldn't hear what was being said, anyway, and I couldn't hear anybody answering. That wasn't like Cutliffe either, because about the only time he ever had a visitor was when somebody came to consult him about the mysteries of carrot cake, which his wife had taught him. Mercifully, she died, and he lives by himself, like me. Anyway, if somebody was in there, he had lost me as a friend, that was for sure, after not letting me see him for weeks.

When I called out to him, I got the usual impatient answer, and I left in a huff.

The following week I tried hiding behind some bushes close to his house after I'd left the package at his door. I wanted at least to see him when he opened it to get the box, to see if he looked okay. He *sounded* all right, God knows, what with his always bellowing at me to leave the hair grower outside.

I had no sooner got behind the bushes than he bawled from inside the house, "I see you behind them bushes, Ned Sturny! Get out of here before I fill you full of shot!"

"Damn it, Cutliffe, this ain't no way to treat a friend!"

"Friends don't squat behind a man's bushes, spying on him!"

"Damn it, Cutliffe, I'm not gonna bring you any more hair grower! From now on I'm gonna put it in your mailbox!"

"Don't make a damn to me. I've got enough now anyway."

"You mean you finished with growing your hair?"

"I will be, when I've used up this boxful."

"You're gonna come outside your house and act normal then?"

"Not for a while. I like it in here mighty fine. Gets me away from people."

"People! What people?"

"Somebody's always coming around here every three or four months, you know that."

I fumed all week. Him treating me like that, me a friend for years. Next to him, I was the longest-living man in the valley since my friend Hiram Walker went away last year. I got so riled up at Cutliffe that that Friday just the sight of another one of his damn hair-growing packages made me lose all control. I threw the damn thing down on the post office floor hard as I could.

Well, a glass bottle inside broke—one of seven bottles in the package, as it turned out. Soon as I had seen what I'd done, I got control of myself, got a rag, and began to wipe up the mess. It was a clear liquid, and, God, did it stink. Smelled like it would grow warts on a horseshoe. Just for the hell of it I wiped my fingers, wet from the stuff, on my bald head. If it would grow hair on Cutliffe's noggin, it ought to grow trees on mine.

The labels on the bottles weren't like any I'd ever seen. Only thing they said was that the stuff was made by Hair Growers, Inc.—that was all. Just "Made by Hair Growers, Inc." And there was no mention of what was in the stuff or how much there was of it or if it had been patented, or any other thing that labels usually have on them.

I didn't take Cutliffe the six bottles on my regular run that Friday. I made a special trip, at night, walking very quietly.

As I crept into his yard, his house was dark except for the light made by his TV. I shushed a dog but one of his horses neighed. I froze. But no light went on and Cutliffe didn't come to the door. Then I knew why. As I got closer to the ranch house, I could hear the set and hear Cutliffe laughing. Now I wasn't about to knock on his door this time and go through all his yelling again. I headed for a window, the one that he'd told me the bears used when they were watching his TV. If there were any bears there tonight watching, they'd have to go find another window. But as I got close I could see that there weren't any there. Must not have been anything on they liked.

Well, when I looked through that window I saw something that, even considering the likes of Cutliffe Starkvogel and what he stood for, was enough to send a sane man out of the woods forever.

Watching TV were Cutliffe, wearing an overcoat, and three black bears wearing what looked like skullcaps. Cutliffe had grown a beard, and I had a hard time not to laugh out loud at that, because his noggin was still barer than mine. If he'd put that stuff on it, it hadn't done him any more good than it had done me. It had made my fingers burn a little is all, the ones I'd used to put the stuff on with.

On the screen was what looked like a zoo, except that people were inside cages, behind bars. Bears were outside, throwing them what looked like peanuts. And laughing and pointing.

That was what Cutliffe and his three friends were doing, too—laughing and pointing—except they didn't have any peanuts. First time I'd ever heard a bear laugh, but, after all, they were Cutliffe's friends.

"Boy, I sure am glad I'm on the outside," Cutliffe said with a big ha-ha.

And then, so help me, I heard one of the bears say in perfect English, "I am too. Now there're only fifty-eight more to go."

Not only that; the voice sounded familiar.

"But it's a damn shame," Cutliffe muttered, "that hair will grow everywhere but on a bald head. That's civilization for you. Getting hair to grow on a bald head is something that even we haven't been able to do yet."

"But we keep trying," the same bear said. "It's the challenge of it."

Then Cutliffe said something I couldn't make out—it sounded like a question—as he looked away from the screen and at the bear who had spoken and then at the other two. I understood what he said next, though. He said, "What do you think, Fulton . . . Sledge?"

Fulton!? Sledge!? I had known a Fulton and a Sledge. And then I knew who the bear who had spoken reminded me of—Hiram Walker. He had lived not far from me until he disappeared last year. So had Fulton and Sledge, except they had disappeared even earlier. And all three had been bald. They'd been my best friends; it had broken me up pretty bad.

I decided I'd had enough of the whole screwy business when I heard their answer and Cutliffe agreeing with it. "That sounds logical," he said. But before I could get the hell out of there the show came to an end and its title flashed across the screen. It read "Bear World."

What really stopped me from leaving, though, was when Cutliffe then turned on the lights. When he did that, what I saw would have turned my hair gray if I'd had any.

Cutliffe wasn't wearing an overcoat. He was covered with hair, except for the top of his head. Even his face was covered with it. And he was bigger and thicker. He had a snout and paws and everything else a black bear has.

Cutliffe Starkvogel had turned into a bald-headed black bear! So had Hiram. And the other two bears—who used to be Fulton and Sledge—were bald, too. They hadn't been wearing skullcaps at all.

I got out of there fast.

The next morning there was a big box sitting outside my front door with a card tied to it. I figured what the card would say even before I read it.

Because during the night I'd kept waking up, and every time I had I'd thought about that "logical" answer to Cutliffe until I'd figured out what his question to the bears must have been. And when I read the card I was sure. "Compliments of 'Bear World,' " it said, followed by "Sponsored by Hair Growers, Inc." Inside the box was a TV set.

Because, you see, what had woken me up during the night were my fingers. They were really burning. And when I'd woken up this morning there were some little black hairs growing out of them—but not out of my head.

Cutliffe must have asked the bears, "Who's next?" Because their answer had been me.

And, sure enough, the following Friday the package that came from Hair Growers, Inc., was addressed to me. By that time I'd thought everything over pretty good and had a change of heart. I mean, when you're a bear lover and your best friends have become bears, what's an old cowpoke to do?

A Bad Cow Market

BY ELMER KELTON

What to say about Elmer Kelton? It's hard to comment on one of the masters. He has won three Spurs, unless I've lost count, was twice awarded the Western Heritage Award, and writes fine books like The Wolf and the Buffalo, The Day the Cowboys Quit, The Good Old Boys *and* The Time It Never Rained.

He says of his fiction, "A majority of my fictional works are based strongly on history, mostly Texas history, my own personal niche. I have chosen various periods of change and stress in which an old order is being pushed aside by the new, and through the fictional characters try to give the reader some understanding of the human reasons for and effects of these changes."

The following story is about change as well. It is a story of the modern "West," and there isn't a shootout in sight. But there is a crisis, and a strong man determined to deal with it. And there is, best of all, Elmer Kelton's smooth, precise prose.

The loudspeaker above the livestock-auction ring carried the auctioneer's chant over the clanging of steel gates and the shuffle of cattle's hooves in the soft sand. Most of the words had no meaning, but George Dixon could hear the price being asked, and he understood *that* meaning all too well: these calves were not going to pay the cost of their raising.

Sitting on a wooden bench high up toward the sale ring's acoustical-tile ceiling, he stared glumly at the last calves of his trailerload, a couple of cutbacks the yard crew had sorted off to keep them from lowering the value of the others. If the rest had been cheap, these were being stolen. He reached to his shirt pocket for cigarettes before he remembered he had given them up, not so much for his health as to save the money.

He jotted the price of the final calves in a shirt-pocket tallybook and reviewed what the other lots had brought. He would have to wait awhile for the bookkeeping staff to make out his check. He dreaded taking it to the production credit office for application against his loans. The PCA manager would not say much, but George could anticipate the look in his eyes. He had seen it many times the last few years as the prices for what he sold kept going down and the prices for what he had to buy kept going up.

Damned sure takes the romance out of the ranching business, he thought sourly.

Two thin crossbred cows came charging into the ring, eyes wide and heads high in anxiety over this unaccustomed place and the noise and the fast handling in the alleyways behind the auction barn. George stood up, glad they weren't his. The market was no kinder to cows than it was to calves. He made his way to a set of steps, begging pardon of other ranchers who pulled their booted feet back to let him pass. They looked no happier than he felt. He walked out into the auction's lobby and glanced at the glass behind which the office staff worked. There was no way he could rush his check. He pushed through a glass door into the restaurant, the smell of fried onions slapping him in the face like a damp, sour towel.

Someone spoke his name. He turned toward a row of booths and saw a man of about his own age, in his early forties, his waist expansive where George's was lean. George wore old faded jeans and a blue work shirt. His hat looked as if it had been run over by his pickup truck. Bubba Stewart resembled an ad in a Western-wear catalog. A big platter of chicken-fried steak and French fries gave off steam in front of him.

"Sit down, George," Bubba invited jovially. When a man had Bubba's wide grin and open manner, it was hard to resent him for being so damned wealthy. "I was havin' a little bite of dinner. I'd like to buy yours and not eat by myself."

George had figured a cup of coffee and a piece of pie would hold him until Elizabeth fixed supper. He didn't spend much these days on café chuck. "You go ahead and eat," he said. "I'll just settle for coffee." He decided against the pie because he didn't want Bubba spending that much on him. He would feel obligated to return the favor the next time.

Bubba stabbed the steak with his fork. "You sellin' today, or buyin'?"

"I'm givin' them away," George responded flatly.

Bubba nodded sympathetically. "I thought last year it couldn't get no worse. So much for my fortune-tellin'." His smile showed his pleasure in the steak. Bubba Stewart had always drawn pleasure from life and seemed never to be struck by the arrows of outrageous fortune. "You sure ought to order one of these. It ain't like Mama makes. It's better."

George looked up as the waitress brought his coffee. "Thanks. This'll do." He blew across the cup.

Bubba said, "Gettin' tougher and tougher to stay a cowman. You thought any more about that proposition I made you?"

George hoped his eyes did not betray how much he *had* been thinking about it. Maybe if Bubba thought he was not interested he would raise the ante. "That ranch has been in the family a long time. My old granddaddy bought it back in ought nine."

Bubba nodded. "Mine was already here. A man could make a good livin' then, raisin' cows on a little spread like that. Now it's like a life sentence to hard labor with no parole."

George could offer no argument.

Bubba talked around a mouthful of steak. "I've given up worryin' about cows. I keep a few for ornamentation, like my wife keeps a pair of peafowl, just to look at their feathers. But recreation—that's where it's at nowadays, George. Cater to hunters out of Dallas and Houston. Not just oilfield roughnecks, either. Go for the rich dudes that just ask where it is, and not what it costs."

Bubba had done well at that. In recent years he had gradually trimmed his livestock numbers and in their place had introduced exotic game animals such as black-buck antelope and sika deer that could legally be hunted the year around. He had built a large rustic hunting lodge where paying guests could rough it with comforts they didn't even have at home. Much of the year he had people waiting in line to get in.

George remembered that local cowboys used to snicker at Bubba because he wasn't much of a hand with cattle and horses. He had been a disappointment to his father and grandfather. But he had been a good student in arithmetic class. Bubba said, "I've got an architect workin' on a second lodge. I could use the extra huntin' acreage your place would give me."

George had lain awake nights, thinking about it. When his restless stirring had roused Elizabeth, he had told her he was having a touch of rheumatism. In reality, it was the cattle that were giving him pain.

He had considered trying to do in a small way what Bubba was doing in a large one, but he knew he could not. He took in a few hunters from East Texas during the fall whitetail deer season, but he could never find financing for facilities like Bubba had built. His ranch was too small.

Bubba said, "I'll raise my offer a little. You could pay off your debts and put the rest out on interest. It wouldn't be a full livin', but you're sure not makin' a livin' now."

George moved his hands from the tabletop and down into his lap so Bubba could not see them tremble. "I don't know. It'd have to be all right with Elizabeth. And I'd have to get approval from my brother Chester in San Antonio. Dad left the place to both of us, you know."

Bubba nodded. "I imagine Chester would be tickled to get shed of the old place and have the cash to put into his business. Plumbin', isn't it?"

"He contracts air-conditionin' and heatin'." George frowned. "If I'd had any judgment, I'd've gone partners with him years ago and left the cow business to somebody else. He offered to take me in."

"Kind of hard to picture you as a city slicker. It fits Chester, a little, but you was always the cowboy of the family."

"And look where it got me." George's voice had a rough edge.

Bubba pushed his empty plate aside and signaled the waitress that he needed his ticket. "Well, you holler if you decide. See you around, George."

George stared absently at the cold gravy on Bubba's plate and did some mental calculations for the hundredth time. He could settle his accounts and buy the family a house in town, maybe San Antonio, where Chester was. Then he could find himself a *paying* job for a change. There were lots of things he could do besides wet-nurse a bunch of feed-loving cows or the runny-nosed sheep that helped subsidize the cows' feed bill.

He sipped the last of his coffee and watched Bubba paying the cashier. Bubba's father and grandfather would turn over in their graves if they knew the direction Bubba had taken their ranch. But financially it was a sensible direction. Bubba was still building and buying while the old-line ranchers who stayed by tradition were losing their butt and all the fixtures. He had the judgment to change with the times. George begrudged him nothing.

He picked up his check and found it was even a bit less than he had expected after commission, feed and yardage. He walked out onto the auction yard to his pickup and long gooseneck trailer. One of the trailer tires had gone halfway down. It was so slick the original tread barely showed. The ranch business had come to a hell of a pass when a load of calves wouldn't even buy a new tire.

He passed Bubba Stewart's ranch entrance before he came to his own. Bubba had built a large stone archway with the Lazy-S brand displayed at top center. Many people used to make a joke of the brand, claiming it fitted Bubba all too well, but some of the scoffers were gone now, while Bubba was growing stronger.

George's entrance had no architect-designed archway. It had only a pair of chest-high stone pillars he and his brother Chester had helped their father to build thirty-odd years ago. They were plain and simple, but each time he drove between them across the cattleguard he remembered his father's pride in a job that had required two days of back-bending work. A mailbox just off the road shoulder was the only thing bearing the Dixon name. George had never thought he needed anything more. About the only people who ever hunted him up were feed and mineral salesmen.

He drove to his barn first and unhitched the trailer, then waded through the mud to a water trough that was overflowing onto the ground. A lifetime of water shortages had given George a contempt for waste. The old float had sprung a leak and filled, leaving the water to run unchecked. He unwired it from the valve and fetched an empty plastic sheep-drench bottle from the barn. It was less efficient than a commercial float, but it did not cost anything.

George had long operated on a principle of thrift: never buy a new nail if a bent one could be straightened. Disgustedly he hurled the old float as far as he could throw it, thinking, *I'm getting damned sick and tired of this*.

He saw a yellow school bus stop on the farm-to-market road. Shortly his fourteen-year-old son Todd came pedaling to the barn on a bicycle he had left hidden in a clump of brush near the cattleguard. The bicycle frightened a couple of calves too young to haul to town, and they stampeded away with tails hoisted.

George's frustration boiled over. He gave his startled son a dressing down for needlessly scaring the stock. "Now you get your clothes changed and start your chores!"

Face red, Todd said, "I've got to be back in town tonight for a 4-H Club meetin'."

"We'll talk about that later. Right now you do what I told you!" Regret arose as he watched the boy walk the bicycle to the house, shoulders hunched under the weight of the reprimand. The boy hadn't deserved that. It had just been one of those days. *Better for all of us*, he thought, *if we get away from this place*.

He tinkered around the barn as long as he could, knowing that when he went to the house Elizabeth would want to know what had made him ride the boy so hard. Todd came back with his old clothes on, milk bucket in his hand. He gave the barn a wide berth as he went to the pen where he had started a new calf on feed for the county stock show next January. Feeding show calves was one thing Todd would have to give up when they moved to town. It was too expensive anyhow; once a boy got past the county show and moved up to the big ones where the real money was, he went against the professional steer jockeys who dominated the circuit. That was simply one more thing gone wrong with the cattle business.

Todd finished milking the Jersey cow and trudged back to the house, followed by a red dog that was like a shadow to him. Presently Elizabeth came out onto the front porch, searching with her eyes. Hands clasped over her apron, she watched George make the long walk from the barn. The sight of her usually lifted his spirit, but not today. He studied the way she looked, framed between the porch posts that George's grandfather had put up. She deserved better than that old house, he thought.

He supposed she saw the answer to her question in his face, but she asked it anyway. "Did the calves sell all right?"

He handed her the sale sheet. "They sold."

She did not look at the paper. "It'll be better next year."

That was always her response to bad news: things'll be better tomorrow, or next week, or next year. He wondered how she found strength for that faith. *His* had about played out.

"Supper's on the table," she said, and moved toward the door. He caught her arm. She turned to face him, but it took a minute for him to bring out the words. "Bubba Stewart made me an offer again today."

He caught a flicker of reaction in her eyes, but she covered it so quickly he could not read it.

She asked, "What did you tell him?"

"Told him I'd have to talk to you, and to Chester. I'll call Chester after supper."

"You're really serious this time?"

"The *times* are serious."

Elizabeth looked past him, toward the barns, the corrals, toward the road that led out to the highway. "Supper's getting cold." She turned abruptly and led him into the house.

Todd was already seated at the table. He avoided his father's eyes. George tried to think of something that would ease the sting of rebuke. "What time's that 4-H meetin'?"

"Seven-thirty."

"We can make it without rushin' our supper."

That was the extent of conversation. Elizabeth offered no comment at all. Finished, George glanced at the clock on his grandfather's old mantel and decided Chester should be home from work by now. He dialed the number. The telephone rang a couple of times. A man answered in a voice George recognized as his brother's, though its tone was oddly somber, as if Chester had just heard bad news, or expected to.

"Hello. Chester? This is George. How's things in the big city?" Chester said he had seen them worse, but he did not remember when. George said, "They aren't good here, either. That's what I'm callin' you about. I was wonderin' if you could come out this weekend. I need to talk to you."

Chester hesitated a long time before saying it would be hard to get away and asking if they couldn't talk about it on the phone.

"No," George told him. "It's not goin' to be simple. We may need time to talk it out."

Chester hedged, saying he did not know how he could leave the business. But finally he relented, though his voice carried no pleasure. "I'll come."

"Bring the family. The kids haven't seen each other in a while."

Chester was silent another long moment. "I'll just have to see about that, George. I can't promise."

Todd brightened as his father hung up the telephone. "You mean Allan'll be out to see us?"

Allan was fifteen, just enough older that Todd had always looked to him for leadership, like the brother he had never had. Allan through the years had always come out from the city each summer to spend a few weeks. Todd would follow him like the red dog followed Todd. This year Allan had not come. Too many things to do, his father had explained to a disappointed Todd. George had reasoned it was natural for boys, even those who had been close, to drift apart as they became older. Each was developing his own interests and pointing himself toward the life-style he would follow as an adult. George remembered a cousin who had been his best friend until they were both about Todd's age. They had not seen each other in ten or fifteen years now, and the cousin rarely even crossed his mind.

He said, "Son, I wouldn't count on Allan. Even if his folks come out, and his sister too, he might not be with them. City boys his age have got football and girlfriends and such as that."

"He'll be here," Todd said enthusiastically.

George frowned. "You ever wish you could live in the city where you could do the things Allan does?"

Todd nodded. "Sure, I've thought about it. I've wished I could go to all the football games and to the picture show when I wanted to. I've wished I could go hang out at the mall like Allan does, and check out the girls." He gave his mother a quick glance. "Just look, though. That's all I'd ever do." He pondered a moment. "But there'd be things I *couldn't* do. I couldn't ride a horse. I couldn't feed our show calves. Those are things Allan wishes *he* could do."

"You might not miss them all that much. You'd have a lot of things you can't get in the country. You'd probably have a bigger and better school."

Todd's eyes widened. "You're not thinkin' about havin' me go live with Uncle Chester and Aunt Kathleen, are you?"

George blinked. He had not expected his son to misread him so badly. "No. That never crossed my mind."

Todd seemed relieved. "I'd probably get tired of the picture show. I might even get tired of hangin' out at the mall. I'd rather have my horse and my show calves."

"We can get used to anything if we want to bad enough."

"I suppose. I just don't think I'd want to." Todd shrugged off the subject as easily as he would slip out of his coat. "You still got any of that pie left, Mama?"

George glanced at Elizabeth. She had that look in her eyes again, that frustrating mask she could draw down at will to cover what she was thinking.

From experience he knew Chester and his family should reach the ranch about noon Saturday. That morning he took advantage of Todd's day off from school to repair a section of the fence he shared with Bubba Stewart's ranch. Some kind of animal had run into it and had broken off an old cedar post, leaving the fence to sag. He could only guess what it might have been; Bubba had a regular menagerie over there. While George put his shoulders into driving a set of posthole diggers against the resisting hard ground, Todd leaned on a crowbar and said, "If we'd waited till afternoon, we could've had Allan to help us."

George answered, "You know how goofy you and Allan get when you start playin' around. One boy can be good help. *Two* boys are like one *good* man had got up and left you."

He heard something crashing through a cedar brake. A long-legged animal with twisting black horns burst into the open, saw the two people and whipped back, disappearing as quickly as it had come. George said, "One of Bubba's exotics. I swear, there are as many on our side of the fence as on his."

"If they come over here, does that make them ours?"

George shrugged. "In a way, I guess. They go where they want to go and eat our feed. But Bubba paid for the breedin' stock. I'd hate to be a judge and jury."

"I still think they're ours."

"It won't matter long anyway."

Todd gave him a quizzical look, but George had said too much already. There would be time enough to tell him when the deal was made. "Here, let's see you hit the bottom of this hole with the point of that bar."

They finished the fence repair a while before noon, and they were still unloading the tools into a frame shed beside the barn when the red dog started barking. George saw Chester's blue automobile raising dust along the graded road. The car was three years younger than the one in George's garage. Todd jumped up into the pickup bed for a better look. "It's Allan!" he exclaimed, and ran toward the house, shouting to his mother. George finished putting away the tools and half-smiled, remembering that he used to make much the same fuss over his own cousin thirty-odd years ago. He paused at the windmill to rinse the dirt and grime from his hands, then walked to the house amid the dust settling from the passage of Chester's car.

Chester had a tired look in his face, as if he had not slept. His voice had the same dark and pained quality George had heard on the phone. "Howdy, George. Good to see you." George reached out, and Chester's handshake startled him. It was strong, almost crushing, but it was not the strength of pleasure; it was like the desperate grasp of a drowning man. George pulled away, looking back to his brother even as he gave sister-in-law Kathleen an obligatory hug. Through the years she had been the bubbly sort, but she also seemed subdued, troubled. The couple's daughter Pamela, at nine too young to play with boys, stuck close beside her mother.

George turned to his brother's son, who had shoulders like a football player. "Allan, we needed your muscles with us this mornin'. We had a couple of mean postholes to dig."

He expected some joking rejoinder, for that had always been the boy's way. Like his mother, he had an answer for everything, and usually a funny one at that. But he offered no reply. He turned away from Todd as if trying to avoid him and stared silently back down the road.

Probably got chewed out about something, and he's pouting, George thought. He had no intention of saying anything to make it appear he was butting in. "You-all come on into the house. I expect Elizabeth's about got dinner ready."

Kathleen and the girl hurried ahead. Chester held back, glancing uneasily at his son. "You made it sound pretty urgent on the phone, George."

George did not know exactly how to start. "It'll keep. Let's go have dinner."

They visited over the table, talking weather and rain and dry spells, exchanging gossip about old friends and acquaintances, studiously avoiding the subject that had brought Chester and his family all the way out here. Nobody smiled much, and nobody laughed. After they had eaten, George and Chester walked out onto the porch and seated themselves on the steps. They were silent for a time. At length George ventured, "I guess business must be pretty bad in the city." That would account for the somber mood in his brother and sister-in-law.

Chester nodded. "But there's a lot of people worse off." He rubbed his hands nervously against his knees. "I think I can guess what you wanted to talk about, George. I keep up with the cattle market. If you want to cut the lease you're payin' me for my half of the ranch, I'd have no objection."

George's jaw dropped. He had not considered that Chester would misconstrue his intentions so badly. He fumbled for words but found none.

Chester went on, "We're brothers, George. Sure, I can use the money, but I don't want it comin' out of your hide." He stared out across the pasture. "Hell, let's just eliminate the lease payment altogether till the cattle market goes up. I wouldn't want you hurtin' this old place by overstockin' it so you could pay me. I remember how much our daddy and granddaddy loved it."

George stared at the ground. He felt as if Chester had punched him in the belly. He had lain awake for hours last night trying to plot out just how he was going to put this proposition to his brother. Suddenly his whole plan had gone up in smoke.

Chester said, "Would you mind drivin' me around, George? Sometimes when the traffic is heavy and all the phones are ringin' at the same time, I get to thinkin' about this ranch. It's like a tranquilizer to me, with no bad side effects."

"The side effects come when you try to raise cattle on it," George said dryly. He stood up. "You boys want to go?"

Todd was eager, but Chester's son seemed distant and cold. Todd grabbed his arm. "Come on, Allan. We'll ride in the back of the pickup, like we used to."

Allan hung back, like a dog reluctant to follow the leash. His father said brusquely, "Come on, son. You've got nothin' better to do."

The boy burst out, "I *did* have, if you'd just left me alone."

"I've left you alone too many times. Get in the pickup!" Chester's face was flushed, his hands clenched. He glanced uncomfortably at George. Allan climbed into the pickup bed, his eyes angry and downcast. Todd hesitantly followed. His questioning gaze touched George, asking for an answer George did not have.

It struck George that Allan looked different, somehow adult, yet somehow lost, even bewildered. *Todd'll be at that stage in another year or two,* he thought. *Damned if I know how we're going to handle it.*

They drove through what had always been known as the horse pasture, now used mostly for young heifers being grown out to join the breeding herd. At one end was a surface tank built to catch runoff after a rain. For the first time since they had left the house, Chester spoke. "Remember how we loved to fish in that tank, George? Never caught much of anything, but we sure did drown a lot of worms."

George nodded soberly. His problem was getting no easier.

Chester said, "Doesn't seem like it took much to keep us happy. A horse to ride, a tank to fish in, a .22 to hunt rabbits with. We never gave Dad a lot of trouble, did we, George?"

George shook his head. "Not much, I guess. We ran some weight off of his calves, learnin' how to rope when he wasn't lookin'. I remember once we ran his pickup into a rockpile and ripped the oil pan out from under it."

"But that wasn't real trouble. Not like today. Livin' out here, George, you've got no idea . . ."

Chester turned away from him and covered his eyes with his hand. "God, George, why couldn't things stay simple like they used to be? Sure, me and you pulled some stunts, but we never really hurt anybody. These days . . ."

George glanced through the back window. Allan was staring moodily to the rear. Todd was watching him in silent disappointment. So far as George was able to tell, there had been little communication between these two boys who used to roll and tumble and tear together. "Is he in trouble, Chester?"

"He *will* be, if he's not already. He's fallen in with a wild bunch. He's usin' somethin'; I can't tell what, but somethin'. You can't talk to him half the time. He flies into a wild rage at nothin'. He's even got his mother and sister scared of him. I'm about at the end of my rope."

Chester went quiet, but George could almost hear him crying inside. "I'm sorry, Chester. I had no idea."

"Wherever these kids turn, there's temptation and trouble. They can buy stuff me and you never even heard of, and do it in the school hallways. Nights, no matter what we tell him, he slips out of the house and is gone. The telephone rings, and I'd rather die than answer it. I'm afraid they've picked him up and hauled him to jail. Or worse, that they've hauled him to a hospital.

"I know even the little towns aren't immune anymore, but at least people can keep track of things better. Where we're at, you don't know who's livin' three houses down the street, or what they're up to. Be thankful you've got Todd out here so you can always know where he is and who he's with."

George could see his brother's hands tremble. He said, "I wish there was somethin' I could say or do. I've never been up against that kind of situation."

"You were always the cowboy, George. I always had two left hands when it came to ranch work. I used to think the happiest day of my life would be when I could go to the city for a nice clean line of work where I'd never have to look another cow in the face. I thought my kids were better off than yours because the city had so much more to give them." He made a bitter laugh. "Look what it gave my boy. I'd've been better off livin' out here somewhere in a line shack, workin' for cowboy wages, and *they*'d've been better off."

George said, "We make our choices the best way we know how. We can never tell what's ahead of us."

"Well, *I* sure made the wrong one. I know I'll never come back here to live; I've got too much of my life invested where I am. But it's a comfort to know I *could*. Maybe somehow we'll pull through this thing with Allan, and he'll outgrow it. Maybe we'll be able to keep his sister from fallin' into the same trap; we'll try our best. But just knowin' this place is out here helps keep me and Kathleen from climbin' the wall sometimes. It's like an anchor in a rough sea.

"So keep your lease payments, George. Even get a part-time job in town if that's what it takes to pull through, so long as you've got this place to come to of a night, and for your boy to come home to. Hang on to our anchor."

George turned to look through the rear window again. Todd was talking, pointing, hopefully enthusiastic. If Allan was even listening to him, he gave no sign.

George said, "I reckon there's worse things than a bad cow market."

No more was said about Allan, or about the low value of cattle. Chester and Kathleen and their two youngsters left Sunday afternoon. Allan had not said fifty words to Todd, so far as George ever heard. Todd ventured, "I think he's probably got girlfriend trouble."

George said, "I expect that's it."

"It'll never happen to me."

George smiled. "No, it probably never will."

He expected to hear from Bubba Stewart by Sunday night, but Bubba did not call. Monday morning Bubba was sitting in front of George's house when George and Todd came out after breakfast. Bubba grinned at Todd as the boy mounted his bicycle and started up to the road to catch the school bus. "Don't let that old bronc throw you," he warned.

Todd laughed. "I've got him broke gentle."

Bubba watched Todd pedal away. "Good boy you got there."

"I know."

"I seen Chester on the road yesterday, headin' back to the city. What did he say about sellin' the place?"

George's face twisted. "I never got up the nerve to ask him."

Bubba pondered a moment, then nodded. "Figured it was somethin' like that."

"He's got troubles. I couldn't burden him with any more."

Bubba gave the old place a long study, from the barn to the corrals and back to the house. "Goin' to try to hang on a while longer, are you?"

"Seems like the thing to do. The market'll turn around one of these days. It always has."

Bubba shrugged. "Well, I'd've liked to add this place to mine. It would've been good for my hunters. But I reckon I know how you feel."

George could see Todd way down by the road, putting his bicycle into a shielding clump of brush. The yellow bus was waiting for him, and Todd trotted across the cattleguard afoot to catch it. "It's not for me, Bubba. It's for *him.*"

Bubba had both hands shoved into his pockets. George had learned years ago that this was his horse-trading stance. Bubba said, "I saw one of my black bucks out yonder by your fence."

"They're all over the place," George replied. "You'll have to put them on a leash if you figure on keepin' them at home."

"It gave me a notion, George. I was thinkin' maybe there's a way for me to add this place to mine without you losin' it. How about you leasin' the huntin' rights to me so I can bring my hunters over? It wouldn't make any difference to them whether I own the place or not, so long as they're in my lodge come dark. I could even pay you to guide them, if you was of a mind to agree to it."

George was enough of a horse trader himself not to let the smile he felt inside come out and betray itself on his face. "I owe you a cup of coffee, Bubba. Come on in the house."

Peaches

BY LENORE CARROLL

*Lenore Carroll is a free-lance writer and editor who teaches college com-
position at the University of Missouri at Kansas City. She lives in Kansas
with her husband, a newspaper editor, and two sons. She is a member of The
Western Writers of America and a founder of the Sacred and Esoteric Order
of the Buffalo, which has two other full members, yours truly and Loren
Estleman.*

*Before you read this story, let me warn you. Have a can of peaches handy.
You'll crave them by the time you're through.*

Coyle Kennedy, a buffalo runner, walked beside the lead ox team as it
pulled the heavy Studebaker wagon loaded with buffalo hides across the
prairie. His skinners sat paired on the wagon seats, taking turns with the
reins. Coyle didn't know what they thought about during the long hours,
but he thought of tinned peaches and his mouth watered.

Although the early springtime sun was high in the sky, the cold, dry
Kansas wind blew his corduroy jacket against his back and tossed his shaggy
brown hair as though it were a sorrel's mane. He was rangy and lean and
had to slow his long strides to match the oxen's pace. Peaches.

Coyle remembered the soft Georgia springtime when he was a boy. The
peach blossoms lay like snow on the branches. Then, after he'd forgotten all
about them, one summer's day when the heat slowed everyone to a walk,
when the women slipped their dresses off upstairs to rest after dinner, when
the gnats hummed in clouds, he climbed a tree in the orchard to dream the
quiet afternoon.

He heard one hard, tiny peach knock against the tree and fall to the grass
with a soft *plop*. Then he noticed the hard little fruits hiding in the leaves.
He tried to eat one, but it puckered his mouth and made him spit and spit
to get the taste away. Then he dreamed of ripe peaches. Skins softer than
velvet. The give when he pressed their ripeness. The sticky juice. The fruity
perfume that rose from the cut slices in the bowl.

He remembered his mother and aunts putting up peach butter in a great flurry. The season was short; the treasure precious. Glass jars tinkling, cook pot steaming, women's voices rising from the summer kitchen. And everywhere the sweet smell of the cooking fruit.

"There's town," hollered Jake Pleasaunce, from his vantage on the seat of the lead wagon.

Coyle looked up and saw smoke rising from the tents and soddies and slapped-together buildings of the raw railhead town.

"Where're we taking this batch?" asked Jake.

"Lobenstein's agent said he'd be at the tracks. Or the nearest saloon."

"Where should we go?"

"Last time there was a boxcar for a depot. Get as close as you can, but don't offload till I settle."

Peaches. Juicy flesh dripping with sugar syrup, fibrous meat raveled where the pit had been pulled away. Sweet, sour, with the fruit's perfume coloring the taste as he chewed the soft flesh. A can of fruit, a jug of cream, a bowl, a spoon—paradise.

The buffalo-hunting party pulled into the little town and the wagons rolled through the churned manure of the main street to the tracks. Coyle palavered with the agent, Hickey, until he got his price. Buffs were starting to get scarce now that the price of hides had gone up and every greenhorn with a few hundred dollars for a kit and wagons was on the prairie, but there were a million buffs left and Coyle had shot his share this month.

He divvied the money with his skinners and took operating expenses to deposit with the storekeeper against reprovisioning for the next hunt. He asked the storekeeper for some canned peaches, but the man shook his head.

"I've got a dozen two-pound tins, but they're spoke for."

"All of them?" Coyle could not believe his heart's longing, so simple, so cheap, would be denied. He had hundreds of dollars in his pockets; he could buy bonded whiskey or the prettiest whore in town. But after a month of buffalo-hump steaks and beans and cornbread, all he wanted was peaches.

"Yes. Got a message last night to hold all the peaches. Miss Polly got a fresh cow in trade for services and all her girls want peaches and cream. They're probably skimming the cream this very minute, waiting till I send the cans over."

Coyle groaned.

"Nothing I can do," said the storekeeper. "Maybe you can go over there, work a deal with them direct."

Coyle stalked out of the store and kicked the hitching post until his toes hurt, then shook himself and walked back inside. He lounged against the glass-front case and said quietly, "I'll carry the case over for you and see what the ladies will agree to."

"I gave my word," said the storekeeper, whose voice said more clearly than words that he thought buffalo runners came off the prairie dauncy from being out alone too long.

"And I give mine." Coyle raised his right hand.

He lifted the wooden box to his shoulder and walked toward Polly's frame house. Polly was the madam, a dark-eyed, curly-haired woman of thirty or so—a pocket Venus, petite but well proportioned. She and several other women had arrived at the little town even before the railroad, with new tents in their wagons. Instead of competing for trade, after a few months they'd pooled their resources, voted Polly in charge and built the house they now occupied. Polly and all the other members of the consortium shared expenses and split the profits. Coyle knew the way.

He had just walked off the covered wooden sidewalk and turned toward Polly's when he stopped. To steal was dishonorable, but perhaps there was another solution.

He turned back to the steps leading from the wooden sidewalk and, holding the box in front of him, pretended to trip and fell forward, his weight against the box, the box against the edge of the top step. The boxwood split and tins nearest the split crashed against the step. It knocked the wind out of Coyle and dented one row of cans. He pulled the splintered wood away from the damaged side, shouldered the box and turned again toward Polly's, whistling as he went. He staged the same accident on Polly's steps and two girls came out to investigate. They found Coyle picking up peach cans and pieces of wood. Among them they got the treasure into the kitchen.

At least half the cans were dented.

"Thank you, Mr. Kennedy," said Polly. She wore a morning dress of soft lilac chambray and shiny, high-heeled button shoes.

"Welcome, ma'am." said Coyle. He turned the damaged cans this way and that on the kitchen table. "Sorry about the accident."

"Those things happen."

"Course, there were some already dented when I got here."

"Mercy."

"Yes." He looked around the sunny kitchen and saw a pan of cream by the sink. "Could be kind of dangerous."

"Yes?" said Polly. She waited for Coyle to finish.

"Yes, ma'am. If the can's been damaged, the peaches might be tainted. Could be deadly." He kept his eyes down as she turned the cans around, pushing the lids, inspecting for damage.

"None of them look broken, just dented."

"You never can tell. Tiny hole you wouldn't even notice, you eat those peaches and you're a goner."

"I hate to think of a whole box of peaches thrown away, especially when the girls have their mouths just set for peaches."

"Well, ma'am, I like peaches, too. Hate to think of them being wasted, myself." Coyle looked out the back door to the tan, winter-weary grass just starting to put out fresh blades fine as hairs. Nothing broke the expanse, which stretched to the far horizon until a farm wagon topped the rise and started down the road to town.

Then he whipped around as though he'd just thought of something. "I've got it! I'll test them! I'll eat the first peach half from each can. If nothing happens to me, then you'll know they're safe. What about that?"

Polly balanced between skepticism and desire. On the one hand, she wanted peaches as much as anybody. In fact, it was her going on and on about peaches that had gotten the girls stirred up in the first place. She was ready to risk lockjaw and ptomaine, she was so hungry for peaches. On the other hand, they could all end up dead if the peaches *were* tainted. Coyle had never lied to her before, but there was something in his manner that made her suspicious. On the other hand (how many hands did this make, now?) he could be right. Besides, he was a handsome man, as lanky and lean as she was small and plump, who laughed with the girls and joked and left before his liquor got to him.

"Let's try this," she suggested, going to the pie safe for some bowls. "We'll open a few tins, take one peach half from each one, eat it and put the rest in a crock. Then if we don't come sick, the others can have their fill."

She handed Coyle a heavy knife and he sawed out the lids of eight cans. Polly carefully spooned out one peach half from each can into two cut-glass bowls.

"That's enough for a start," she said. She strained cream from the pan into a pitcher and brought it to the table. The sight and smell of the peaches was nearly overwhelming. Coyle's mouth watered so much he couldn't speak. He kept his eyes on the gleaming yellow hemispheres, afraid to meet Polly's eyes. Without a word each pulled a chair toward the table. Almost furtively, each drew his bowl toward him across the bare wood. Polly laid a spoon beside each bowl.

With silent concentration, her tongue protruding from between cherry-red lips, she poured the creamy libation over each bowl in turn. Her breathing quickened as she picked up her spoon. She looked at Coyle. He licked his lips and swallowed, his breath coming faster now. Their eyes locked for a moment. She broke a peach half into bites with the side of her spoon, then lifted a brimming mouthful to her lips. She paused.

Then Coyle remembered he was supposed to be testing the peaches for corruption. He quickly cut a bite and slurped it up. Peach exploded in his mouth. He chewed slowly, felt the juices and cream flow around his tongue. His stomach gave a demanding growl and he swallowed, sending the creamy sweetness down his grateful throat.

"Tastes okay," he said, looking at Polly. She took a deep breath and plunged in with a little animal noise of satisfaction. Neither spoke. They spooned the sweet mixture into their mouths slowly, savoring each moment, until their portions were gone.

Polly sighed and pushed her bowl away.

"That was wonderful," she purred.

"Wonderful for me, too," said Coyle. They sat in contented silence at the table and watched the flies buzz around the empty peach tins.

"Well, I guess we better wait a day, see if we take sick." She covered the crock of peaches with a dish towel.

"Yes, ma'am." Coyle looked at the woman, looked *into* her. He had bedded her, but had never eaten with her. He felt they had shared something indescribable.

Then his conscience smote him.

"Miss Polly," he began, then had to clear his throat, "there's nothing wrong with those peaches."

"I didn't think so," she admitted.

"I dented them myself on the way over."

"Now why would you do that, Mr. Kennedy?"

"It was just . . . I'd been thinking of peaches for days, all the way in with the hides. 'Scuse me, ma'am. I didn't even get cleaned up before I came. I went straight to the mercantile, then came here."

"Why are you confessing, Mr. Kennedy?" Polly smiled, not at all angry at Coyle's admission.

"I've been running buffalo a month and my mind got fixed on peaches. But now that I've had some, I can think of something even better than peaches."

Miss Polly smiled and took his hand, still sticky with peach juice, and led him up the stairs.

Judas and Jesus

BY THOMAS SULLIVAN

Taking an old theme and making it fresh is an extremely hard thing to do. Unless your name is Thomas Sullivan, Sully to his friends; then it's no trouble at all. The following story has an old tradition at its roots, but the fruit it bears is quite unexpected.

Thomas Sullivan lives in Michigan and teaches high school. His short fiction has appeared in Omni, Midnights, Cold Sweat *and other top markets. One of his stories won third prize in a recent Hemingway Days Literary Contest.*

Blunt. Cold. Wordless. Bloodless. That was Carson Reddner. That was the image. It made sense, because the only moments of his thirty-seven years that the Territory had preserved in its collective memory were the twenty-four seconds or so it had taken him to face down and shoot dead nineteen of his own breed.

He had been a miller's assistant, a powder boy, a sodbuster, a pony stringer, a drifter. He had a mother who still loved him, a father who didn't. He had put eight years in school, two in the army. He had buried a wife and a baby. And all this was unremarkable and uninteresting. All this hid behind twenty-four seconds of calling out death and the fractions therein of outdrawing it.

It was Easter and it was raining and his hemorrhoids were killing him as he rode up on Three Wells. He couldn't actually see the town. But it would be there, a little stain of humanity at the foot of the palisade. The other time he had been through he had been unremarkable and uninteresting. *Lord Jesus, let me be unremarkable and uninteresting,* he prayed fervently, but it wasn't going to happen this time. If Christ himself had ridden in at his elbow, they would have gotten even billing this Easter, the second coming for each.

The storm played games with its wind-driven veils—white, gray, black—right up until the last. He smelled the blacksmith's fire and still couldn't see the town. Despite the rain, he caught that, because the forge was on the eastern edge. He didn't actually see the forge until he was even with it, and the smith didn't see him until after he had walked his Appaloosa under the overhang and shed a small lake.

The smith looked like a hippopotamus in a leather apron, but something about his expression got very small as he peered at the stranger. Carson had seen the nuances of that look too many times not to know it. It wasn't reasoned fear in the face of lethal force, it was an uncertain fear bubbling out of the gut, a fear of snakes and spiders and aberrations in the night. The smith had no right to be afraid like that. The stranger before him was a drowning rat come out of the storm, his guns hidden by a tattered duster, a sodden lump of homespun and leather and weary flesh.

"Hotel's right up the street, mister," came out at last. "Reckon you're soaked through to the bone."

"Obliged if I could just dry out by your fire a spell," he answered.

An extra second or two hung between them before the smith's face lit up with false hospitality. "My pleasure," he said.

Carson tethered his mount to one of the poles supporting the overhang and moved to the side of the forge. He avoided the smith's eyes when he stripped off his duster, revealing the mismatched peacemakers—one short-barreled for clearing leather, one long for accuracy. He hovered over the stones that bedded the hot ash then, and for a while the rain made all the noise that was necessary between them. The smith fussed with a roan the whole time, as if he was afraid to come near the forge. And then the storm relented to a soughing wind and the eerie, pointless fear became too loud for Carson. He spun around to catch the blacksmith's chilled soul staring at him from out of those same small eyes.

"You know me?" he demanded.

Blinking, the smith shook his head.

He knew him.

Was it the telegraph this time? Was it some pony gossip riding his balls off out of Lodestock to say that Carson Reddner had survived another challenge and was headed this way? Look for the stranger. He changes hats, he changes horses, but he cannot change his guns. They are his Judas and his Jesus all at once. Call in your women and children, little towns. Call out your fools and your fantasizers. He will give you a funeral.

It is Easter, and I am not ready to rise again, thought Carson.

Rather than ride, he walked his horse through the mud of the street. He did not know why. Maybe it was an act of deference to the town. Maybe it was the hemorrhoids. Maybe it was just to lower his profile. He was used to an empty street, but this emptiness wasn't any of his doing. No one could have seen him ride in, the blacksmith had been his captive host, it had to be the weather. Gray rags fluttered across the sky. White light pooled from somewhere and didn't seem to illuminate anything but puddles.

And then he heard it. To the left. Behind the wooden pillar holding up the millinery porch. A year ago he would have been crouching already, the short-barrel smoking in his hand. But now he listened.

It is Easter, and I want to stay dead, echoed in his head.

It was what a soul-weary, thirty-seven-year-old gunfighter thought. It was why he wouldn't see thirty-eight. Because he had thoughts. Thoughts and second thoughts before he pulled triggers. Maybe it was suicide. Maybe it had always been suicide. *Come on, you whoring bastards, how many years will it take you to silence my rage?* This one fit behind the pillar of a millinery, and Carson Reddner waited for the click as his feet sucked one more time out of the mud.

But the crucial sound, when it came, was different, and it was that difference which kept his trigger finger on the daylight side of murder. He twisted in the mud and cleared the short gun and covered the spot. But he never fired. Because a small hand holding a block of L-shaped wood was aiming around the pillar. The sound, repeated now, came out of the throat of his would-be assassin.

"What the hell are you doing?" he growled tightly.

Elfin eyes emerged in a face that seemed all roundness and circles. "You didn't even get a shot off," came evenly out of a rosebud mouth.

Carson was not charmed. This was obscene. "You know what you damn near did, boy?"

"I *did* do it," averred the boy. "I outdrew Carson Reddner."

"The hell you did. You damn near got your brains splattered all over that storefront."

The boy's eyebrows took tiny twists. "I *did* do it," he insisted petulantly.

Carson holstered his gun. "How old are you?"

"Eight."

"How do you know my name?"

"Ma said you were comin'."

Ma. *Happy Easter, ma'am. Was this your boy I shot dead?*

"Everybody's expectin' you, but I'm the first one got to draw on you, and I beat you fair," the boy prattled on.

Carson hated this child. Everything that was wrong with his life was summed up there. "How many hotheads like yourself are you referring to?" he asked.

"What?"

"Skip it." He knew he really didn't care how many. It might be one, it might be ten. However many he avoided, however many he survived, there would always be another, as long as there were days and towns. He dragged like stone between them, and the prickle of excitement that preceded this latest sudden move and the revelation that followed it had exhausted him. There was never a respite. It didn't matter that it was Easter, didn't matter that he couldn't take off his guns to squat in a bush or close both eyes or pull his shirt off without—

"Wanta do it again?"

It was the boy, slogging along beside him. He stopped, staring malignantly down on the child. "Do it again?"

"For real. You let me have one of your guns and we'll draw."

Carson leaned menacingly forward. "You oughta be gelded, you know that?"

"You know I beat you fair," the boy concluded smugly.

Carson wanted to take him by the shoulders and shake salvation into him, but he said, "Okay. You shot me. Never mind if it was a fluke or I sneezed or a bee stung me just as I was drawing. Let's just say you're lightning in a bottle. So it's done. Your bullet did something to my brain and I'm vomiting breakfast. My whole body's convulsing, and the shit and the piss and the blood are pouring out of me, and you're standing there proud as a new mother, grinning. Now what? You going home to supper? Not likely. 'Cause even if you can stomach it after killing a man, you won't settle for long. You don't want to be around family when the others come— the others like you who think they want everybody to be afraid of 'em. Trouble is the ones is afraid is the ones you'd be comfortable living with. The ones isn't is the ones you can't trust. And you won't live it down. Once you've killed a man that way, the world never forgives. The world never forgives, boy."

He straightened slowly and turned to go on, but the child came out with "The reason you're trying to scare me is because you don't want to draw against me."

Carson felt as though he'd just emptied both revolvers at the moon. He took two more steps, turned. He lifted one boot out of the mud, let it back down. "Does it set right with you, shooting Sunday school teachers, boy?"

"You're not a Sunday school teacher."

"May interest you to know, I was exactly that once."

"Was. You're not a Sunday school teacher now." Their eyes locked. "I know what you are."

Carson nodded, kept nodding. "Well. I don't work on Easter. So you're out of luck."

"You'll have to fight, if you keep going that way!" the boy hollered after him. "The Butler brothers got *real* guns."

Again he stopped, stopped at the behest of this child with killing in his heart. Butler brothers, Armstrong brothers, Billy Wayne, Frank Taylor, Johnny Oldfield—there was always a cast of supporting characters. He didn't need them today, didn't need a kill, didn't need to die.

"Any Butler brothers that way?" He nodded at the street's lone juncture, which he had already passed.

"You really are afraid, aren'tcha?"

Carson led his Appaloosa around in the street. He was only buying time. Just an Easter Sunday. Sooner or later the flies would come humming to the carrion of his history, and either they would land in his face or they would just buzz around like so many did, hoping to share in someone else's carnage. Sometimes he was tempted to be slow in slapping them down, to think the second thoughts. One lazy draw and he would have peace for eternity. Defeat was nothing he feared anymore. What was there between now and the inevitable worth having? But giving a victory to another of his breed, that still drew his passion to the surface. Because he hated the breed as he hated himself. And if he could have taken their tainted, snarling souls to hell with him, he would have galloped all the way.

"You really are," the boy said again.

"Really what?"

"Really afraid."

He wanted to murder this child. This wasn't an eight-year-old boy. It was a disease. What kind of youngster voiced such grotesque notions to a dangerous stranger? He would be dead by fifteen, or, if he really was fast, Lord help the innocents who crossed his path. The child was a disease, and if he died today it would be a blessing.

"I knew you'd be afraid," said the boy, "just like I knew I could outdraw you."

"You didn't outdraw me."

"You're afraid!"

Carson gave him another deep stare. The little bastard was actually goading him.

"Fear is what makes young fools pick up guns in the first place," he murmured.

"Sure."

"If you weren't afraid, it wouldn't take a gun to make you feel safe. Real men only need a plow or a storekeeper's apron or a smile to feel safe. You ever smile, son?"

"If you'd let me use one of your guns, I'd show you who was afraid."

Precocious son of a bitch. Carson was half-tempted to oblige him.

"You know, if there's any hope at all for you, it's that you actually kill a man face-to-face while you're still young enough for the world to forgive."

"Huh?"

Carson sized up the town ahead. "I suppose, the minute I hole up, you're gonna run around like a blue jay letting everyone know I'm here."

"I'm not leavin' sight of you, I reckon."

The boy damn well meant it, and the gunman felt yet another weight on himself as he considered the child at his hip. "You also figuring on snatching one of those guns, son?" No answer. " 'Cause if you are, you ought to know that one of them is named Judas and the other Jesus. Make sure you get the right one."

"I'll take either," the boy piped up hopefully.

"I believe you would." There was something like expectation in the young face, and Carson felt the chill of witnessing an obscenity again. "How come you're the only one in the street? Even dogs have the good sense to stay out of the rain and the wind."

"I've been hanging around the edge of town for two days," the youngster said proudly. "And I was glad for the rain, 'cause it meant I'd be first to get a chance at you."

Incredible. *Two days . . . the first to get a chance.* How many more when the sun came out? God, he was weary. He looked at the boy long and hard then, and he knew he could not take another step without silencing him. "All right," he said

For just a wisp of a moment he thought he saw fear wash down the boy's face, and he knew—he thought he knew—that the youngster was feeling it in his bowels for the first time, that taste which flutters there and sinks like a spade in the gut. That was good. He was human after all. Maybe he wouldn't go to hell. Maybe when today was done, the boy would understand what it meant and take a different road.

"Tell you what. I'll let you draw on me with an unloaded gun. We'll both draw. And if my trigger clicks before yours, you go home and forget you ever saw me." He gave eternity some play before he said the next thing, but the boy's face remained eager. "And if yours clicks first, we load the guns and do it again for real."

The boy actually grinned, and that was the most obscene thing of all.

Carson Reddner turned away. He had just understood that it would be possible for him to shoot a child and have no regrets.

They went behind the telegraph office then. The sky was racing like it was in a hurry to bring on the night, and the only lights on the face of the earth were the unexplainably brilliant puddles whose mirrored mosaics caught God's startled eye.

"I'm giving you Judas," Carson said, pulling the cartridges out of the short-barreled peacemaker. "It's the faster of the two, and you'll have to draw it out of your waistband."

"It ain't as accurate," the boy noted.

Carson glowered. "That's right."

"When we do it for real, I want to be close to you, then."

"If we do it for real, you can stand on my toes and aim for the center of my chest. You can aim, can't you?"

The boy didn't answer.

Carson closed the cylinder, handed it to him. Then he took out the full-length peacemaker. "This one's Jesus," he said. He freed the cylinder, but the boy was intent on the heavy weapon in his own small hand. The gunman caressed the primers of the six disciples under his thumb and closed the chamber with a snap. Then he slipped the long barrel into his right holster and once more regarded the cartridges he had taken from the other in his left palm.

"Set," he said.

The boy was nesting the weapon gently into his waistband, and he had a look on his face that utterly disgusted the man he faced. It was a look of power. It was a look of breathing ether. The one redemption left Carson Reddner was sending that look to hell, and he was glad that it would be gone in a roar and a flash.

"Now," he said, and there was a roar and a flash.

The roar was heaven's outrage, and the flash united the shards of a holy eye broken on the earth, as each puddle became more brilliant still. It was a blasphemy, this thing, the blasphemy of a child murdering a man. Because it was Carson Reddner who lay dead behind the telegraph office of Three Wells, shot exactly where he had told his killer to shoot. In his tightly rolled left hand were *five* cartridges, and in his right holster Jesus slept on Easter.

The nine-year-old boy looked down at the crude marker. There was no ether to breathe this Easter. A year had come and gone, and still he could not think of that moment without the taste that fluttered and sank like a spade in the gut. He had tried to tell everyone that it was an accident, that he hadn't known about the single bullet. But no one believed him. Whatever they imagined the evil man had been attempting to do to him when he somehow got the gun, that was more plausible than the truth. It didn't matter. He was a hero to them, and to hell with his deep, dark doubts. Would he have gone through with a second confrontation that day? The relentless unfolding of those possibilities would haunt him all his mortal life. But he didn't carry a wooden gun anymore. And whenever they lay for him —those cruel companions of his boyhood—leaping out with their sticks drawn and foolish sounds coming from their pulsing cheeks, he saw only Judases in their hands.

"Sallie C."

BY NEAL BARRETT, JR.

The following story could only have been written by Neal Barrett. That may sound like a stupid statement on the surface, but consider this: Haven't you read stories that were good, yet you realized that a dozen other writers could have written them? Not exactly the same way, mind you, but easily as well.

Not so with the story that follows, "Sallie C." No one but Neal Barrett could have written it. No one but Barrett would have thought of it. And had another writer miraculously thought of it and written the story, well . . . it would have been a failure.

This is Barrettese, a special sauce seeped down from the gray matter (perhaps overly heated in the Texas sun) of Mr. Barrett's head, out through his fingertips and into his pen (he writes first drafts longhand), to be ultimately transformed into this ingenious little jewel.

Neal Barrett is an Austin writer. He looks a bit like Robin Hood, without the bow and arrow. Most of his work has been science fiction or fantasy, and I recommend heartily to you Stress Pattern, *a minor science-fiction classic; the Aldair series, four books about a feisty . . . uh, pig; and* Westward Trail, *a novel about Daniel Boone. Under other names, he has written numerous Western novels, most of them to pay the bills. He's abandoned all that now. Only his work and his name from here on out. So watch out, here comes a literary locomotive, Neal Barrett.*

Will woke every morning covered with dust. The unfinished chair, the dresser with peeling paint were white with powdery alkali. His quarters seemed the small back room of some museum, Will and the dresser and the chair an exhibit not ready for public view. Indian John had built the room, nailing it to the hotel wall with the style and grace of a man who'd never built a thing in all his life and never intended to do it again. When he was finished he tossed the wood he hadn't used inside and nailed the room firmly shut and threw his hammer into the desert. The room stayed empty except for spiders until Will and his brother moved in.

In August, a man had ridden in from Portales, heading vaguely for Santa Fe and having little notion where he was. His wife lay in the flatbed of their wagon, fever-eyed and brittle as desert wood, one leg swollen and stinking with infection. They had camped somewhere and a centipede nine and three-quarter inches long had found its way beneath her blanket. The leg was rotting and would kill her. The woman was too sick to know it. The man said his wife would be all right. They planned to open a chocolate works in Santa Fe and possibly deal in iced confections on the side. The railroad was freighting in their goods from St. Louis; everything would be waiting when they arrived. The man kept the centipede in a jar. His wife lay in the bed across the room. He kept the jar in the window against the light and watched the centipede curl around the inner walls of glass. Its legs moved like a hundred new fishhooks varnished black.

The man had a problem with connections. He couldn't see the link between the woman on the bed and the thing that rattled amber-colored armor in the jar. His wife and the centipede were two separate events.

The woman grew worse, her body so frail that it scarcely raised the sheets. When she died, Indian John took the centipede out and killed it. What he did, really, and Will saw him do it, was stake the thing down with a stick Apache-style. Pat Garrett told the man to get his sorry ass out of the Sallie C. that afternoon and no later. The man couldn't see why Garrett was mad. He wanted to know what the Indian had done with his jar. He said his wife would be fine after a while. He had a problem with connections. He couldn't see the link between burial and death. Indian John stood in the heat and watched ants take the centipede apart. They sawed it up neatly and carried it off like African bearers.

Will thought about this and carefully shook his trousers and his shoes. He splashed his face with water and found his shirt and walked out into the morning. He liked the moment suspended, purple-gray and still between the night and the start of day. There was a freshness in the air, a time before the earth changed hands and the sun began to beat the desert flat.

Behind the hotel was a small corral, the pen attached to the weathered wooden structure that served as work shed, stable and barn. The ghost shapes of horses stirred about. The morning was thick and blue, hanging heavy in the air. Saltbush grew around the corral, and leathery beaver-tail cactus. Will remembered he was supposed to chop the cactus out and burn it.

Indian John walked out on the back steps and tossed dishwater and peelings into the yard. He took no notice of Will. The chickens darted about, bobbing like prehistoric lizards. Will opened the screen and went in. The hotel was built of wood but the kitchen was adobe, the rough walls black with smoke and grease. The room was hot and smelled of bacon and strong coffee. Will poured himself a cup and put bread on the stove to make toast.

"John, you seen my brother this morning?" Will asked. He didn't look up from his plate. "He get anything to eat?"

"Mr. Pat say your brother make a racket before noon, he goin' to kill him straight out. Like that." John drew a finger across his throat to show Will how.

"He hasn't been doing that, John."

"Good. He gah'dam better not."

"If he *isn't*, John, then why talk about it?"

"Gah'dam racket better stop," John said, the menace clear in his voice. "Better stop or you brother he in helluva big trouble."

Will kept his fury to himself. There was no use arguing with John, and a certain amount of risk. He stood and took his coffee and his toast out of the kitchen to the large open room next door. He imagined John's eyes at his back. Setting his breakfast on the bar, he drew the shades and found his broom. There were four poker tables and a bar. The bar was a massive structure carved with leaves and tangled vines and clusters of grapes, a good-sized vineyard intact in the dark mahogany wood. Garrett had bought the bar up in Denver and had it hauled by rail as far as he could. Ox teams brought it the rest of the way across the desert, where Garrett removed the front of the hotel to get it in.

There was a mirror behind the bar, bottles and glasses that Will dusted daily. Above the bottles there was a picture of a woman. The heavy gilt frame was too large for the picture. The woman had delicate features, deep-set eyes and a strong, willful mouth. Will imagined she had a clear and pleasant voice.

By the time he finished sweeping, there were pale fingers of light across the floor. Will heard steps on the back stairs and then the boy's voice talking to John, and then John speaking himself. John didn't sound like John when he spoke to the boy.

Will looked at the windows and saw they needed washing. It was a next-to-useless job. The sand ate the glass and there was no way to make them look right. The sight suddenly plunged him into despair. A man thirty-six with good schooling. A man who sweeps out and cleans windows. He wondered where he'd let his life go. He had scarcely even noticed. It had simply unraveled, coming apart faster than he could fix it.

The boy ran down the steps into the yard. He walked as if he owned the world and knew it. Will couldn't remember if he'd felt like that himself.

The front stairs creaked and Will saw Garrett coming down. This morning he wore an English worsted suit and checkered vest. Boots shined and a fresh linen collar, cheeks shaved pink as baby skin. The full head of thick white hair was slicked back and his mustache was waxed in jaunty curls. Will looked away, certain Garrett could read his every thought. It made him furious, seeing this ridiculous old fart spruced up like an Eastern dandy. Before the woman arrived, he had staggered around in moth-eaten dirty longhandles, seldom bothering to close the flap. At night he rode horses blind drunk. Everyone but John stayed out of his way. Now, Will was supposed to think he had two or three railroads and a bank.

Garrett walked behind the bar and poured a healthy morning drink. "Looks real nice," he told Will. "I do like to see the place shine."

Will had rearranged the dust and nothing more. "That Indian's threatening my brother," he announced. "Said he'd cut his throat sure."

"I strongly doubt he'll do it. If he does, he won't tell you in advance."

"What he said was it was you. I assure you I didn't believe him for a minute. I am not taken in by savage cunning."

"That's good to know."

"Mr. Garrett, my brother isn't making any noise. Not till after dinner like you said."

"I know he's not, Will."

"So you'll say something to John and make him stop?"

"If you've a mind to weary me, friend, you've got a start. Now how's that wagon coming along?"

"Got to have a whole new axle, like I said. But I can get it done pretty fast."

Garrett looked alarmed. "What you do is take your time and do it *right*. Fast is the mark of the careless worker, as I see it. A shoddy job is no job at all. Now run out and see that boy's not near the horses. I doubt he's ever seen a creature bigger than a fair-sized dog."

Garrett watched him go. The man was a puzzle and he had no use for puzzles of any kind. Puzzles always had a piece missing and with Will, Garrett figured, the piece was spirit. Someone had reached in and yanked it right out of Will's head and left him hollow. No wonder the damn Injun gave him fits. A redskin was two-thirds cat and he'd worry a cripple to death.

Garrett considered another drink. Will had diminished the soothing effects of the first, leaving him one behind instead of even. He thought about the woman upstairs. In his mind she wore unlikely garments from Paris, France. John began to sing out in the kitchen. *Hiyas* and such strung together in a flat and tuneless fashion. Like drunken bees in a tree. Indian songs began in the middle and worked out. There was no true beginning and no end. One good solution was the 10-gauge Parker under the bar. Every morning Garrett promised himself he'd do it. Walk in and expand Apache culture several yards.

"I'll drink to that," he said, and he did.

The boy was perched atop the corral swinging his legs. John had given him sugar for the horses.

"Mr. Garrett says you take a care," Will told him. "Don't get in there with them now."

"I will be most careful," the boy said.

He had good manners and looked right at you when he talked. Will decided this was a mark of foreign schooling. He walked past the horses to the barn. The morning heat was cooking a heady mix, a thick fermented soup of hay and manure; these odors mingled with the sharp scent of cleanly sanded wood, fuel oil and waxy glue.

Will stopped a few feet from the open door. The thing seemed bigger than he remembered. He felt ill at ease in its presence. He liked things with front and back ends and solid sides to hold them together. Here there was a disturbing expanse of middle.

"Listen, you coming out of there soon?" Will said, making no effort to hide his irritation. "I'm darn sure not coming in."

"Don't. Stay right there." His brother was lost in geometric confusion.

"Orville, I don't like talking to someone I can't even see."

"Then don't."

"You sleep out here or what? I didn't hear you come to bed."

"Didn't. Had things to do."

"Don't guess you *ate* anything, either."

"I eat when I've a mind to, Will, all right?"

"You say it, you don't do it."

"One of those chickens'll wander in, I'll eat that. Grab me a wing and a couple of legs."

Will saw no reason for whimsy. It didn't seem the time. "It isn't even eight yet, case you didn't notice," he said shortly. "I promised Mr. Garrett you wouldn't mess with that thing till noon. John raised Ned with me at breakfast. Me, now, Orville, not you."

Orville emerged smiling from a tortuous maze of muslin stretched tightly over spars of spruce and ash, from wires that played banjo as he passed, suddenly appearing as if this were a fine trick he'd just perfected.

"I am not to make noise before noon," he told Will. "Nobody said I couldn't work. Noise is forbidden but toil is not."

"You're splitting hairs and you know it."

Orville brushed himself off and looked at his brother. "Listen a minute, Will, and don't have a stroke or anything, all right? I'm going to try her out tomorrow."

"Oh my Lord!" Will looked thunderstruck.

"I'd like for you to watch."

"Me? What for?"

"I'd like you to be there, Will. Do I have to have a reason?"

Orville had never asked him a question he could answer. Will supposed there were thousands, maybe millions of perplexities between them, a phantom cloud that followed them about.

"I don't know," he said, and began to rub his hands and bob about. "I can't say, maybe I will, I'll have to see." He turned, suddenly confused about direction, and began to run in an awkward kind of lope away from the barn.

Helene kept to herself. Except for her usual walk after supper, she had not emerged from the room since her arrival. Herr Garrett sent meals. The savage left them in the hall and pounded loudly at her door. Helene held her breath until he was gone. If he caught her he would defile her in some way she couldn't imagine. She ate very little and inspected each bite for foreign objects, traces of numbing drugs.

Garrett also sent the Indian up with presents. Fruits and wines. Nosegays of wilted desert flowers. She found these offerings presumptuous. The fruit was tempting, she didn't dare. What rude implication might he draw from a missing apple, a slice of melon accepted?

"God in Heaven help me!" she cried aloud, lifting her head to speed this plea in the right direction. What madness had possessed her, brought her to this harsh and terrible land? The trip had been a nightmare from the start. A long ocean voyage and then a train full of ruffians and louts. In a place called Amarillo they said the tracks were out ahead. Three days' delay and maybe more. Madam was headed for Albuquerque? What luck, the stranger told her. Being of the European persuasion, she might not be aware that Amarillo and Albuquerque were widely known as the twin cities of the West. He would sell her a wagon cheap and she would reach her destination before dark. Albuquerque was merely twenty-one miles down the road. Go out of town and turn left.

Her skin was flushed, ready to ignite. Every breath was an effort. Her cousin would think she was dead, that something dreadful had happened. She applied wet cloths. Wore only a thin chemise. The garment seemed shamefully immodest and brought her little relief. Sometimes she drifted off to sleep, only to wake from tiresome dreams. Late in the day she heard a rude and startling sound. Mechanical things disturbed her. It clattered, stuttered and died and started again.

Before the sun was fully set, she was dressed and prepared for her walk. Hair pale as cream was pinned securely under a broad-brimmed hat. The parasol matched her dress. In the hall she had a fright. The savage came up the stairs with covered trays. Helene stood her ground. Fear could prove fatal in such encounters; weakness only heightened a man's lust.

The savage seemed puzzled to see her. His eyes were black as stones. "This your supper," he said.

"No, no, *danke,*" she said hurriedly, "I do not want it."

"You don't eat you get sick."

Was this some kind of threat? If he attacked, the point of the parasol might serve her as a weapon.

"I am going to descend those stairs," she announced. "Do you understand me? I am *going* down those stairs!"

The Indian didn't move. Helene rushed quickly past him and fled. Outside she felt relatively secure. Still, her heart continued to pound. The sky was tattered cloth, a garish orange garment sweeping over the edge of the earth. Color seemed suspended in the air. Her skin, the clapboard wall behind her were painted in clownish tones. Even as she watched, the color changed. Indigo touched the faint shadow of distant mountains.

So much space and nothing in it! Her cousin's letter had spoken of vistas. This was the word Ilse used. Broad, sweeping vistas, a country of raw and unfinished beauty. Helene failed to see it. At home, everything was comfortably close. The vistas were nicely confined.

"Well now, good evening, Miz Rommel," Garrett said cheerfully, coming up beside her to match her pace, "taking a little stroll, are you?"

Helene didn't stop. "It appears that is exactly what I am doing, Herr Garrett." The man's feigned surprise seemed foolish. After four days of popping up precisely on the hour, Helene was scarcely amazed to see him again.

"It's truly a sight to see," said Garrett, peering into the west. "Do you get sunsets like this back home? I'll warrant you do not."

"To the best of my knowledge, the sun sets every night. I have never failed to see this happen."

"Well, I guess that's true."

"I am certain that it is."

"I have never been to Germany. Or France or England either. The Rhine, now that's a German river."

"Yes."

"I suppose you find my knowledge of foreign lands greatly lacking."

"I have given it little thought."

"I meant to travel widely. Somehow life interceded."

"I'm sure it did."

"Life and circumstance. *Herr,* now that means mister."

"Yes, it does."

"And missus, what's that?"

"Frau."

"Frau Rommel. In Mexican that would be *señora. Señor* and *señora.* I can say without modesty I am not unacquainted with the Spanish tongue."

"How interesting I'm sure."

"Now if you were unmarried, you'd be a *señorita.*"

"Which I am not," Helene said, with a fervor Garrett could scarcely overlook.

"Well, no offense, of course," said Garrett, backtracking as quickly as he could. "I mean if you were, that's how you'd say it. You see, they put that *ita* on the end of lots of things. *Señorita's* sort of "little lady." Now a little dog or little—Miz Rommel . . . you suppose you could see your way clear to have supper with me this evening maybe nine o'clock I would be greatly honored if you would."

Helene stopped abruptly. She could scarcely believe what she'd heard. "I am a married woman, Herr Garrett. I thought we had established this through various forms of address."

"Well now, we did but—"

"Then you can see I must decline."

"Not greatly I don't, no."

"Surely you do."

"To be honest I do not."

"Ah well! All the more reason for me to refuse your invitation! To be quite honest, Herr Garrett, I am appalled at your suggestion. Yes, appalled is the word I must use. I am not only a married woman but a mother. I have come to this wretched land for one reason, and that reason is my son. As even you can surely see, Erwin is a boy of most delicate and sickly nature. His physician felt a hot and arid climate would do him good. I am no longer certain this is so."

"Miz Rommel," Garrett began, "I understand exactly what you're saying. All I meant was—"

"No, I doubt that you understand at all," Helene continued, her anger unabated, "I am sure you can't imagine a mother's feelings for her son. I can tell you right now that I see my duty clearly, Herr Garrett, and it does *not* include either the time or the inclination for—for illicit suppers and the like!"

"Illicit suppers?" Garrett looked totally disconcerted. "Jesus Christ, lady . . ."

"*Language*, Herr Garrett!"

Garrett ran a hand through his hair. "If I've offended you any, I'll say I'm sorry. Far as that boy of yours is concerned, you don't mind me saying he looks healthy enough to me. If he's sickly, he doesn't show it. John says he takes to the desert like a fox."

"I would hardly call that an endorsement," Helene said coolly.

"John knows the country, I'll hand him that."

"He frightens me a great deal."

"I don't doubt he does. That's what Indians are for."

"I'm sorry. I do not understand that statement at all."

"Ma'am, the Indian race by nature is inured to savage ways. Murder, brutalizing and the like. When he is no longer allowed these diversions, he must express his native fury in some other fashion. Scaring whites keeps him happy. Many find it greatly satisfying. Except, of course, for the Sioux, who appear to hold grudges longer than most."

"Yes, I see," said Helene, who didn't at all. The day was suddenly gone; she had not been aware of this at all. The arid earth drank light instead of water. Garrett's presence made her nervous. He seemed some construction that might topple and fall apart.

She stopped and looked up and caught his eye. "My wagon. I assume you will have it ready quite soon."

The question caught Garrett off guard. This was clearly her intention.

"Why, it's coming along nicely, I would say."

"I don't think that's an answer."

"The axle, Miz Rommel. The axle is most vital. The heart, so to speak, of the conveyance."

He was fully transparent. He confirmed her deepest fears. She could see his dark designs.

"Fix it," she said, and the anger he had spawned rose up to strike him. "Fix it, Herr Garrett, or I shall take my son and *walk* to Albuquerque."

"Dear lady, please . . ."

"I will *walk*, Herr Garrett!"

She turned and left him standing, striding swiftly away. He muttered words behind her. She pretended not to hear. She knew what he would do. He would soothe his hurt with spirits, numb his foul desires. Did he think she didn't know? God preserve women! Men are great fools, and we are helpless but for the strength You give us to foil them!

There was little light in the west. The distant mountains were ragged and indistinct, a page torn hastily away. Garrett had warned her of the dangers of the desert. Rattlesnakes slithering about. He took great pleasure in such stories. She had heard the horrid tale of the centipede. From Garrett, from Will, and once again from Erwin.

Turning back, she faced the Sallie C. again. How strange and peculiar it was. The sight never failed to disturb her. One lone structure and nothing more. A single intrusion on desolation. A hotel where none was needed, where no one ever came. Where was the woman buried, she wondered? Had anyone thought to mark the grave?

Drawing closer, she saw a light in the kitchen, saw the savage moving about. Another light in the barn, the tapping of a hammer coming from there. She recalled the clatter she'd heard that afternoon. Now what was that about? Erwin would surely know, though he had mentioned nothing at all. The boy kept so within himself. Sometimes this concerned her, even hurt her deeply. They were close, but there was a part of this child she didn't know.

Helene couldn't guess what made her suddenly look up, bring her eyes to that point on the second story. There, a darkened window, and in the window the face of a man. Her first reaction was disgust. Imagine! Garrett spying on her in the dark! Still, the face made no effort to draw away, and she knew in an instant this wasn't Garrett at all but someone else.

Helene drew in a breath, startled and suddenly afraid. She quickly sought the safety of the porch, the protecting walls of the hotel. Who was he then, another guest? But wouldn't she have heard if this were so?

She smelled the odors of the kitchen, heard the Indian speak, then Erwin's boyish laughter. Why, of course! She paused, her hand still on the door. The savage had carried *two* covered trays when she met him in the hall. At the time, she had been too fearful of his presence even to notice. The other tray, then, was for the man who sat in the window. He, too, preferred his meals in his room. Something else to ask her son. What an annoying child he could be! He would tell her whatever she wanted to know. But she would have to ask him first.

It was Pat Garrett's habit to play poker every evening. The game began shortly after supper and lasted until Garrett had soundly beaten his opponents, or succumbed to the effects of rye whiskey. Before the game began, Garrett furnished each chair with a stack of chips and a generous tumbler of spirits. Some players' stacks were higher than others. A player with few chips either got a streak of luck or quickly folded, leaving the game to better men. Bending to the harsh circle of light, Garrett would deal five hands on the field of green, then move about to each chair in turn, settle in and study a hand, ask for cards or stand, sip from a player's glass and move on, bet, sip, and move again. After the first bottle of rye the game got lively, the betting quite spirited, the players bold and sometimes loud in their opinions. Will, lying awake in the shed out back, and on this night, young Erwin at the bottom of the stairs, could hear such harsh remarks as "Bet or go piss, McSween," "You're plain bluffing, Bell, you never saw kings and aces in your life . . ."

More than once, Will had been tempted to sneak up and peer in a window to assure himself Garrett was alone. He thought about it but didn't. If Garrett was playing with ghosts, Will didn't want to know it.

Sometime close to three in the morning, Helene awoke with a start. There was a terrible racket below, as if someone were tossing chairs and tables across the room, which, she decided, was likely the case. Moments later, something bumped loudly against the wall outside her window. Someone muttered under his breath. Someone was trying to climb a ladder.

Helene woke Erwin, got him from his bed and brought him to her, holding the boy close and gripping her parasol like a saber.

"God save us from the defiler," she prayed aloud. "Forgive me all my sins. Erwin, if anything happens to me, you must get to Cousin Ilse in Albuquerque. Can you ride a horse, do you think? Your father put you on a horse. I remember clearly he did. At Otto Kriebel's farm in Heidenheim?"

"*Nein, Mutti,*" he assured her, "it is all right, nothing is going to happen."

"Hush," she scolded, "you don't know that at all. You are only a boy. You know nothing of the world. You scarcely imagine the things that can happen."

At that moment, a most frightening shout came from just below the window. The cry receded, as if it were rapidly moving away. The ladder struck the ground, and half a second later something heavier than that. The night was silent again.

"Perhaps someone is injured," Erwin suggested.

"Go to sleep," Helene told him. "Say your prayers and don't forget to ask God to bless Papa. We are far away from home."

There was no question of sleeping. To the usual morning noise of men stomping heavily about, of chickens clucking and horses blowing air was now added the hollow ring of timber, of hammering and wheels that needed grease. Helene dressed quickly, recalling her promise to Erwin the night before. Before she could sweep her hair atop her head he was back, eyes alight with wonder, those deep, inquisitive eyes that seemed to see much more than a boy should see.

"Komm schnell, Mutti!" he urged her, scarcely giving her time to pause before the mirror. Holding tightly to her hand, he led her quickly down the stairs and out into the brightness of the morning. The Indian leaned against the wall, drinking a can of peaches from the tin, practicing looking Mescalero-mean. Garrett slumped in a rocker, his leg propped testily on a stool.

Helene could not resist a greeting. "Are you hurt, Herr Garrett? I do hope you have not had an accident of some sort."

"I am in excellent health, thank you," Garrett said shortly.

"Well. I am most pleased to hear it." The man seemed to have aged during the night. His flesh was soft as dough. Helene wondered if he would rise, swell like an ungainly pastry in the heat.

"There, *Mutti*, see?" said Erwin. "Look, they are coming. It is most exciting, yes!"

"Why yes, yes, I'm sure it is, Erwin," Helene said vaguely. In truth, she had no idea what she was seeing. The strange sight appeared around the corner of the hotel. It seemed to be an agricultural device. Helene framed a question for Erwin but he was gone. "Have a care," she called out, but knew he didn't hear.

Two men guided the wagon toward the flats. One of the two was Will. She guessed the other was his brother. Will looked stricken, a man pressed into service who clearly hoped no one would notice he was there.

As Helene watched, the first flash of morning touched the horizon, a fiercely bright explosion that scarred the earth with light and shadow. A silver lance touched the strange device; the thing seemed imbued with sudden magic. Light pierced the flat planes of muslin and spruce, and Helene imagined transparent flesh and hollow bones. A dragonfly, a golden fish in a dream.

"Oh. Oh, *my,*" she said aloud, deeply touched by the moment. "Looks to me like a medicine show hit by a twister," said Garrett.

"*I* think it has a certain grace," said Helene. "The rather delicate beauty one associates with things Oriental."

"Chink laundry," Garrett countered. "Got in the way of a train."

"They say strong spirits greatly dull the imagination," Helene said coolly, and took herself to the far end of the porch.

Out on the flats, Will and his brother carefully lifted the device off the wagon onto the ground. Broad wooden runners, which might have come from a horse-drawn sleigh, were attached to the contraption's undercarriage. Helene knew about sleighs. The runners seemed strangely out of place. Snow was clearly out of the question.

Suddenly, the engine in the device began to snarl. The latticed wooden structure, the wires and planes of fabric began to shake. In the rear, two enormous fans started churning plumes of sand into the air. Orville donned a long cotton duster and drew goggles over his eyes. He climbed aboard the device, perched on a bicycle seat and looked carefully left and right.

"Erwin, *nein,*" Helene cried out, "get back from that thing!"

Erwin, though, was too engrossed to hear. He held a rope attached to the lower muslin plane. Will held one on the other side. The engine reached a shrill and deafening pitch. Orville raised a hand. Erwin and Will released their hold.

The contraption jerked to a start, a dog released from its chain. Helene made a small sound of surprise. Somehow, the possibility of motion hadn't occurred. The device moved faster and faster. Orville leaned hard into the wind. His hands clutched mystical controls. Muslin flapped and billowed. Suddenly, with no warning at all, the thing came abruptly off the ground.

"Holy Christ Colorado," said Garrett.

Helene was thunderstruck. The device, held aloft by forces unseen and unimagined, soared for ten seconds or more, then wobbled, straightened, and gently kissed the earth. The engine fluttered and stopped. Will and Erwin ran frantically over the flats waving their arms. Orville climbed to the ground. Will and Erwin shook his hand and clapped him firmly on the back. Then all three made their way to the hotel.

Erwin was elated. He might explode from excitement any moment. Even

Will seemed pleased. Orville was curiously restrained. His goggles were pushed atop his head. His eyes were ringed with dust.

"*Mutti,* it was something to see, was it not!" Erwin cried.

"It certainly was," said Helene.

"I've got to admit," said Garrett, "I never saw a man ride a wagon off the ground."

"Now I can fix that," Orville said thoughtfully. "I know exactly what happened. This was only the first trial, you understand."

Garrett seemed confused. "You planning on doing that again?"

"Why yes, sir. Yes, I am."

Garrett pulled himself erect. "Not till after noon you're not, Orville. That racket assaults the nerves. I doubt if it's good for the digestion." He turned and went inside.

"It was most entertaining," Helene said, thinking that she ought to be polite.

"The elevator needs more weight," said Orville, as if Helene would surely agree. "That should keep the front firmly down. And I shall tilt the sail planes forward. Too much vertical lift the way they are."

"Yes, of course," said Helene.

"Well, we had best get her back to the barn," Orville said. "Lots of work to do. And thank you for your help, young man."

Erwin flushed with pride. "Sir, I was honored to assist."

Will and Orville walked back into the sun.

"*Mutti,* it is a marvel, is it not!" said Erwin.

"Yes, it is," Helene agreed. "Now you stay away from that thing, do you hear? I want you to promise me that."

Erwin looked stricken. "But Herr Orville has promised that I shall have a ride!"

"And *I* promise that you shall do no such thing," Helene said firmly. "Just get that out of your head."

Erwin turned and fled, holding back the tears that burned his eyes. Helene released a sigh, wondering how she would manage to handle this. Everyone was gone. She seemed to be all alone on the porch.

The sounds of Orville's labor continued throughout the day. When Helene returned from her regular evening walk, a lantern still glowed within the barn. Orville disturbed her more than a little. The man had a fire in his eyes. Such a look frightened her in a man. Her husband's eyes were steady and reassuring. When she saw the two together, Orville and her son, a vague disquieting shadow crossed her heart. Erwin had such a light as well.

"Evening, Miz Rommel," said Garrett. The glow of his cigar came from the porch.

"I did not see you standing there," said Helene. Her tone was clearly distant.

"I suppose you're put out with me some."

"With reason, I should think."

"I guess there is."

"You only guess?"

"All right. I would say you have some cause."

"Yes, I would say that indeed."

"Look, Miz Rommel—"

"Is this an apology, then?"

"I was getting to that."

"Then I shall accept it, Herr Garrett."

Garrett shifted uncomfortably. "That wagon will be ready in the morning. Now Albuquerque's a hundred and twenty miles through real bad country in the heat. There can be no question of such a trip. On the other hand, it is only fifty miles down to Roswell and the train. I shall have Will ride along and see that you get there safely."

"I am grateful, Herr Garrett."

"You don't have to be at all."

"Perhaps you could pack a nice lunch."

"I don't see why I couldn't."

"And rig some kind of shade for the wagon."

"I could do that, yes."

"How nice. A very thoughtful gesture."

"Miz Rommel—"

"Yes, Herr Garrett?"

Garrett was on the brink of revelation. He had steeled himself for the moment. He would bare the fires of passion that burned within. She would be frightened and appalled but she would know. He saw, then, as the words began to form, that her skin matched the pearly opalescence of the moon, that her hair was saffron-gold, spun fine as down from a baby duck. In an instant, his firm resolve was shattered. He muttered parting words and turned and fled.

A most peculiar man, thought Helene. A drunkard and a lecher without a doubt, yet God was surely within this wayward soul, as He is within us all.

She had meant to go directly to her room. Yet she found her steps taking her to the barn and knew the reason. Erwin was surely there. The matter must be settled. She loved the boy intently. Anger struggled with the pain she felt in her heart. They had never quarreled before as they had that morning. She had sternly forbidden him to have anything to do with Orville's device. Yet he had openly disobeyed. Helene had no desire to quell his spirit. Still, she could not brook open rebellion in her child.

The moon was bright with chalky splendor. The broad backs of the horses moved like waves on a restless sea. A man came toward her through the dark. From his quick, awkward gait she knew at once that it was Will.

"Good evening," she said. "Can you tell me if my son is back there, please?"

"Yes, ma'am, yes, he is," said Will. "He's surely there, Miz Rommel."

Why did the man act in such a manner? He was ever bobbing about like a cork. As if there might be danger in standing still.

"He is *not* supposed to be there." Helene sighed. "I am afraid he has disobeyed."

"That wagon will be ready in the morning," said Will.

"Yes. So Herr Garrett has explained." She felt suddenly weary, eager to put this place behind her. "Do you know Erwin well? Have you talked to him at all?"

"No, ma'am. Not a lot. He mostly talks to Orville."

"He feels some kinship with your brother."

"Yes, he surely does."

"He is a free spirit, your brother. I see that in him clearly."

"I guess he's that, all right."

"A man pursuing a dream?"

"He has never been different than he is. The way you see him now. When we were boys he'd say, 'Will, there is a thing I have to do.' And I'd say, 'What would that be, Orville?' And he'd say, 'Man sails boldly before the wind across the seas. I would set him free to sail the land.' And I'd say, 'Orville, why would you want to do that?' Lord, I guess I've asked that question a million times."

"And what would Orville say?"

"Same thing every time. 'Why not, Will?' "

"Yes. Yes, of course," Helene said softly. Oh, Erwin, have I lost you to your dreams so soon!

"Miz Rommel . . ."

"Yes, Will?"

Will bobbed about again. "Maybe I have no business speaking out. If I don't, you just tell me and I'll stop. That boy wants to ride in Orville's machine. Wants it so bad he can taste it. I hope you'll relent and let him do it. He's a boy bound and determined is what he is."

"I think I know that, Will."

"I am a man of practical bent, Miz Rommel. I will never be anything more. I used to see this as a virtue in myself. In some men maybe it is. In me it is a curse, the great failing of my life. Mr. Garrett thinks Orville is a fool. That I am a man who's lost his spirit. Perhaps he is right about us both. But he does not know the truth of the matter at all. It is not my brother's folly that brought us here but mine alone. *I* failed. *I* brought us down. We had a small shop where we repaired common household items. Coffee mills, lard presses, ice shavers and the like. Not much, but it kept us going. I felt there was something more. I reached for a distant star and invested quite heavily in the windmill accessory business. I think Orville sensed that I was wrong. Out of kindness, he did nothing to dissuade me. When we left Ohio we had nothing but our wagon. A few days' food and the clothing on our backs. And Orville's wood and muslin and his motor. Our creditors demanded these as well. I have never stood up for myself. Not once in all my life. But I stood my ground on this. Your Erwin is a good boy, Miz Rommel. Let him be what he will be."

"Yes. Yes," said Helene, "I understand what you are saying. And I am grateful to you, Will."

Helene was taken aback by this long and unexpected declaration. She hadn't dreamed the man owned so many words, or that he had the passion within him to set them free. Now, as he tried to speak again, he seemed to see what he had done. He had tossed away countless nouns and verbs, spent whole phrases and contractions he couldn't retrieve. Clutching his hat, he bolted past her and disappeared. Helene listened to the horses stir about. Orville laughed and then her son. It seemed one voice instead of two. She made her way quickly to her room.

Erwin's mother had asked him if knew about the man and Erwin did. He knew John took him all his meals. He knew the man never left his room. He was much too angry at his mother to tell her that and so he lied. The lie hurt. It stuck in his throat and stayed, no matter how hard he tried to swallow. Late the night before, when he came in from working in the barn, she was sitting waiting quietly in the dark. They burst into tears and cried together. Erwin told her he was sorry. She said that it was over now and done. He didn't feel like growing up and yet he did.

It took all the courage he could muster. Just to stand in front of the door and nothing more. What if John came up the stairs? He wasn't afraid of John and yet he was.

The door came open with ease. Erwin's heart beat wildly against his chest. The room was musty, heavy with unpleasant odors. Stale air and sour sweat. Food uneaten and chamber pots neglected. Mostly the smell was time. The room was layered with years. Erwin saw yesterdays stuffed in every corner.

A window centered the wall. The morning burned a harsh square of brightness, yet the light failed to penetrate the room. It was stopped, contained, it could go no farther than this. The sound of Orville's machine worried the quiet, probed like a locust through the day.

"You stand there, boy, you'll turn to stone. Or is it salt? I can't recall. Salt or stone one. Get over here close so I can see."

Erwin jumped at the voice. He nearly turned and ran.

"It's salt. Salt for certain. Lot's wife. Sodom and Cincinnati. Lo, the wicked shall perish and perish they do. I have seen a great many of them do it."

Erwin walked cautiously to the window. The man sat in shadow in a broken wicker chair. The chair had once been painted festive yellow. Down the arms there were eagles or maybe chickens in faded red. Cactus the pale shade of leafy mold. For a moment it seemed to Erwin that the man was wicker too, that the chair had fashioned a person out of itself, thrust brittle strands for arms and legs, burst dry backing from Chihuahua, Mexico, for springy ribs. The whole of this draped with tattered clothes of no description. Hair white silk to the shoulders and beyond. The head newspaper dry as dust, crumpled in a ball and tied with string about the brow, a page very likely blown six hundred miles from Fort Worth across the flats. Eyes and nose and shadow mouth vaguely nibbled into shape by friendly mice.

Or so it all seemed on this attic afternoon.

"Well, what's your name, now?" the man asked, in a voice like rocks in a skillet.

"Johannes Erwin Eugen Rommel, sir," said Erwin, scarcely managing to find his voice at all.

"By God. That's more name than a boy needs to have, I'll tell you sure. What do they call you for short?"

"Erwin, sir."

"Erwin sir and two more. Might be handy to have a spare at that. Knew a man called Zero Jefferson White. Couldn't remember who he was. What does your father do?"

"He is a schoolmaster, sir."

The paper mouth crinkled in a sly and knowing way. "I am aware of that, you see. John has told me all. I am kept informed, and don't forget it."

"Are you a hundred, sir?" The words came out before he could stop them.

The mouse-nibble eyes searched about. "I might be, I couldn't say. What year you think it is?"

"Nineteen hundred and three, sir."

"It is? Are you sure?" The man seemed greatly surprised. "Then I am likely forty-four. I have lived a fretful life and half of that in this chair less than a man. It's a wonder I look no worse. How old are you?"

"Eleven, sir. I shall be twelve in November. When I am eighteen I shall become a *Fahnenjunker*. I will be a fine officer cadet, and I shall excel in fencing and riding."

"I doubt a soldier's life would have suited me at all. Parades. Lining up and the like. That kind of nonsense and wearing blue shirts. Never trust a man in a blue shirt. You do, I can promise you'll live to regret it."

The man seemed intrigued by the sight beyond his window, by the sleek muslin craft cutting graceful figure eights across the sand. The engine clattered, the fans roared, and Orville sped his dream across the desert raising great plumes of dust in his wake. The dust rose high in the still, hot air and hung above the earth like yellow clouds.

"Charlie Bowdrie and old Dave Rudabaugh would go pick the best horses they could find and start out from Pete Maxwell's place and ride the mounts full out. Ride them full out without stopping, you understand, until one or the other dropped dead, the horse still running being the winner. The other horse, too, would generally die, as you might expect. A senseless thing to do. Dangerous to the man and plain fatal to the horse."

"I am sorry that you are ill, sir."

"What? Who said that I was?" The paper eyes came alive. "Definitions, boy. I am done, mortally hurt. That is not the same as ill. Ill, as I recall, is simply sick. Taken with disease. An affliction or discomfort of the body. I am mortally hurt is what I am. Cut down, stricken, assaulted by violent hand. Felled with a bullet in the spine. God in Oklahoma, that's a wonder," the man said, following Orville's path. "A marvel of nature it is. I wish Charlie Bowdrie could see it. I would give some thought to the army. I can think of nearly thirty-two things I'd rather do. Course that's entirely up to you. I went to Colorado one time, me and Tom O'Folliard, driving horses. Came back quick as I could. The cold there not to my liking at all."

"You got to go now," said John, and Erwin wasn't sure just how long he'd been standing there in the room.

"That canopy will shade you from the sun," said Garrett. "I don't expect the heat will be bad. You'll reach Roswell before dark and Will'll see you settled before he leaves."

"Thank you," said Helene, "we are grateful for your help."

Will sat straight as a rod beside Erwin and his mother. He was proud of this new if only temporary post as wagon driver, and was determined to see it through. Orville wore his duster and his goggles. Earlier, after he had taken Erwin racing over the flats for nearly a full half hour, he had given him a finely rendered pen-and-ink sketch of his muslin craft. John gave him two brass buttons, which he said had belonged to a U.S. Army major prior to a misunderstanding with Apaches in the Sierra Diablo country, which is south of the Guadalupe Mountains in Texas.

Garrett extended his hand. "Take care of your mother, boy. I have confidence that you will make yourself proud."

"Yes, sir," said Erwin.

"Well, then." Garrett extended his hand again, and Helene laid white-gloved fingers in his palm for just an instant. He studied the fair lines of her face, the silken hair swept under her bonnet. Strangely enough, he found he no longer regretted her departure. To be honest, he was glad to see her go. Keeping real people and phantoms apart was increasingly hard to do. Delusions he'd never seen were lately creeping into his life. An old lady crying in the kitchen. A stranger at the table betting Queens. The woman only served to cause confusion, being real enough herself while his fancy made her something she never was.

"I'm giving you the shotgun, Will," said Garrett. "I don't see trouble but you use it if there is."

"Yes sir, I surely will."

"You know where the trigger is, I guess."

"I surely do."

"And which way to point it, no doubt."

"Quite clearly sir, yes, I do."

"Then make sure you—"

"Oh. Oh, my!" said Helene, and brought a hand quickly to her lips.

Garrett turned to see her concern. The sight struck him in the heart. "Christ Jesus California!" he said at once, and stepped back as if felled by a blow. John stood in the door with the wicker chair, his great arms around it like a keg, the chair's pale apparition resting within. Garrett was unsure if this image was whiskey-real or otherwise and greatly feared it was the latter.

"John," he managed to say, "what in *hell* is he doing out here!"

"Mr. Billy say he ride," John announced.

"Ride what, for God's sake?"

"Ride that." John nodded. "He say he ride in Orville's machine."

"You tell him he's lost his senses."

"Mr. Billy say to tell you he going to do it."

"Well, you tell Mr. Billy that he's not," Garrett said furiously. "This is the most damn-fool thing I ever heard."

"Tell Mr. Garrett I can kill myself any way I want," Billy said. He looked right at Garrett with a wide and papery grin. "Tell him I do not need advice from a fellow can't shoot a man proper close up."

"So that's it, is it," said Garrett. "You going to come downstairs every twenty-odd years now and pull *that* business out of the fire. By God, it's just like you, too. I said I was sorry once; I don't see the sense in doing it twice."

"Miz Rommel," said Billy, "I do not think your boy ought to look to the army. That is a life for a man with no ambition or gumption at all, and it is clear your boy is a comer. Bound for better things. May I say I have greatly enjoyed watching you take your evening walk. I said to Sallie Chisum once, you've likely seen her picture inside if Mr. Garrett hasn't thrown it out or burned it, which wouldn't surprise me any at all, I said, 'Sallie, a woman's walk betrays her breeding, high or low. She might be a duchess or the wife of a railroad baron or maybe even a lady of the night, a woman dedicated to the commerce of lust and fleshly delight, but the walk, now, the walk of a woman will out, the length and duration of her stride will tell you if she comes from good stock in a moment's glance.' Now am I right or am I not?"

"I would—I would really—I would really hardly—" Helene looked helplessly at Garrett.

"Will, Miz Rommel is sitting around in the heat," Garrett said firmly. "Would you kindly get this wagon headed south sometime before Tuesday?"

Will bobbed about with indecision, then flicked the reins and started the team moving with a jerk. Erwin waved. Garrett and John and Orville waved back.

Billy waved too, though in no particular direction. "If you are headed for Roswell," he advised, "there was a fair hotel there at one time. Of course it may have changed hands, I can't say. Mr. John Tunstall and I stopped there once and I recall that the rates were more than fair. A good steak is fifty cents, don't spend any more than that. The cook is named Ortega. His wife cooks a good *cabrito,* if you can find a goat around that's not sick. Don't eat a goat that looks bad or you'll regret it. The coffee's too bitter, though I've known those who prefer it that way to any other. Mr. John Chisum took four spoons of sugar. I could never fathom why. He kept an owl in a cage behind his house. That and other creatures, some considerably less than tame . . ."

When the wagon reached the rise slightly east of the Sallie C., Erwin looked back and heard the engine running strong and saw the white planes of muslin catch the sun, saw the runners racing swiftly over the sand. Orville's duster flew, his goggles flashed, his hands gripped the magic controls. John gripped the chair at Orville's back, and though Erwin from afar couldn't see Billy at all, spiderweb hair like a bright and silken scarf trailed past the wicker arms to whip the wind.

The Nighthawk Rides!
(A Teleplay)

BY WILLIAM F. NOLAN

The following story by William F. Nolan is the most traditional in the book. It is the least traditional in form. It's a teleplay.

Nolan's teleplays are written with the broad, imaginative strokes of a water colorist, or to cut the flack, he is one of those rare writers who writes a screenplay you can enjoy reading, not just seeing performed. I'm of the opinion that had this story been in any other form—short story, novel—it would have been old hat. But the teleplay form gives this type of broadly played, slightly tongue-in-cheek story a zest that is addicting.

I'm also convinced that as mental television, it will do much better here than it would have on the tube. No hammy actors to fluff the lines, no silly camera shots and angles, no commercials advertising soft toilet paper and take-out burgers. Just good old-fashioned, action-packed story of the sort Max Brand used to write, and a movie for the head.

William F. Nolan (known to a rare few as The Blue Hat Kid) lives in the Los Angeles area. He writes for television frequently, is the author of many novels, short stories and nonfiction books. Among his better-known efforts are Logan's Run, *written in collaboration with George Clayton Johnson, and made into a rather indifferent film;* Hammett, a Life on the Edge, *an excellent biography of Dashiell Hammett;* Space for Hire, *a wild science-fiction/ detective farce. He is also the editor of two fine volumes,* Max Brand's Best Western Stories, 1 *and* 2.

Settle back now, switch on the mental television in your head, put any actors you wish in the roles, and have a merry, ole time.

Author's Preface

As you read this teleplay, if my character of the Nighthawk in Old Texas reminds you of Zorro in Old California, the resemblance is purely intentional. And therein lies a tale. . . .

In October of 1977 I met director David Greene in his office at MGM Studios in Culver City. I was there to discuss an idea generated at the top executive level at ABC, calling for a fast-action ninety-minute Western series patterned after the adventures of Zorro. To star a new hero I would create.

The first question I asked was "How *much* like Zorro does he have to be?"

Greene was firm in his reply: "Almost exactly—with one exception."

"Which is?"

"ABC doesn't want this series set in Old California. They kind of like the idea of setting it in Old Texas. With this Zorro-type guy fighting local corruption. A sissy by day, a masked hero in the dark, you know?"

"Oh, I know."

"He needs a name. Something with some zass to it."

I nodded. "How about calling him the Nighthawk?"

"Terrific!" said Greene. "And there's another thing."

"What's that?"

"The network's really *hot* on this one and they need it fast. The outline in a week, the teleplay in two weeks."

"That's fast," I said.

"Can you do it?"

"I can do it."

And I did it. I had the outline on Greene's desk just seven days after our initial meeting. He okayed it with enthusiasm and set me to my task of writing the teleplay.

"Remember," he cautioned me as I left his office, "this guy has to be just like Zorro."

I was excited by the challenge. I had never read any of the early Zorro tales by Johnston McCulley, but when I was twelve I'd flipped over *The*

Mark of Zorro, starring Tyrone Power (1940), had seen it three or four times, and still remembered almost every frame of it. Then there were the Zorro serials from Republic, the Zorro radio show, and (later) Zorro on television. I knew precisely what the network wanted. Also, more than a hundred hard-galloping Westerns by Max Brand had fired my teenage years, and I thought it would be great fun to develop some of my action scenes and characters as Brand might have handled them had *he* been given this assignment.

Two weeks later I was back in Greene's office with my completed teleplay. He read it that afternoon. "Terrific," he told me. "You're a hundred percent on target. ABC will *love* it."

Then silence. Weeks of silence. Finally I called Greene at MGM. "It's a dead monkey," he said sadly.

"Huh?"

"They're not going to produce your script."

"But why? There's got to be a *reason.*"

"There is," he replied in a mournful tone. "They said, and I quote, that it was 'too much like Zorro.' "

End of tale.

The teleplay you are about to read has never been produced. Or printed. Until now. When the Nighthawk rides out of these pages and across the private TV screen inside your head, he will finally reach his audience. I'm very happy about that. I had a ball writing him, and I think you'll find fun and thrills aplenty in his Zorro-like adventures. Happily, the Hawk is in the saddle at last, ready to do battle against "local corruption" in Old Texas— with a tip of his sombrero to Johnston McCulley, Ty Power and Max Brand.

Thank you, gentlemen.

FADE IN:

ESTABLISHING SHOT—NIGHT

A passenger ship steaming sluggishly through the Gulf of Mexico under a Texas moon.

ON SHIP—EXTERIOR UPPER DECK—NIGHT

We come upon what seems to be a shipboard attack. A tall, rugged IN-DIAN wields a long-bladed knife against a gold-headed cane in the hand of a slim, dapper-suited DANDY. The young Dandy drops to one knee under the Indian's charge, twisting aside the head of the cane to produce a sword. He thrusts upward—but the Indian sidesteps.

They circle each other warily. Then the Indian lunges, his knife adroitly blocked by the sword blade. They silently feint and thrust at one another, eyes locked, intense. . . . (The deck is deserted except for this fighting pair.)

Then, surprise! The Indian casually tosses his knife to the Dandy while he, in turn, tosses his sword-cane to the red man. The duel goes on—with each of them an obvious expert in the use of sword and knife. Their speed and footwork are dazzling.

CLOSER

The dapper youth is JAMES "JAIMIE" HEWETTSON—in his early twenties, as slimly built as the blade of his sword. He is clean-shaven, with a strong "American" face.

The Indian is CHAKA, a muscled Comanche dressed in tribal garb, with huge shoulders and wise, alert eyes.

JAIMIE: *(tossing back the Indian's knife)* Enough, Chaka. It's late. We've had our exercise.

Chaka nods, returning the sword-cane to Jaimie. The Indian belts the heavy knife—then "talks" with swift hand gestures to his young master. (It can be seen that the red man is mute.)

JAIMIE: *(continuing)* Yes . . . We should be there by sunup. *(hesitates)* One thing . . . With that last sword thrust . . . you were wide open. I could have gutted you.

The Indian allows a faint smile to cross his wide, solemn face. He makes a single, sharp hand gesture.

JAIMIE: *(nodding)* Ah . . . then you *wanted* me to go for your belly. *(grins)* I apologize, old friend! *(gripping the Indian's right arm)* I should *never* underestimate you!

CUT TO:

EXTERIOR BOAT-DOCK AREA—FULL SHOT—DAY

This is Herrick's Landing—on the Gulf Coast of Texas, 1832—a cross-mix of buckskin-clad colonists, boatmen, long-skirted town ladies, Mexican settlers, soldiers . . . A scene of busy humanity.

We see Jaimie Hewettson moving down the gangplank from boat to shore, grandly outfitted in a tailored European silk-and-velvet suit, top-hatted, and carrying his gold-headed cane. The crowd regards him with a mixture of awe and contempt. Such a dandified European gentleman is rare in these parts, but Jaimie seems unaware of the stir he is causing.

Directly behind him, the Indian, Chaka, follows his master ashore, easily balancing a heavy wooden steamer trunk on each massive shoulder. He, too, rates some attention—although there *are* "friendly" Indian servants and he is not all *that* unique. It is his size and manner that mark him.

Now a hush in the crowd as a magnificent stallion follows them both down the gangplank. This is DIABLO, obviously a thoroughbred, with a silk-black coat and white forelegs. He requires no one to lead him as he steps ashore with grace and confidence, nuzzling his proud head against Jaimie's shoulder. He begins fishing for an apple in Hewettson's long-tailed coat.

JAIMIE: You shameless beggar!

Jaimie gives him the apple, ruffling the stallion's mane. There is affection between them.

Now Chaka moves close to Hewettson, lightly touches his arm. Jaimie turns toward

HIS POINT OF VIEW—RIDERS AND WOMAN

Two MEXICAN SOLDIERS are riding past, with a frightened young INDIAN GIRL stumbling on foot behind them. Her wrists are tied with rawhide, and there's a "lead rope" around her neck. The second rider jerks at the rope from time to time to make her move faster. Each time he does she's thrown off stride, almost falling.

The two Mexicans are drunk, and the first officer is waving a bottle of whiskey in one hand. They laugh roughly as the girl loses her balance and falls. They gleefully continue trotting their horses, dragging her along the ground. She is choking under the tight noose at her throat.

CLOSE ON JAIMIE

His eyes burn with anger at this display of cruelty.

WIDE SHOT—FEATURING JAIMIE

as he charges forward, Chaka at his side—to grab the neck rope, jerking it

hard enough to pull the drunken Mexican from his horse. He crashes into
the dust, stunned and blinking.

The second officer, with an angry bellow, levels his saddle musket at them.
Jaimie slams his cane across the man's wrist, knocking the weapon from his
hands, while Chaka's knife slashes the rope that is choking the girl. He
helps her to stand.

JAIMIE: *(to the mounted officer)* You almost *killed* her!

The girl is coughing violently, hands to her throat.

OFFICER: She belongs to us!

JAIMIE: *(accepting the truth of this)* Then let her ride behind you. Human
property must be respected.

And he helps the wide-eyed girl to mount up behind the angry Mexican—
as the first soldier also remounts.

OFFICER: *(in a fury)* I'll have your *name!*

JAIMIE: You'll have nothing! Now . . . *move!*

He slaps the horse across the withers with the flat of his cane, while Chaka
whacks the rear of the second horse, putting both animals into a run.

CLOSE ON JAIMIE'S EYES
burning with frustration and anger, as we

DISSOLVE TO:
RANCH WAGON—MOVING-DAY
A two-horse wide-bodied ranch wagon bumps over a rutted Texas road.
Chaka rides in the wagon bed with the trunks, while Diablo trots behind on
a loose rope attached to the wagon's rear section.

Jaimie sits with the driver, "DOC" PRITCHARD, grizzled and gray-
bearded—an old family friend come to fetch them home. His face is troubled as he talks of current problems.

PRITCHARD: . . . Lot bad has happened since you took off for Europe,
Jaimie. Whole area's under martial law now. . . . There's no trial, no

justice. . . . Americans are no longer allowed to immigrate. Bustamante closed down the borders two years ago. We're cut off here. While he enjoys himself, living like a king in Mexico City, we suffer under the boot heel of his new Governor. They've even got several colonists jailed at San Antonio!

As they have been talking, the CAMERA SLOWLY PANS BACK, and we see that someone is coming hell-bent . . . at first, specks on the horizon, but now seen as two riders on fast horses, galloping toward the wagon. They rein up sharply in a plume of road dust, as Doc halts the team.

ANGLE ON THE TWO RIDERS—A MAN AND A WOMAN
The man is JONATHAN WHEATLEY—a boy, really, barely out of his teens. He looks untamed, like the horse he rides.
The woman is also very young, a year or two older than her brother. She's SUSANNAH WHEATLEY, in wide hat and buckskins. Her flashing eyes bespeak a strong will, but there is a steady quality about her, wholly lacking in Jonathan.
The girl leans across the saddle to kiss Jaimie on the cheek.

SUSANNAH: Welcome home, Jaimie! *(to the Indian)* I see you took good care of him, Chaka!

Chaka allows her one of his faint smiles.

JONATHAN: *(shaking Jaimie's hand)* How did you like Europe? Is Paris as wild as they say?

JAIMIE: Even wilder! . . . *(chuckles)* You'd do well there, Jonathan.

SUSANNAH: What grand clothes! . . . Did you buy them in London?

JAIMIE: Yes, I had them tailored. No choice, really. Buckskins seem to be out of fashion there. . . .

They all laugh at this—except Jonathan.

JONATHAN: *(serious)* Did Doc tell you how bad things are?

JAIMIE: Yes . . . it's absolutely *rotten!*

JONATHAN: There are those of us who don't intend to go on this way. . . . We're going to *fight!*

JAIMIE: *(questioning)* That's all well and good—but with *what?* . . . Sticks against cannon?

JONATHAN: We can get guns! . . . The point is we *must* act.

JAIMIE: Looks as if I got home just in time!

JONATHAN: *(eagerly)* Then you're *with* us?

JAIMIE: Of course . . . but we'll have to use common sense. When the time is right we can—

JONATHAN: *(overriding hotly)* "Common sense" won't get our lands back— or free those prisoners at San Antonio! The Mexicans crack the whip, and we jump. Well, I'm through playing dog for them! *(a beat)* You're either with us—or you're not!

SUSANNAH: Jonathan . . . give Jaimie a chance! You can't expect him to—

JONATHAN: I'll expect him to *fight* when we do . . . *(a beat, as he wheels his horse around)* . . . and that time is coming soon, *very* soon!

And he rides off.
There is a strained silence.

SUSANNAH: I guess he hasn't grown up so much after all. *(a beat)* It's just that he feels so strongly about things.

JAIMIE: I understand.

In an effort to lighten the mood, Susannah dismounts, walks over to Diablo.

ANGLE AT REAR OF WAGON—ON DIABLO
as the girl pats his silken neck. His eyes flash at her.

SUSANNAH: What a beauty! . . . *(a beat)* Did you get him in Europe?

JAIMIE: Austria. *(proudly)* He's a show horse . . . trained by a Czar.

SUSANNAH: We'll have to ride together soon. The country's changed in four years . . . lots of new settlers. *(climbing back into the saddle)* I have to go. Things to do at the ranch. *(a beat)* We *will* be seeing each other, won't we, Jaimie?

JAIMIE: Positively!

She smiles and gallops off, waving back at them, as we

DISSOLVE TO:

EXTERIOR VERANDA OF HEWETTSON RANCH—DAY

Jaimie mounts the wide porch steps *(as Chaka sees to the trunks)*. At the door to greet him is WILLIAM QUINCY HEWETTSON, a gaunt, straight-backed man in his sixties, with a brush mustache and gunmetal-gray eyes. He is very happy to see his son.

HEWETTSON: *(stepping onto the porch)* James, son! So *good* to have you home again!

And they embrace with much warmth.

JAIMIE: It's good being home, Father!

HEWETTSON: *(to Pritchard)* Come on in, Doc—we'll celebrate!

WIDER—FEATURING PRITCHARD

as he calls up to them from the wagon.

PRITCHARD: Got some sick folks to cure. No time for celebrations. *(whipping up the horses)* Besides, I've ordered myself to quit drinking . . . saves the liver!

And he's off, dust clouding behind the wagon as it heads out for the main road. Coming in as he leaves, several MEXICAN SOLDIERS ride into the yard. While Jaimie waits on the porch, the elder Hewettson goes down to face them.

ANGLE AT BOTTOM OF STEPS—GROUP
The lead officer dismounts as his men wait on horseback.

OFFICER: I have a personal message from Colonel Madero.

HEWETTSON: *(stern-faced)* Then deliver it and get off my land.

The officer's face tightens.

OFFICER: *(with stiff formality)* My Colonel wishes me to warn you regarding certain statements you have made against the policies of Governor Francisco Portilla. . . . My Colonel wishes me to say that such statements will no longer be tolerated.

HEWETTSON: *(heatedly)* Your Colonel can be damned! And the Governor with him!

The officer strikes Hewettson across the face, knocking him back against the steps. Blood flecks his cheek.

CLOSE ON JAIMIE
his eyes fired with anger. We see him surge forward toward the officer, hands fisted—only to confront

SOLDIERS
with their muskets up and cocked, trained on Jaimie and on his father.

BACK TO JAIMIE
realizing that, unarmed as he is, he'll be shot if he goes for the officer. Very reluctantly he backs off, eyes still bright with anger.

ANGLE ON CHAKA
watching all this from the doorway. His impassive face tells us nothing of his emotions.

FEATURING HEWETTSON
as he staggers upright. He swings his head toward the Indian at the door.

HEWETTSON: *(in a shout)* Chaka! Fetch my pistol!

JAIMIE
again looking at

SOLDIERS
ready to fire if this command is obeyed.

BACK TO JAIMIE

JAIMIE: No, Chaka! I'll handle this.

and he moves toward the officer, forcing a smile. To save his hotheaded father he's made a decision—to placate the officer. His manner becomes mild; his tone softens.

ANGLE ON GROUP
as Jaimie faces the officer.

JAIMIE: I must apologize for my father's words. He is a strong-tempered man. *(a beat)* I shall personally see to it that he heeds Colonel Madero's warning.

The officer is furious—grabs Jaimie by the front of his London shirt.

OFFICER: You'd best see that he does!

Jaimie sniffs, as if offended. He steps back, adjusting his shirt. His father is looking at him, amazed at this sudden change in Jaimie's manner.

JAIMIE: You need not abuse my person, Lieutenant. As a gentleman, I deplore physical violence.

The officer grunts out a harsh, abusive laugh, turns to remount his horse. The soldiers gallop from the yard, leaving Hewettson to stare at his son.

ANGLE ON FATHER AND SON

HEWETTSON: *(hotly)* You've disgraced my name by apologizing to that cur!

JAIMIE: They mean what they say, Father. They have the power to imprison you!

HEWETTSON: I'm not afraid of Madero! *Or* of the Governor. *(a beat)* And I didn't think *you* would be either.

JAIMIE: *(flatly, telling the truth)* I'm not.

Hewettson stares at him.

HEWETTSON: *(in a tone of disgust)* I don't know what four years in Europe did to you, but you act like no son of mine!

And he mounts the steps to enter the house, slamming the door behind him.

ON CHAKA AND JAIMIE
as the tall Indian awaits Jaimie on the porch. There is pain in Chaka's eyes.

JAIMIE: *(intense voice)* I know—you think I failed him! Actually, I saved his life. *(grips Chaka's shoulder)* But fear not, my friend! Today you see me bleat like a lamb, but soon—when the time is right—you'll see me swoop like a hawk!

We CLOSE on Chaka's face. He reveres Jaimie Hewettson. The trust is there.

CUT TO:
INTERIOR MAIN BALLROOM—GOVERNOR'S HOUSE—FULL NIGHT
A gala affair is in progress. A band plays waltz music as couples swirl about the room in grand style. The ladies are in low-cut, full-skirted gowns; the men are in formal attire, with a considerable number of uniformed Mexican officers among them. In fact, Jaimie Hewettson is one of only two Americans in the group.

IN ON JAIMIE AND PARTNER
He is dancing with DOLORES MARIA BERNADOTTA DE ESCANDON. She was never pretty, even as a girl. She is now well past thirty and the faded bloom of youth has left her dumpy and plain-faced. Her movements are clumsy and self-conscious, and it is obvious that she is utterly entranced with this handsome young man.
Jaimie grunts as she accidentally steps on his foot.

DOLORES: Is something wrong?

JAIMIE: Oh, no. You . . . uh . . . you dance beautifully.

DOLORES: Father taught me. He says it's important to be schooled in the social graces!

JAIMIE: Indeed! A woman like you belongs in Paris. *(a beat, as he makes a sweeping gesture)* I see you on the Champs Élysées.

DOLORES: *(dumbly)* Is that in France?

JAIMIE: *(momentarily thrown off stride by her stupidity)* Yes . . . it is. And I—

DOLORES: *(overriding)* Oh, there's Father now! *(waves rather wildly)* He loves to see me have a good time!

ON HER FATHER
DOMINGO DE ESCANDON, awkward, gross-bellied, coarse-featured. He stands near the arched doorway and, seeing his daughter, boorishly returns her wave, managing in the process to spill some wine on the front of his ill-fitting officer's uniform.

BACK TO DOLORES AND JAIMIE
as their dance continues.

DOLORES: *(proudly)* Father's in charge of the prison compound at San Antonio!

JAIMIE: So I'm told. I imagine he's been kept quite busy of late . . . what with all the recent arrests. . . . *(casually)* How many prisoners does he have there now?

DOLORES: A dozen or more, I suppose. *(sniffs)* Rebels are so tiresome! Always causing a disturbance.

JAIMIE: Well, I'm sure your father can handle them.

DOLORES: He'll want to meet you, Mr. Hewettson.

JAIMIE: *(chiding tone)* Ah, but you must call me James . . . *(smiles, all charm)* And I shall call you Dolores!

DOLORES: How charmingly informal! *(giggles)* It's almost wicked . . . the way we're so *alike!* I, too, am bold and unconventional!

And she gives him a suggestive look meant to be sexually alluring. For a moment he stares at her, at a loss for words, but fortunately, at that moment the waltz ends, and he escorts her back to the punch table.

ANGLE AT TABLE
as Jaimie is in the act of dipping out some punch for Dolores, a hand touches his shoulder. He turns and is startled to face a trim young American wearing a Mexican Army Captain's uniform. This is ANSON HUBBARD.

HUBBARD: *(in a tentative tone; not sure of what reaction he'll encounter)* Hello, Jaimie.

JAIMIE: *(cool)* Well, Anson . . . or should I address you as Captain Hubbard?

HUBBARD: I wrote you in Europe, about my promotion, but you never answered my letters.

JAIMIE: *(ignoring this remark)* From an Ohio schoolboy to Texas immigrant to an officer for Mexico. *(a beat, with irony in his voice)* You've come a long way, Anson.

Hewettson finds it impossible to conceal the scorn he feels regarding the turncoat activities of his former friend.

HUBBARD: I'm afraid dirt-farming never really appealed to me, Jaimie. *(smiles tightly)* But then, Ohio's a long way behind *both* of us.

They stare at one another until the awkward silence is broken by a Governor's AIDE, who comes up to Jaimie.

AIDE: Excuse me, sir, but the Governor wishes to greet you.

Jaimie excuses himself to Dolores and goes off to

THE GOVERNOR

a hard-eyed, heavy-bodied man well into middle age, with the look of corruption in his thick jowls: RAFAEL FRANCISCO PORTILLA. He smiles as Jaimie approaches.

PORTILLA: Ah, Mr. Hewettson. I must tell you how gratified I am that you were able to accept my invitation.

JAIMIE: *(with a slight bow)* My pleasure, Governor Portilla.

PORTILLA: Considering the unfortunate problems we are encountering here in the Texas colony, very few Americans are friendly toward us. *(a beat)* Our collection of the new customs tax, vitally needed to support our army of brave soldiers, is not an easy task to accomplish.

JAIMIE: I can appreciate your job is a difficult one.

PORTILLA: *(oily smile)* I would hope that your father, who is highly regarded in the colony, could also be persuaded to appreciate my position.

JAIMIE: Father's good sense will prevail, I'm sure. With my help.

PORTILLA: *(beaming)* Splendid, splendid! And now—to more pleasant matters. *(a beat)* I am told that you are proficient in the musical arts!

JAIMIE: To a degree . . . *(with a modest shrug)* A minor talent, I assure you.

Portilla nods toward the musicians' area.

PORTILLA: Please . . . favor us!

Hewettson smiles, walks over to the musicians, CAMERA PANNING, and bows to a mustached violinist.

JAIMIE: If I may?

The man nods, handing over his instrument.

ANGLE ON JAIMIE

as he tucks the violin smoothly under his chin, raises the bow, and begins to play expertly, and with spirit, a European dance tune.

DISSOLVE TO:

CORRAL AT HEWETTSON RANCH—JAIMIE AND DIABLO—DAY

He is in riding clothes (but since they are London-cut, they are still quite regal for the area). With swift strokes he brushes down Diablo's sleek black coat, as Susannah rides up in background.

She dismounts, walks over to Jaimie and the thoroughbred. The horse nuzzles her shoulder.

JAIMIE: Diablo fancies you, Susannah! Usually he's quite cool to strangers.

SUSANNAH: *(rubbing the stallion's neck)* He's a fine animal! Are you riding him today?

JAIMIE: *(shocked tone)* Oh no! I'd never risk Diablo over this kind of terrain. He's strictly a show horse. *(proudly)* I plan to exhibit him in New Orleans.

Susannah looks sad.

SUSANNAH: I wonder if he likes being pampered.

JAIMIE: What he likes or doesn't like is of no concern to me. He does exactly what I command him to do.

And he steps back, snapping his fingers.

ANGLE ON DIABLO

Jaimie claps his hands twice, and Diablo spins in a circle, then prances backward around the corral, with high, mincing steps.

ON SUSANNAH

She is not pleased.

SUSANNAH: I think he's too beautiful to be turned into a performing clown!

And she strides toward the veranda.

⸱F THEM

.he corral after her.

ou going?

drink. A glass of your father's best wine will do nicely.

young ladies don't drink in the morning.

m *not* a proper young lady. *(a beat)* I not only drink, but I also
ammit!—when I get angry.

ou've changed, Susannah.

ops to look at him.

sANNAH: *(with a soft note of regret)* So have you, Jaimie.

ANGLE ON VERANDA

as Chaka comes out the door, leading a long-haired French poodle. The dog
is nervous and high-strung.

SUSANNAH: *(smiling up)* Morning, Chaka!

The Indian nods solemnly. Now Susannah comes up the steps to pet the
dog.

SUSANNAH: She's new, isn't she?

JAIMIE: *(joining them)* Yes, a gift of Dolores de Escandon . . . knowing
my weakness for superior animals. Her name's Choo-Choo, and she—

He breaks off, peering at the dog, then frowning at Chaka.

JAIMIE: *(continuing)* I told you to keep her brushed! She's picked up a
bramble from the yard.

Chaka makes a small "sorry-about-that" hand movement, but Jaimie continues to berate him.

JAIMIE: I simply won't have it, Chaka! Your laziness will not be condoned. Take Choo-Choo inside and comb her out. Now!

The Indian leads the nervous poodle back inside.

ANGLE ON SUSANNAH AND JAIMIE
Now she's *really* annoyed at him.

SUSANNAH: You treat your horse and dog better than your servants!

JAIMIE: *(with a faint smile)* But, dear Susannah, my animals are thoroughbreds.

She stares hard at him; she can't believe the things she's hearing.

SUSANNAH: What happened to you in Europe?

JAIMIE: I don't understand.

She sits down on the top step, looks out over the rich spread of land.

SUSANNAH: I thought that when you got home *(a beat)* that you'd help us against Portilla. Instead, you attend his parties . . . accept gifts from wastrels like that Escandon woman—

JAIMIE: *(sternly)* That kind of talk is uncalled for. I really don't—

But he pauses as his attention is taken by

RIDER—FULL SHOT
as, at that moment, Captain Anson Hubbard rides into the yard, dismounting to approach the porch.

PORCH—ALL THREE
Jaimie is not pleased to see him, and Susannah flushes, looking disturbed.

HUBBARD: *(nodding coolly to Hewettson)* Jaimie . . . *(then to the girl)* I thought we were to ride together this afternoon, Susannah.

SUSANNAH: I told you, Anson, that I did not wish to see you again.

HUBBARD: Then your brother's been talking against me?

SUSANNAH: And why not? How can you continue to wear that uniform after the way Madero's been treating the colonists? *(a beat)* Maybe Jonathan is right! Maybe we should stand up and fight!

HUBBARD: I'm surprised to hear you say that, Susannah. Your brother's a hothead. I'm saddened to hear you echo his sentiments.

JAIMIE: Personally, I see nothing but folly in any form of open rebellion. Like it or not, we're under Mexican rule here, and our grievances must be processed through proper channels. *(a beat)* And Anson is right about Jonathan's being hotheaded. As for me, I pride myself on being a realist.

SUSANNAH: No, I'll tell you what you are, Jaimie. *(tight)* You're a spineless fop! . . . And I've had quite enough of you both!

And she turns her back on them, moving down the steps to her horse. Hubbard quickly follows. Jaimie watches them go, then looks toward

CHAKA
in the doorway. He exchanges a knowing look with Jaimie as we

DISSOLVE TO:
INTERIOR PRISON SECTION OF SAN ANTONIO GARRISON—ON ESCANDON
Domingo de Escandon is tipped back in a chair, against the wall, snoozing like an immense pig.
A soldier comes up to nudge him.

SOLDIER: Wake up! . . . It's the Colonel!

Escandon lumbers to a standing position, the chair falling behind him. He puffs and sputters, trying to awaken himself.

ANGLE ON OUTER CELL DOORS
as a loud offstage voice is heard.

VOICE: *(offstage)* Open up here! . . . *Open,* I say!

Escandon is there, fumbling a key ring from around his swollen neck.

ESCANDON: *(wheezing)* The keys are here, my Colonel! They never leave my body.

He keys open the door to admit
AUGUSTIN JOSÉ MADERO. He's a formidable-looking man in his early forties, with iron-gray hair and dark eyes. There is no slackness to his trimly uniformed body; he is all military steel—an officer of strength and purpose. Madero moves close to Escandon, sniffs his breath.

MADERO: Lieutenant Escandon . . . I smell whiskey!

The fat man crosses himself.

ESCANDON: In the name of San Antonio himself, I swear it is of the previous evening! To drink on duty is a crime beyond imagining!

The Colonel squints at him.

MADERO: I'll let it go this time. But if I ever smell whiskey on your breath again, I'll have your bloated head on the end of my sword!

Escandon tenderly fingers his neck. Nods mutely.
CAMERA FOLLOWS them, as they proceed deeper into the cell block. Again, Escandon takes the key ring from his neck to unlock a second door. The third key on the ring is for the prisoners' cells.
Madero directs him to open one of them.

ANGLE ON CELL
as Madero steps inside, scowling down at

PRISONER
sprawled on a wooden cot, pale and breathing heavily. He looks very sick indeed.

WIDER
as Madero jostles him with a boot tap.

MADERO: Up, you lazy swine!

The prisoner blinks dully at the tall officer.

PRISONER: I . . . can't . . . *sick* . . . very sick . . . need . . . doctor . . .

MADERO: What you need is a lash across your back! *(turns to Escandon)* I won't have a prisoner here who refuses to work. . . .

ESCANDON: But . . . my Colonel, as you can see, he cannot stand! I have tried to—

MADERO: *(cutting him off)* You are a fool, Escandon—to let a lazy dog deceive you. Have him up and on work duty by tomorrow morning, or else I'll—

Before Madero can finish the threat, a soldier approaches him, leans close to deliver a message (which we cannot hear) in a low, urgent voice.

MADERO: *(continuing)* Of course. At once.

And he wheels from the cell—with Escandon hurrying after him to open the outer doors. . . .

CUT TO:
INTERIOR BEDROOM OF GOVERNOR'S HOUSE—ON PORTILLA—DAY
A servant is with the Governor, preparing to dress him in one of Portilla's flashy dress uniforms.
There is a KNOCK at the door.

PORTILLA: Enter.

The door opens and Madero is there.

MADERO: You sent for me, Governor?

PORTILLA: Ah yes, Augustin . . . come in, come in. We can talk while I dress.

The Governor is being dressed during the scene, with the servant performing in the manner of one who is dressing a matador. Portilla is a proud man when it comes to his attire—and we see this pride demonstrated here.

PORTILLA: I sent for you to ask a simple question. . . . What has happened to the taxes?

MADERO: They are being collected, day by day. But as you know, I am overextended . . . the area is large . . . there are many colonists. . . .

PORTILLA: You give me excuses—yet with each passing week El Presidente grows more impatient. . . . He inquires about his tax, Augustin. What am I to tell him?

MADERO: The colonists are stubborn and uncooperative. . . . They claim poverty . . . crop failure . . . that they cannot pay us. . . . *(a beat)* My men warn them, even *beat* them, but often we come away empty-handed. The stone will not give blood! Also . . . *(a beat)* they have leaders who urge resistance.

PORTILLA: Ah yes . . . such men as William Quincy Hewettson. . . . He is an influential force here. . . . If we seize his land . . . imprison him . . . we risk a wave of colonial unrest which would be most unpleasant.

MADERO: I have warned him! More than once. *(a beat)* At least his son appears no threat to us.

A laugh begins deep in Portilla's belly—and rumbles up to his throat.

PORTILLA: Ha! . . . That violin-strumming milksop has no stomach for rebellion! In fact, he may even be able to handle his father for us.

MADERO: I doubt that anyone can reason with old Hewettson. We may be forced to act against him.

CLOSE ON PORTILLA
as he finishes the ritual by slipping into his ornate gold-button uniform coat.

PORTILLA: I sincerely hope not, but . . . what must be . . . must be. *(a pause, as he sees a flaw in the coat)* You! *(to the servant)* Look at *this!* *(holds up the sleeve)* A *spot!* . . . How dare you allow such a thing to happen! . . . I do *not* wear soiled clothing!

He grabs a riding quirt from a nearby table, slashes it across the servant's face, as we

CUT TO:
INTERIOR HEWETTSON RANCH—SITTING ROOM—DAY
Jaimie and Chaka are feinting at one another in the middle of the room, each armed with a foil. (Jaimie is in fencing tights, but Chaka is dressed in his normal attire.)

JAIMIE: *(as they fence)* Father absolutely *insists* that I take lessons, and so . . . *(he lunges, driving Chaka back)* . . . although I made it clear to him that I consider the sport barbarous . . . *(and he executes a dazzling bit of foilwork)* . . . I agreed to humor him. Although I have *no* skill or affinity for such weapons . . .

And he forces Chaka into a corner in a quick series of brilliant assault strokes.

JAIMIE: *(continuing)* . . . I shall, as a gentleman, do my best to learn!

And he whip-spins the foil from Chaka's grasp—has the point of his blade at the Indian's heart.
They both exchange a slight smile as Jaimie steps back, allowing Chaka to pick up his foil. They are about to resume when FOOTSTEPS are heard in the hall.
Chaka instantly racks his foil, resuming the role of "servant" as the door opens and the fencing instructor enters.
He is HENRI BERTRON, thin, dour, long-faced, with sad, drooping eyes. His hands are narrow and long-fingered. His mouth is a down-drawn line.

JAIMIE: *(saluting him with the foil)* Monsieur Bertron!

And he bows. Bertron returns the bow.

BERTRON: *(thick French accent)* I see that you are eager to begin our little session.

JAIMIE: Yes . . . I was just—what is it called?—limbering up. *(laughs)* En garde!

And he executes a series of hopelessly awkward, flat-footed moves—slashing the foil wildly in several directions.

Bertron clears his throat delicately and unracks the second foil from its place on the wall. Takes up his fencing stance—with the look on his face telling us that he *knows* this young clod will *never* make a swordsman. Still, one is paid, so . . .

They begin, as we

CUT TO:

EXTERIOR LOG CABIN—FULL SHOT—NIGHT
as a group of five Mexican soldiers ride up to a modest log cabin belonging to one of the Texas colonists.

They dismount, and their leader, a wolfish man with a thick voice, LIEUTENANT DOMINGUIZ, pounds on the cabin door.

ANGLE AT DOOR
as it is unlatched and a young, raw-faced COLONIST peers out at them.

COLONIST: What . . . do you want?

DOMINGUIZ: You have not paid your customs duty. . . . We are here to collect it.

The man's wife, an attractive young woman, hovers at his shoulder, eyes wide.

COLONIST: It has been a hard year for us. . . . Our crop has failed. . . . We have only enough to buy corn for the winter. . . .

DOMINGUIZ: *(gruff-voiced)* I'm not here to waste time listening to your troubles. . . . Give me what you have. Quickly!

COLONIST: But . . . without corn for bread . . . we'll starve!

Dominguiz crashes past him into the cabin. The soldiers follow him.

INTERIOR LOG CABIN—GROUP
as Dominguiz grabs the trembling wife of the colonist and throws her to one of his men.

DOMINGUIZ: The money—or we take *her* instead.

The soldiers grin at one another, looking greedily at the young woman. The colonist hastily takes down a jar from a shelf, pulls out a small cloth bag of coins, hands the bag to Dominguiz. The Lieutenant shakes the money into the palm of one hand.

DOMINGUIZ: Not enough! *(a beat, as he smiles)* But I am a man of compassion. . . .

And he nods to the soldier holding the wife. She is released—rushes over to her husband.
The soldiers leave.

EXTERIOR YARD OF CABIN
as the group mounts up. Dominguiz swings the bag of coins above his head, laughing with his men—but the laughter is cut off abruptly as a whirlwind descends upon them: A masked rider on a tall black horse explodes into their midst, grabbing the sack of coins from Dominguiz, then galloping off into darkness as quickly as he appeared.

DOMINGUIZ: *(in shock)* We've been *robbed! (suddenly roaring to the men)* After him!

And they thunder away in pursuit.

ON COLONIST AND WIFE
watching all this in awe from the door of their cabin. As the soldiers thunder off into the woods, they turn to go back inside—but pause, listening. There is the DRUM of hoofbeats coming up behind the cabin—a lone horseman—and we realize that the NIGHTHAWK has led the soldiers in *one* direction, then tricked them by circling *back* in the other.

WIDER—THE HAWK
as he rides INTO the SHOT, pulling Diablo to a halt. The colonist and wife get their first clear view of him as he towers above them on the black stallion. He's in red and black: a red silk bandanna covers his face (except for mouth and chin); his shirt is black silk stitched in silver; topping dark riding pants and gleaming thigh boots. A brace of pistols are tucked into the sash at his waist.

NIGHTHAWK: *(from the saddle)* This is yours!

And he tosses the cloth bag of coins to the startled colonist.

NIGHTHAWK: If the soldiers come back, deny that you have seen me. . . .
They must not know your money has been returned.

COLONIST: But . . . why do you help us? Who are you?

NIGHTHAWK: A hawk from the sky . . . who strikes against injustice.

And he wheels the great black stallion around—galloping off into darkness.

CLOSE ON COLONIST AND WIFE
as they stare numbly at one another, then down at the bag of coins in his hand.

CUT TO:

EXTERIOR WHEATLEY RANCH—ON HAWK—NIGHT
as he rides into the ranch yard, taking Diablo close to the side of the house. Now he stands up in the saddle—reaching an open window. With a fluid move, he is through the window.

NIGHTHAWK: *(offstage) (from inside house; a sharp whisper)* Go, Diablo.

ON THE HORSE
We see him wheel about, and trot off to hide himself in the nearby edge of the woods.

INTERIOR HOUSE—ON HAWK
moving through the dark toward

INTERIOR SITTING ROOM
Light seeps from the closed door. Slowly, *very* quietly, the Hawk eases it open, seeing

SUSANNAH
She is seated at a small desk, in her nightrobe, working on some papers. Sensing something, she pivots to face the Hawk. Her eyes widen with shock.

WIDER
as he crosses the room to her.

NIGHTHAWK: Don't be afraid. I won't harm you.

SUSANNAH: Who are you?

NIGHTHAWK: A friend.

Now they both HEAR a thudding of hoofs—and the Hawk moves quickly to the window.

HIS POINT OF VIEW—MEXICAN SOLDIERS
The same group of Mexican soldiers who pursued him earlier. They CLATTER into the yard, dismount, to POUND at the door.

BACK TO HAWK AND SUSANNAH
as he whispers to her:

NIGHTHAWK: Send them away!

SUSANNAH: *(hesitating)* I don't—

NIGHTHAWK: Tell them you've seen *no one! (with urgency)* Trust me!

She looks at him for a long moment as the POUNDING continues. Then she hurries from the room. We STAY WITH the Hawk as he listens, unmoving in the darkness. Below him, the mutter of voices. Finally, he breathes easier as he HEARS the soldiers mount up and ride from the yard.

ANGLE AT DOOR
as Susannah returns.

SUSANNAH: They've gone. Now . . . *(a beat)* Who are you?

NIGHTHAWK: I'm not a bandit.

SUSANNAH: You wear a *mask!*

NIGHTHAWK: Only because I must.

SUSANNAH: What do you want here?

NIGHTHAWK: To warn your brother. *(a beat)* I know that he's attempting to foster rebellion among the colonists. . . .

SUSANNAH: Jonathan hates what's being done to us. . . .

NIGHTHAWK: I understand that. But *he* can't fight Madero's army. *(a beat) I* can. *(intense)* You must make him understand that what he is doing can lead only to his imprisonment. Will you talk to him?

SUSANNAH: I'll . . . try.

She is very close to the Hawk, her face soft in the moonlight. He tips up her chin, kisses her trembling lips.

NIGHTHAWK: Tell your brother to leave the men of Madero to me . . . ! Tell him that a hawk has come to hunt them!

And he moves to the window, whistles once. Diablo gallops up to the side of the house, and the Hawk vaults into the saddle, waves, and is gone.

CLOSE ON SUSANNAH
as she holds her fingers tentatively against her lips . . . her eyes luminous.

DISSOLVE TO:
MONTAGE
Here we see the Nighthawk versus the men of Madero—in a quick blend of action NIGHT SHOTS. Chaka (also masked) rides with him on these forays. We feature trick riding, as Diablo's special talents are seen: spinning in a circle, answering the Hawk's call, weaving in a zigzag pattern as the Hawk rides low-slung along the side of the great horse, et cetera. These MONTAGE SHOTS involve the Hawk and Chaka attacking, stealing tax money, escaping Mexican pursuit.

DISSOLVE THROUGH MONTAGE INTO:
INTERIOR OFFICE OF COLONEL MADERO—TIGHT ON HIS FACE—DAY
It is pearled with sweat. The Colonel grunts, grits his teeth, making a supreme physical effort—as CAMERA BACKS to reveal that he is wres-

tling a huge black man, attempting to apply a neck hold to his massive opponent.

The black man breaks Madero's hold, springs away—and they slowly circle each other in a half-crouch, hands open. . . . Both are stripped to the waist, and sweating.

Lieutenant Dominguiz is also in the room, talking to Madero about the Hawk as the Colonel continues to wrestle. Their entire dialogue in this scene is spoken *as the match proceeds,* with Madero's eyes always on his opponent, never on Dominguiz. Often, the Colonel's words are half-grunted as he engages or breaks a hold.

MADERO: . . . And why has he not been shot or captured?

DOMINGUIZ: We have tried many times . . . and many times we have *almost* had him, until—at the last moment—he slips magically away into darkness.

MADERO: *Almost* is not good enough! He makes fools of us . . . steals our tax . . . routs our soldiers. . . . *(hard; spitting the words)* You are *women. . . . /* That you cannot stop *one* bandit and a stupid Indian!

Dominguiz, as he talks with Madero, keeps circling the wrestlers in an effort to confront his Colonel.

DOMINGUIZ: He has many weapons . . . and his horse is a *devil. . . . /* We place our men in one area, to trap him, and he strikes from another like a ghost!

MADERO: Or a *hawk. . . . /* I want his name! I want that mask torn from his face!

Madero's anger at the thought of the Hawk inspires him to greater effort. Gripping his opponent at the waist, Madero lifts him in a spin, to send him crashing to the floor, as the brutal match continues.

DOMINGUIZ: I know he could not be one of the colonists. . . . They are like frightened sheep. . . . No one of them would dare attack us.

MADERO: Well, what of this Jonathan Wheatley? *He* is a firebrand, a troublemaker. . . . *(a beat)* or William Hewettson. . . .

DOMINGUIZ: Hewettson is too old for such escapades. And I have men watching young Wheatley. . . . He is not the Nighthawk.

MADERO: Whoever he is, he *must* be stopped! Capture him or kill him—I don't care which—but stop this bandit! *(a beat)* I'll take no more excuses. My head is on the block—and so is yours.

And as Madero says these final words, he pins the black man's massive shoulders to the mat—*winning* the contest.

DISSOLVE TO:
EXTERIOR COUNTRY ROAD—FULL SHOT—DAY
Jaimie is returning from town with a wagonload of supplies for the ranch, when he sees a buckboard approaching.

JAIMIE'S POINT OF VIEW
The buckboard is driven by Dolores de Escandon—who waves at him, urging her horse forward.

ANGLE FROM ROADSIDE
as the wagon and buckboard meet, both drivers reining their horses to a stop.

JAIMIE: Dolores! . . . What a *pleasant* surprise.

DOLORES: Shame on you, James! . . . You promised to visit me! *(pouting)* I thought we were friends!

JAIMIE: And so we are! My life has been quite impoverished without a sight of your delicate beauty!

Only a person as stupid as Dolores de Escandon could believe that any man could find *her* beautiful—but the words enchant her.

DOLORES: You make me blush, sir! *(a beat; she giggles)* And how is little Choo-Choo? Are you caring for her properly?

JAIMIE: Ah . . . that delightful minx! . . . She's quite spoiled. Demands to be fed at the supper table. . . .

DOLORES: I'd *really* like to see more of you, James.

JAIMIE: Then we must ride together soon. *(smiles; all charm)* A romantic gallop through the high grasses under the moon!

DOLORES: *(drawing back in alarm)* Oh, no . . . *never* after dark! Not with that dreadful Nighthawk person terrorizing the countryside. *(flouncing her skirt)* No decent woman is safe after dark with that *bandit* running amok!

JAIMIE: *(nodding agreement)* He *is* rather a frightful rogue. I hear that he laughs at bullets, that he fairly *swallows* them like hens' eggs. And that no sword can penetrate his skin.

DOLORES: *(shuddering)* The man's a demon!

JAIMIE: He'll soon be lodged in one of your father's cells, I'll wager.

DOLORES: It would be a feather in Daddy's cap—having the Nighthawk under lock and key!

JAIMIE: You must be very proud of him. . . . I hear that your father is trusted with the only set of keys to the compound!

DOLORES: That's true. And they *never* leave his body, day or night!

JAIMIE: A man of true devotion to duty. *(picking up the reins)* And now . . . regretfully—I must take my leave.

DOLORES: I shan't allow you to go until you *promise* to visit us . . . and bring your violin!

JAIMIE: A promise, then! . . . I've mastered a *smashing* new piece—Maximus Scarmini's Concerto for Stringed Instruments in E minor, Opus 36 *(a beat)* I'm quite sure you're familiar with it.

DOLORES: Ah . . . *(blank-eyed)* I'm quite sure I *am.*

JAIMIE: Splendid! . . . See you soon! *(whips up the wagon, waving)*

DOLORES: *(attempting a French farewell) Oh revere!*

DISSOLVE TO:

INTERIOR BARN—CLOSE ON HOE HANDLE—NIGHT

Against a babble of angry VOICES, the wooden handle is being banged against the floor of the barn in the manner of a courtroom gavel.

FARMER'S VOICE: *(offstage) (loudly)* Friends! . . . Please! . . . We *must* begin.

CAMERA BACK to FULL SHOT—showing us a wide barn, lit by flickering oil lamps.

The barn is filled with two dozen Texas colonists, including Susannah and Jonathan, along with Jaimie and his father.

The group gradually lapses into silence, facing the farmer.

FARMER: You all know why you've been called here tonight. . . . In the last six months our taxes have doubled. . . . Several of our people have been brutalized . . . we have no right to an honest trial . . . farms are being taken away from the poorest among us . . . our women are being mistreated. . . .

SECOND FARMER: We know all that! . . . But what are we going to *do* about it?

JONATHAN: *(a ringing declaration)* We'll take up *arms!* We'll *fight* their tyranny!

A general rumble of discontent among the others; they obviously do not favor Jonathan's radical approach.

THIRD FARMER: Violence is no answer! . . . This bandit who calls himself the Nighthawk has harmed *all* of us with his attacks. He's stirring up a hornet's nest . . . turning the soldiers against us. *(a beat; growing in passion)* We are treated much worse because of him. They think that we encourage him, offer him support, hide him from their patrols. . . .

SUSANNAH: *(breaking in)* The Nighthawk is our *friend!* . . . He stands against the injustice we suffer. . . . I *know* he is good . . . I have met him, talked with him—and I declare him a brave man!

THIRD FARMER: You *defend* a common bandit!

JONATHAN: *(taking up the argument)* He steals for *us!* . . . returning that which Madero's soldiers take away. . . . He keeps nothing for himself. *(a beat)* While we shrink and whimper—he stands up to these brutes with pistol and sword!

A fresh babble of voices . . . until

HEWETTSON: I wish to speak. . . . Hear me!

The voices fade to silence. All eyes are on old Hewettson, who stands grave-faced before them.

HEWETTSON: I condemn violence—but I also condemn passive submission to unjust laws which reduce us to oxen . . . denying us our human rights. *(a beat)* Up to now, I have been preaching passive rebellion . . . I have urged many of you to refuse tax payments . . . but now we need to do *more*.

SECOND FARMER: Short of armed rebellion, what other course do we have?

HEWETTSON: I propose that, here tonight, we elect a delegation to travel to Mexico City—where we can directly confront El Presidente . . . lay out our problems to Bustamante. Surely he will—

JONATHAN: *(leaping in)* He will spit in our faces! *(turning to the others)* Protest has accomplished nothing. Delegations will accomplish nothing. . . . We must *fight!*

Jaimie steps forward.

JAIMIE: The Mexicans have cannon. . . . They have many armed soldiers here and will not hesitate to call in more at the first hint of an armed rebellion in this colony. Texas belongs to them. We *came* to the territory with this knowledge. My father's plan is a sound one. Listen to him . . . *(turns toward Jonathan)* . . . and not to firebrands. Leave it to bandits

such as this Nighthawk to battle Madero's men. Let *him* divert their
attention until justice can be restored. But we must at least *try* to speak
truth to Bustamante.

Jonathan glares at the crowd.

JONATHAN: You're all fools and weaklings! I want no more to do with you.
. . . *(a beat)* I'll raise an army on my own! There are many in this colony
who will support my views.

And he stalks from the barn to a mutter of voices.

ANGLE AT BARN DOOR
No sooner has Jonathan stepped through it than he's seen walking *back-
ward*, into the barn again, a shocked look on his face. His hands are raised.
We discover the reason: Colonel Madero enters—holding a pistol aimed at
Jonathan's stomach.

MADERO: *(eyes on Jonathan, but loudly to all)* This meeting is over! . . .
And Jonathan Wheatley is under official arrest for the crime of armed
resistance to the Government of Mexico.

The fact that Jonathan carries no weapon does not seem to bother Madero.
WIDER as several soldiers, muskets at the ready, enter the barn behind the
Colonel.
We SEE Susannah on the sidelines, watching in desperation. Jaimie's father
surges forward, enraged.

HEWETTSON: Colonel, you cannot do this! . . . I absolutely forbid you
to—

Madero reacts by swinging the barrel of his heavy pistol in a sweeping arc
hard against the skull of William Hewettson—who falls onto the barn floor.

ANGLE NEAR FALLEN HEWETTSON
as Jaimie rushes to kneel beside him—joined by Susannah. In the background the soldiers raise their muskets to a loud rumble of protest from the
colonists. It is clear that Madero's men will fire on anyone who provokes
them.

JAIMIE: *(to Susannah)* He's unconscious. . . .

SUSANNAH: *(looking up at Madero)* You *swine!*

FEATURING MADERO
He chooses to ignore this insult—prodding Jonathan ahead of him with the pistol, toward the outside horses.

CLOSE ON JAIMIE
as he holds the head of his unconscious father in his lap. His eyes are coals of fire. . . .

DISSOLVE TO:
INTERIOR HEWETTSON RANCH—BEDROOM—DAY
William Hewettson lies in his bed, eyes closed—as Doc Pritchard completes his examination, turning to face Jaimie. Chaka stands in background.

PRITCHARD: *(with a sigh)* He's still in a deep coma. . . . *(a beat)* That blow to the head induced a severe concussion.

JAIMIE: But it's been *two days!* How much longer will he stay like this?

PRITCHARD: There's no real way to tell. *(a beat)* He could regain consciousness anytime within the next twenty-four hours, or . . .

JAIMIE: Or what?

PRITCHARD: Jaimie, I don't—

JAIMIE: Doc . . . I want to *know!*

PRITCHARD: If he doesn't come out of this coma in the next twenty-four hours . . . he'll die. *(a beat)* I've done everything I can. It's up to *him* now.

EXTERIOR PORCH OF HEWETTSON RANCH—DAY
as Jaimie bids Pritchard good-bye.

JAIMIE: Thanks, Doc!

PRITCHARD: You don't have to thank me, Jaimie. He's your father—but he's *my* oldest friend.

And as he rides out of the yard, CAMERA PANS to pick up Susannah, who gallops up to the edge of the veranda, vaults down from the saddle.

ANGLE AT STEPS
as the girl rushes up to Jaimie. Her face is tense and strained, her eyes clouded with worry.

SUSANNAH: I've been to the garrison. . . . They won't release Jonathan. They wouldn't even *listen* to me!

JAIMIE: *(bitterly)* Madero doesn't listen to anybody. *(a beat)* Come inside.

INTERIOR HEWETTSON LIVING ROOM
Jaimie brings her some wine as she paces, unable to sit. She takes the wine, sips it.

SUSANNAH: How's your father? Will he be all right?

JAIMIE: We don't know. Everything depends on his coming out of the coma. . . .

She nods—meeting his eyes in a steady gaze.

SUSANNAH: I'm here to ask a favor, Jaimie . . . a very important favor . . . it's about my brother. *(a beat)* Will you help free him?

JAIMIE: I'll do everything I can. I know Governor Portilla. . . . I'll personally petition him on Jonathan's behalf.

SUSANNAH: No, no! . . . Petitions are useless. *(a beat)* The colonists respect your father. They respect the Hewettson name. You could rally them . . . lead them against the garrison. . . .

JAIMIE: Me?!! . . . against musket and cannon? Why, I'd be cut to pieces before I could reach the gates.

SUSANNAH: *(standing; fierce-eyed)* Then you refuse to act like a *man!* . . . And with your own father a victim of Madero!

JAIMIE: Susannah, I assure you—

SUSANNAH: *(overriding)* Oh, if only I knew where to reach him! . . . There's one man who'd do it, who isn't afraid of *any* of them!

JAIMIE: If you mean that bandit . . . who hides behind a mask and strikes from the dark . . . you'd be well advised to stay clear of such a fellow.

She glares at him.

SUSANNAH: You're not one *tenth* the man he is! *(a beat)* I should have known that my asking you for any *real* help would be a waste of breath. . . . Jonathan's in prison . . . maybe being beaten . . . tortured . . . and you talk of *petitions!*

Bitterly, she leaves. Jaimie's face is dark and disturbed. Chaka enters the room, makes a quick gesture.

JAIMIE: Then you heard what she said?

The Indian nods. Makes several more quick flashing hand movements.

JAIMIE: *(continuing)* Yes . . . I *know* she's right. The Nighthawk has to act to save Jonathan . . . although the boy's a bigheaded fool. *(a beat)* Did our new weapons arrive?

Chaka nods.

JAIMIE: Good. I need to know what the four-barrel can do. . . . Also, I want to test the saddle guns. *(crisply)* Fetch the horses. We'll use the clearing at Twin Forks. Should be safe enough.

The Indian moves away quickly.

CUT TO:

EXTERIOR CLEARING IN WOODED AREA—ON BOTTLES—DAY

Four whiskey bottles are lined up on a log, gleaming under the sun. CAM-

ERA PANS to Jaimie, standing a good distance away. A very odd-looking "scatter" pistol is in his right hand—with *four* barrels fanning out from a single hammer.

We SEE him final-check the weapon, then slip it into a special holster at his waist. (He is dressed in ranch attire, *not* as the Nighthawk.)

ANOTHER ANGLE

to include Jaimie and the four bottles (with CAMERA BEHIND the bottles, shooting through at Jaimie).

In one sudden, flowing movement, Jaimie draws and FIRES.

In an abrupt EXPLOSION of glass, all four bottles shatter at the same moment INTO CAMERA.

WIDER ANGLE

as Jaimie exchanges a tight smile of satisfaction with Chaka, who holds a long bullwhip looped in his hand.

Now it's the Indian's turn.

CAMERA PANS to a stuffed-clothing dummy, tied to the saddle of Jaimie's black stallion.

JAIMIE: Forward, Diablo!

The shining thoroughbred breaks into a trot, heading straight for Chaka—who steps aside deftly—and snaps out the whip with a sharp CRACK. The whip wraps itself around the dummy, and as Chaka lunges back, the man-figure is jerked violently from the saddle.

JAIMIE: Bravo! . . . That should give Madero's men a surprise or two.

Now Jaimie slips on a pair of soft kidskin gloves and vaults lightly into the saddle, putting Diablo into a circular gallop around the clearing.

We see that several bottles have been placed on logs around the clearing's perimeter, at widely spaced positions.

Jaimie dips both hands downward, snapping two pepperbox pistols from custom saddle holsters and FIRING with either hand as he rides. With each shot, a bottle explodes into fragments.

ON JAIMIE

as he holsters the two weapons and dismounts, slapping Diablo's neck with affection. The horse rears up, pawing air, and makes a full turnaround on its back feet.

The stunt amuses Jaimie.

JAIMIE: When *we* show off, you've got to get into the act, eh?

Diablo paws the ground, eyes flashing.

JAIMIE: *(to Chaka)* Maybe we should just send *him* after Jonathan!

And on the Indian's faint grin, we

DISSOLVE TO:
EXTERIOR HOUSE OF ESCANDON—FULL SHOT—NIGHT
It is deep night, very late. The moon flushes a wash of pale silver over the sleeping house.

ANGLE AT SIDE OF HOUSE
as the Nighthawk scales a heavy vine that twists upward to an iron balcony. He vaults easily over the railing, landing as lightly as a cat.

EXTERIOR BALCONY—UPPER ANGLE
as he moves to the window, works a slim bit of steel beneath the catch, flips it open—and enters a darkened bedroom.

INTERIOR BEDROOM
as the Hawk stops just inside, allowing his eyes to adjust to the gloom. We hear a heavy offstage snoring. Hawk looks toward

HIS POINT OF VIEW
the sprawled figure of Domingo Escandon. The great-bellied officer sleeps like a land-bound ship in a huge canopy bed. His jaw hangs open, as thick snores issue from his slack lips.
CAMERA IN—to feature the ring of three jail keys looped around his fat neck, below double chins. The keys TINKLE faintly as he snores.

ON HAWK
as he glides ghostlike across the chamber to the bed. He reaches into his jacket, extracts an object: a bar of softened soap.
Now, holding the bar in his left hand, he leans forward and delicately lifts

the first key, easing it up to separate it from the others. He presses the key (CAMERA CLOSE) firmly into the soft bar.

We see a perfect impression of the key in the soap.

WIDER

as he begins to repeat the procedure with the second key, Escandon snuffles, coughs—seems about to wake!

The Hawk leaps back, hand to the pistol in his sash. But the danger passes, as the fat man adjusts his position and lapses back into heavy snoring.

The Hawk resumes work, taking his impressions of the other two keys, but as he finishes, crouched over the bed to return the final key to the ring, CAMERA PANS to show us

the bedroom door (from the hall) opening.

ON HAWK

as light from the doorway spills across his boots, he springs instantly away from the bed into corner darkness.

ANGLE AT DOOR

Dolores is there, holding a glass of water in one hand, two pills in the other.

DOLORES: *(starting into the room)* Papa! . . . Time for your stomach pills! . . . Wake up, Fath——

A hand clamped abruptly across her mouth cuts off the word—as the Hawk drags her back into the hall. With his booted foot, he eases the door shut behind them.

INTERIOR HALLWAY

as the glass falls from her hand, rolls along the strip of rugging. The pills also drop to the floor as she claws at the Hawk's arm, which encircles her body.

NIGHTHAWK: *(hand still over her mouth)* Scream—and it will be the last sound you make!

She nods. No scream. He removes his hand from her mouth, still holding her.

CLOSER ON THE PAIR
as she looks at him with wide, puffed eyes.

DOLORES: Are you here to . . . *rob* us?

NIGHTHAWK: I'm a thief, aren't I? *(makes a sweeping bow)* . . . you may
lead me to your room.

Dolores is suddenly all a-twitter. She is mightily intrigued with the idea of
having a man in her bedroom.

DOLORES: Just what . . . do you intend to *do* with me?

NIGHTHAWK: Why . . . *rob* you, of course.

DOLORES: *(hopefully)* Of my virtue?

NIGHTHAWK: No, dear lady, of your jewels. *(in a firm tone)* That is *all* I shall
take, I assure you.

DOLORES: *(really disappointed)* Oh. *(pulling herself together)* But . . . I'm
only a poor jailor's daughter. I *have* no jewels.

And we CUT FROM her face TO an open jewel box in the hands of the
Hawk.
CAMERA BACK to show her bedroom, all wildly overdone in feminine
bad taste. Dolores stands facing the Hawk as he empties her jewels into a
velvet sack.

DOLORES: *(hot-eyed)* Are you *sure* there's . . . nothing else you want?

And she moves her body, allowing a nightdress strap to fall from one of her
meaty shoulders.

NIGHTHAWK: Nothing! *(as he pushes the strap back into place)* I have what I
came for.

She stomps her foot and bursts into tears, as he leaves the room, locking the
door behind him.

CUT TO:

EXTERIOR WOODS—ON HAWK AND CHAKA—MOVING SHOT—NIGHT
as they ride through the dark woods back to the Hewettson ranch. Chaka is asking his master some questions with quick gestures.

NIGHTHAWK: No . . . he didn't wake. He'll never know the keys were touched. *(pulling forth the jewel bag)* But *these* were a bonus I did not expect. We can dispose of them in New Orleans, then put the money to proper use here. *(chuckles)* I'd say we've done a good—

Chaka raises a hand for silence. He is listening. They pull their horses to a stop.

NIGHTHAWK: What do you hear?

More signs from the Indian.

NIGHTHAWK: *(straining his ears)* Are you certain . . . ? I don't hear anything.

Chaka smiles thinly.

NIGHTHAWK: *(light tone)* Meaning that *I* do not possess the wisdom of the woods?

Chaka nods. Indeed, the Indian's senses are sharpened beyond that of any white man.

NIGHTHAWK: All right, then, let's head over there . . . we may be needed.

And they urge their mounts forward.

NIGHTHAWK: Now . . . walk *softly*, Diablo.

ANGLE ON DIABLO
Amazingly, we see the great animal actually respond to this command by raising and lowering his hooves with *great care* (in a kind of controlled prance through the woods).

EXTERIOR CLEARING IN WOODS—FULL SHOT—NIGHT

In the bright moonlight, a group of Madero's soldiers are riding in a circle around a man on foot in the middle of the clearing.

The man is JAMES BOWIE (later to die at the Alamo). His face is streaked with blood, and his buckskins are ripped from saber cuts, baring his wide chest. Bowie is weaponless—and is being toyed with by the soldiers— the way a dozen cats might toy with a single mouse.

As they circle him on their horses, they taunt and challenge him, knowing they have the man totally in their power. Their sabers are out, and as they ride past Bowie, they slap at him playfully with the flat of their blades. He's exhausted, but still nimble enough to avoid most of their saber strokes, dancing backward at the last instant.

A slain deer lies at the clearing's edge, its life ended by Bowie's knife.

SOLDIER: Perhaps you will learn not to hunt in the woods of Portilla!

BOWIE: *(defiantly)* These woods belong to those who *use* them. I hunt to live.

SECOND SOLDIER: *(fierce; with a sweeping gesture)* All of this land belongs to the Government of Mexico. And El Presidente forbids hunting here!

A LIEUTENANT in charge of the men, a mean-faced, snarling fellow, rides out of the circle and over to Bowie. He draws a pistol from his belt, cocking it.

LIEUTENANT: . . . Let us show this one what we do to those who flaunt our laws.

In the background, the others have halted. The circle falls silent as the Lieutenant aims the pistol at Bowie's head.

ON BOWIE

as he stands defiant, eyes tight on the officer's face. He is looking at death. A muscle jumps along his jaw, but there is no fear in Jim Bowie.

CLOSE ON PISTOL

as the Lieutenant's finger tightens on the trigger, the weapon is suddenly jerked from his hand by the looping end of a CRACKING bullwhip.

WIDER—ON HAWK AND CHAKA

as they charge straight at the soldiers. Chaka has the whip, and the Hawk waves a sword as he rides.

MONTAGE OF BATTLE SHOTS

as Bowie joins his two rescuers in dealing with the soldiers. Bowie pulls the startled Lieutenant to the ground, nailing him with a single punch; he is an incredible fighter, pulling one soldier after another from the saddle and dispatching them with savage blows.

It is soon clear that the men of Madero want no more of the battle—and they take off at a gallop, leaving the three men alone in the clearing.

ANGLE ON BOWIE

as he walks over to the slain deer and retrieves his massive bowie knife, jamming it into his belt, then turning to the others.

BOWIE: Name's Bowie . . . Jim Bowie. And I'm only half a man without this. *(as he pats the blade at his belt)*

They shake hands.

NIGHTHAWK: I've heard of you, Jim.

BOWIE: And I of you. *(a beat; he chuckles)* They say you can take the form of a hawk when need be—fly right away from danger!

The Nighthawk smiles.

NIGHTHAWK: They say a lot of things about me—most of them untrue.

BOWIE: I owe you . . . for saving my life. How do I pay the debt?

NIGHTHAWK: Join us on a mission. We need a man like you.

BOWIE: And what's your mission?

NIGHTHAWK: We're paying a little visit to San Antonio, where some rebel colonists are imprisoned. The tax money Portilla took away from them is there, too.

BOWIE: I'm not a rebel . . . and I don't ride for causes. At least I haven't up to now. *(thinking it over)* Still . . . after what was done to me here tonight . . .

NIGHTHAWK: Then . . . you'll join us?

BOWIE: *(flatly)* You saved my life.

And the Hawk smiles, as we

DISSOLVE TO:
INTERIOR HEWETTSON BEDROOM—ON HEWETTSON—DAY
CLOSE on the face of William Quincy Hewettson. And, for a long moment, he seems as he was when last we saw him—deep in the coma, eyes closed, his skin gray and unhealthy.
But now a change begins: the eyelids flutter open. His mouth moves in soundless words. Suddenly, he sits half-up in the bed, crying out his son's name.

HEWETTSON: *(strangled voice)* James! . . . *Jaimie!*

PAN TO bedroom door as young Hewettson bursts in, a smile on his face. He rushes to the bed, to clasp his father's trembling hand.

ANGLE AT BED

JAIMIE: Father! . . . You—you've come out of it!

The old man looks up at him, blinking.

HEWETTSON: *(weakly)* I . . . need . . . water.

Chaka is quickly there with a glass of cold water. Jaimie takes it, holds the glass to his father's trembling lips. The elder Hewettson swallows, coughs, swallows again.

HEWETTSON: I . . . had a terrible dream. Or perhaps . . . it was real. . . . Madero's men, it was . . . they came with guns . . . the Colonel . . . he arrested Jonathan. . . . *(a beat)* I . . . tried to stop them . . . but Madero . . . he—

JAIMIE: No dream, Father. It really happened. You were struck down. You've been unconscious for many hours.

HEWETTSON: But . . . what of Jonathan?

JAIMIE: They took him. He's in the prison garrison at San Antonio.

HEWETTSON: *(angry)* It's too much! That brute Madero has gone too far!

JAIMIE: Petitions have been sent to Mexico City . . . President Busta-mante will intervene, I'm sure.

A grim voice from behind them:

PRITCHARD: *(offstage)* If he does . . . he'll be too late.

ON DOC PRITCHARD
at the doorway. He walks to them, CAMERA PANNING.

PRITCHARD: Governor Portilla has ordered Jonathan's death. *(a beat)* He'll personally be there to supervise the execution.

Jaimie's eyes blaze. He exchanges a hard look with Chaka (in background).

JAIMIE: *When . . . ?*

PRITCHARD: At sundown. Today. *(a beat)* But there's more. They've taken Susannah to the garrison. She'll be forced to witness her brother's execution. *(bitterly)* Colonel Madero calls it "an object lesson."

Jaimie starts from the room.

HEWETTSON: *(weakly)* Jaimie! . . . Where are you going?

He hesitates, looks back at his father.

JAIMIE: *(gentle tone)* Everything will be all right, Father. I promise you. *(a beat)* I'm going to find the Nighthawk.

And he leaves with Chaka, as we

DISSOLVE TO:

EXTERIOR WALL OF SAN ANTONIO GARRISON—CLOSE ON BRASS CANNON—DAY
The fading rays of the late-afternoon sun dazzle on the cannon's barrel.
CAMERA MOVES along wall to reveal several armed soldiers stationed
near other cannons. They scan the area carefully, ready to loose a deadly
barrage on any who might attempt an attack.

There is the SOUND of boots.

A squad of smartly uniformed Mexican soldiers march into the area. Jonathan accompanies them, his wrists and ankles shackled to heavy chain. He
finds it very difficult to maintain the marching pace with his legs hobbled—
and now falls heavily into the packed dirt of the courtyard.

He is instantly dragged to his feet by Lieutenant Dominguiz, and is pushed
forward again by a soldier who uses his musket to prod Jonathan in the
back.

Dominguiz walks close to Jonathan, taunting him.

DOMINGUIZ: Can you *taste* it, rebel? . . . Is it on your tongue, like sour
brine? . . . The taste of death . . . and the smell of it . . . *(laughs)*
Already you are a dead man—a walking corpse. Even as you move, your
soul prepares itself for hell!

Jonathan glares at him.

DOMINGUIZ: *(continuing)* I want to see how defiant you are when I give the
order to fire! . . . And with your sister looking on. *(a beat)* I will enjoy
that sight, I promise you. I will treasure it like gold. *(smiling)* And it will
be *soon!*

Dominguiz squints at the sky.

HIS POINT OF VIEW—THE SUN
almost at the edge of the horizon. The day is rapidly winding to a close.

BACK TO SCENE

DOMINGUIZ: Are you thinking that perhaps I am wrong? . . . That at the
last moment your miserable friends will come running in to save you?
(snorts) Ha! Let them try. Our cannon will scatter them like grain in the
wind. . . . *(a beat)* So pray to the Madonna . . . to the saints . . . or

perhaps God Himself will save you. *(laughs)* He is the only one who could storm those gates!

Now the squad has halted. Dominguiz steps to one side and orders Jonathan tied to a wooden post sunk deep in the dirt of the yard.

ANGLE AT POST—ON JONATHAN
He is sweating; his bravado has finally deserted him. The muscles along his jaw are tight with strain as he attempts to contain his fear.

WIDER
as we see Dominguiz, who stands in charge of the firing squad, squint his eyes and then smile.

DOMINGUIZ: Ah . . . the Governor *(a beat)* . . . with our guest of honor!

HIS POINT OF VIEW
We see Portilla, dressed for this state occasion, emerging from the inner garrison, followed by Colonel Madero, who walks Susannah Wheatley forward, his hand gripping her arm tightly.
Susannah's stride is firm, her chin high, her back held as straight as that of any soldier.

ON JONATHAN
as he sees his sister, his eyes widen; he strains wildly at his ropes.
Dominguiz walks close to him, grinning.

JONATHAN: Why did you bring Susannah here?

DOMINGUIZ: What better witness for us? After what she sees, she'll warn any others who might wish to rebel. . . . She can tell them how you died.

CLOSE ON SUSANNAH
as she stares at her brother, her eyes tear up; the mental pain is intense for both of them.

WIDER—THE GROUP
The Governor nods to Dominguiz.

PORTILLA: You may retire, Lieutenant . . . Colonel Madero will order the execution.

Dominguiz salutes Madero and steps back, as the Colonel goes forward to stand beside the assembled firing squad. He draws his saber.

MADERO: *(commanding voice)* Prepare . . . arms!

The squad brings up their muskets. Again, Madero squints at the sky.

HIS POINT OF VIEW
as the sun drops below the horizon. Sunset.

BACK TO SCENE
Madero brings up his saber.

MADERO: Prepare . . . to fire.

As each musket is COCKED, PAN TO:

SOLDIERS ON GARRISON WALL
There is agitation in their ranks, as they peer toward

THEIR POINT OF VIEW
A rising cloud of dust beyond the garrison, growing larger, accompanied by an immense drumming SOUND. . . .

BACK TO SOLDIERS
as one of them shouts down to Madero.

SOLDIER: My Colonel! . . . Someone . . . *something* . . . is coming . . . very fast!

ON MADERO
as his eyes narrow with resolve. Whatever is happening, he does not intend to let anything halt this execution.

MADERO: *(shouting at soldiers)* Then *deal* with it!

And he turns back to the squad, again raising his saber.

WIDER—GROUP
as the Colonel's commanding voice cracks over the courtyard:

MADERO: *Aim!* . . .

Each member of the squad sights along his leveled weapon. But now the
NOISE has become very loud inside the garrison. It is like ROLLING
THUNDER—and a sense of alarm is spreading through those in the yard.
Hope flares in Susannah and Jonathan.
Again, Madero hesitates.

ON WALL
as the soldiers fearfully stare at

THEIR POINT OF VIEW
a herd of Texas longhorns, coming like hell itself, straight at the wooden
gates of the garrison.

BACK TO COURTYARD SCENE
as the group realizes that they are all standing directly in the path of a
rampaging herd (since, by now, they do not have to be *told* what is coming
at them).
The firing squad begins to break . . . first one man . . . then another. . . .

ON MADERO
furious, shouting:

MADERO: Stand fast! . . . I *command* you to stand fast!

FULL SHOT
Despite Madero's order to hold, the soldiers break rank in a desperate dash
for the safety of the inner garrison.

ANGLE—FEATURING GOVERNOR PORTILLA
as he, too, starts trotting for safety. Dominguiz and Madero also join the
mass run.

ON SUSANNAH
who rushes over to her brother, begins frantically tugging at the ropes that
bind him to the post. The stout ropes defy her attempts to untie them.

SERIES OF ACTION SHOTS

as the guards FIRE down hopelessly from the wall, into the THUNDER-ING HERD, trying to stop them before they reach the gate. Even a cannon is FIRED—but the longhorns SMASH through, a galloping wall of flesh which splinters the heavy gates like matchwood.

ANGLE AT REAR OF HERD

as three riders, their bodies slung low over their saddles, FIRE pistols to keep the herd in panic movement.

It is, of course, the Hawk, Jim Bowie and Chaka. They ride straight into the garrison behind the herd.

ON HAWK

as he gallops into the courtyard, he sees Susannah and Jonathan, surrounded and battered by the stampeding cattle.

WIDER—FULL SCENE

as the Hawk fights his way through the steers to reach the Wheatleys, leaning from the saddle to slash Jonathan's ropes. Chaka is with him, and the strong arms of the Indian pull Jonathan onto the back of his mustang, just as the Hawk lifts Susannah into the saddle behind him.

They ride through a narrow arch to the inner garrison area as the longhorns, energy spent, mill about in the central courtyard. Their run has ended, but with their wildly tossing horns, they are still dangerous.

EXTERIOR INNER GARRISON—ON GROUP

They all dismount, as Bowie joins them. Suddenly, four soldiers on the wall above begin FIRING down at them.

ON HAWK

as he unlimbers his four-barrel "cannon"—swings it to shoulder level, and FIRES.

ON WALL

as *all four* of the soldiers topple like ninepins from the single blast!

BACK TO GROUP

It is still a very tense situation, and the Hawk snaps out words like gunshots.

NIGHTHAWK
Jim and I are going inside to free the other prisoners . . . *(to Chaka)* You know what to do!

The red man nods, moves off toward an inner door.

NIGHTHAWK: *(to Jonathan)* You and Susannah stay here with the horses. . . . We'll be back.

JONATHAN: I want to go with you!

NIGHTHAWK: And leave your sister? *(handing him a pistol)* Take this. Self-revolving barrel . . . five shots to a load.

Jonathan nods.

BOWIE: Hurry! We're losing time!

And the Hawk takes off with him, sprinting for the prison area.

CUT TO:
EXTERIOR GARRISON POWDER ROOM
as Chaka reaches the room of explosives. He FIRES a charge at the door, blowing off the lock. Quickly, he enters.

INTERIOR POWDER ROOM—ON CHAKA
Using his knife, he splits one of the stacked powder barrels, scoops out a handful of black powder—begins making a trail with it to the door.
A soldier appears in the doorway, musket raised.

SOLDIER: You! *Indian!* Get away from that—

Chaka wheels to FIRE, dropping the man, then aims at the powder along the floor, FIRES again, his shot igniting the edge of the powder line.

ON POWDER
SIZZLING and burning toward the stacked barrels.

CUT TO:
INTERIOR GARRISON PRISON—ON BOWIE AND HAWK

as they break through the outer door, there is a thunderous EXPLOSION offstage. Chaka has done his work well.

NIGHTHAWK: That ought to keep most of them busy for a while!

And he turns to face

ANSON HUBBARD
Jaimie's ex-friend from Ohio, the turncoat officer. Hubbard faces the Hawk and Bowie with a sword in his hand.

HUBBARD: This is as *far* as you go, gentlemen!

WIDER—THE TRIO
The Hawk smiles.

NIGHTHAWK: Stand aside, Hubbard! We're going in.

HUBBARD: Can you walk through steel? Escandon is off duty—and the only set of keys is with *him*.

NIGHTHAWK: *(grinning)* Not the *only* set!

And he holds up his own ring of three. (Made from the soap molds.) Furious, Hubbard lunges at the Hawk, slashing his jacket along one sleeve.

NIGHTHAWK: *(tossing the keys to Bowie)* Use these, Jim! . . . Free the men. *(a beat, as he pulls his sword)* I'll deal with our treacherous friend.

We see Bowie unlock the first door, then head for the second.

ON HAWK AND HUBBARD
as Jaimie advances, blade in hand.

NIGHTHAWK: You should have stayed with farming. . . . A living farmer is better than a dead soldier.

HUBBARD: It's you who'll die—with my blade in your heart! *(a beat)* You'll find that I fence quite well. It's rather a hobby of mine.

And they clash to a SOUND of ringing steel.

MONTAGE—THE DUEL
In a series of ACTION SHOTS, we stage a furious fencing duel between
two men equally skilled in the use of a blade. Theirs is a deadly game of
thrust-and-parry, but while Hubbard is coldly serious about it all, the Hawk
finds it satisfying to have, at last, found a fencer who calls on his full skills.
Now they have battled their way out along the wall of the garrison—and a
soldier rushes at the Hawk from behind. He spins to dispatch the fellow,
wheeling back to catch Hubbard's thrust. Anson is beginning to tire, and is
retreating along the ledge of the high wall.

CLOSE ON THE PAIR
as they play out the final death duel. The Hawk stumbles on a loose stone,
and Hubbard, seeing his chance, lunges in for the kill. But at the last half-
second the Hawk twists his body aside—and the fury of his charge sends
Hubbard over the edge. With a sharp, choked cry, he falls.

DOWN ANGLE—AT HUBBARD'S BODY
sprawled below, unmoving.

CUT TO:
EXTERIOR BACK GATE OF GARRISON—FULL SHOT—NIGHT
as we see Governor Portilla and Colonel Madero, carrying a large metal box
between them. They exit the gate with this box and move to the Governor's
four-horse coach.
Lieutenant Dominguiz is on the high seat, at the reins—and now they all
heave and tug the metal box into place on top of the coach, lashing it tight
with rope.
Madero and Portilla scramble inside, as Dominguiz whips the horses into
swift motion. PAN BACK TO exit gate where Chaka, having just arrived,
watching the coach RATTLE off at a fast clip. He ducks back inside the
garrison as we

CUT TO:
EXTERIOR GARRISON INNER COURT—JONATHAN AND SUSANNAH—NIGHT
They are still with the horses, where the Hawk left them—but there is
trouble. . . .
Jonathan is busy fighting off three soldiers who have discovered them. With
a pair of well-placed bullets from his revolving pistol, he downs two of the

Mexicans. As he pivots to face the third of the trio, the Mexican soldier FIRES, striking the boy in the right shoulder. Jonathan reels back, dropping the pepperbox pistol, as Susannah cries out at his wound.

The girl tries to grab up the weapon, but the grinning soldier kicks it away from her. He is about to finish them off when a strong arm is looped about his neck.

CLOSE ON KNIFE
in Jim Bowie's hand. He brings up his arm in a short, killing arc.

WIDER
as the soldier grunts; his eyes roll up and he falls loosely to the dirt.
The Hawk, who is with Bowie, checks Jonathan's shoulder.

NIGHTHAWK: Flesh wound. The ball came out clean.

BOWIE: *(nodding)* He'll be all right. I know how to tend those things. Had more than one myself!

SUSANNAH: Did you free the other men?

NIGHTHAWK: Jim did. They went out the side gate on some "borrowed" horses.

Chaka pads up, gestures quickly to his master.
The Hawk nods, turns to the others.

NIGHTHAWK: The money's gone. On the coach with Portilla and Madero. They took the King's Highway.

BOWIE: Then we'll go after them!

NIGHTHAWK: No, not you, Jim. I want you to look after Jonathan's shoulder —then get him and Susannah out of here. . . . . *(a beat)* We'll all meet later tonight at Stone Creek.

ON SUSANNAH
as she rushes forward—to kiss the Hawk. A kiss of gratitude *and* passion.

SUSANNAH: We all owe you our lives!

WIDER
as the Hawk and Chaka mount up and ride OFF with a wave.

CUT TO:

EXTERIOR KING'S HIGHWAY—FULL SHOT—NIGHT
El Camino Real, although grandly named, is of rough dirt, rather narrow, and flanked by trees and rocks.
We are into a SERIES OF INTERCUTS—showing the Hawk and Chaka at full gallop, gradually drawing closer to the Governor's coach.
At first Dominguiz is not aware that they are being pursued, but when he finally sights the two riders behind him, he lashes the coach horses forward with a curse.

INTERIOR COACH (MOVING)—PORTILLA AND MADERO—NIGHT
as Madero cants his head through the coach window, like a turtle from a shell.
He pops his head back inside, face ashen.

PORTILLA: *(demanding)* Well? . . . Who are they?

MADERO: *(checking his pistol)* It's *him*—with the Indian.

PORTILLA: *Madre de Dios!*—the Devil himself!

MADERO: If we can reach the garrison just beyond Sutter's Bridge, we're safe. *(a beat)* We should be able to keep ahead of them for that distance

PORTILLA: Ah . . . then we have a chance to clip the wings of this Hawk after all!

And he settles back into the seat, pulling a small wooden lever near the floor of the coach.

PORTILLA: This should give us ample protection.

EXTERIOR COACH (MOVING)
We SEE a surprising thing happen: iron shutters slide up to protect the windows on each side. Another shutter seals the door. The coach is now literally an armored vehicle!

CUT TO:

HAWK AND CHAKA (MOVING)

as the Indian hand-signals "this way"—and takes off into the rough beyond the road. Obviously, he knows the terrain, and a shortcut is in order. The Hawk gallops after him.

SERIES OF SHOTS

as they pound across country—through a narrow ravine, emerging shortly at an angle in the road which puts them almost directly behind the thundering coach.

Dominguiz half-turns in the high seat and FIRES his pistol at Chaka, who is now riding alongside—but the shot misses, and the Indian pulls a knife from his belt, whips it away in a killing throw . . . into the back of Dominguiz, who drops the reins and pitches headlong from the high coach seat.

WIDER

as we SEE that the vehicle is now "wild"—since the horses are without rein. They gallop mindlessly toward the upcoming bridge.

ON HAWK (MOVING)

as he rides along the opposite side of the coach, spotting the metal tax-box tied to the roof.

CLOSE ON BOX

held in place by a stout rope.

BACK TO HAWK

as he jerks a pistol up from the saddle and FIRES.

ON BOX

as his shot severs the rope. The heavy box tumbles from the roof onto the road.

The money is there, but the pursuit continues.

ANGLE AT BRIDGE—SHOOTING TOWARD COACH

as the runaway horses THUNDER onto Sutter's Bridge, which rises above a RUSH of swift river water.

INTERIOR COACH

Madero and the Governor are in a panic. The Colonel pushes the Governor aside to claw at the inner door handle. He gets it open and jumps from the vehicle just as it sways heavily into one of the bridge supports. The impact snaps the wooden "tree" between coach and horses, and the vehicle is now on its own (as the four animals gallop on ahead).

ANGLE AT RIVER—SHOOTING UP AT
the heavy coach as it SMASHES through the wooden rail of the bridge and plunges downward into the river.

ON HAWK AND CHAKA
shocked at the sight. They look downward at the scene.

THEIR POINT OF VIEW—THE COACH
Floating on its side, with Governor Portilla riding it like an upturned canoe. Coach and man are being carried downriver by the current.

WIDE
as the Hawk shouts to Portilla.

NIGHTHAWK: I'll see you on another day, Governor!

Portilla shakes his fist in the air (in the manner of Bligh of the *Bounty*).

PORTILLA: *(shouting)* When next we meet, I'll have you before a firing squad! . . .

His voices fades in the ROAR of the current as we

CUT TO:
MADERO—ON BLUFF OVER RIVER
who has survived his jump at the bridge. Now he pulls a pistol from his coat, aims it carefully at his enemies, and FIRES.

ON HAWK AND CHAKA
The Indian is hit in the thigh and falls from his mustang. The Hawk wheels around on Diablo and charges straight at Madero.

FULL SCENE
as the Hawk leaps from the saddle to engage the Colonel in a fierce hand-to-hand, unaware of the man's strength and skill as a wrestler.

In their battle (SERIES OF SHOTS) the Hawk locks both hands at Madero's throat, his fingers closing, but the Colonel easily breaks the hold with an abrupt body twist. He deftly applies a crushing right-arm elbow lock on the Hawk, who gasps with pain, managing to drive his left fist into Madero's face, breaking the hold.

They circle one another, with Madero looking confident, a thin smile curving his lips. It is clear that the Hawk cannot match Madero's superior wrestling skills. Indeed, with an agile surge of power, the Mexican tosses the Hawk into a bed of rocks, some feet below the bluff. In falling, the Hawk is stunned.

CLOSER ANGLE—FAVORING MADERO
as slowly, with gusto, he reloads his pistol and aims it down at the sprawled figure.

MADERO: You have caused me much trouble. Now all that is about to end—with your life!

But Chaka grabs Madero from behind before he can fire the pistol, knocking it from his grasp. Despite his wound, he grapples with the powerful Mexican. The battle is totally one-sided. Weak from loss of blood, his left leg numb from Madero's bullet, Chaka has no chance against the Colonel.

ANOTHER ANGLE
as they grapple—and Madero puts the Indian into a stranglehold. Chaka's eyes bug as he struggles for breath. He is being choked to death. Suddenly the Hawk's voice from below:

NIGHTHAWK: *(offstage) Madero!*

The Colonel swings his head toward the rocks.

ON HAWK
Having pulled his own gun from his sash, he holds it on the Colonel.

NIGHTHAWK: Let him go!

MADERO: *(enraged) After* I've snapped his neck!

CLOSE ON CHAKA
eyes bugged, tongue protruding from his mouth.

WIDE
as the Hawk FIRES. Madero's hands fly up loosely, allowing Chaka to spill into the dirt, gasping for air. Madero swivels toward the Hawk, eyes slitted.

MADERO: Damn you!

And he topples dead to the grass.

DISSOLVE TO:
EXTERIOR WOODED AREA—FULL SHOT—DAY
Jaimie is with Susannah as they say good-bye to Jonathan (his shoulder bandaged) and to Bowie.

JAIMIE: Please don't thank me for the money. Father wants you both to have it as much as I do. *(a beat)* At least it's enough to give you a start in New Orleans.

JONATHAN: We've had our differences . . . but this loan—and your finding the Nighthawk the way you did—more than squares things. *(a beat)* I hope we're friends now, Jaimie.

JAIMIE: We are.

SUSANNAH: You never *did* tell us how you found him. . . . No one else seems to be able to. *(a beat)* And if you *hadn't* found him . . .

JONATHAN: *(grinning)* I wouldn't *be* here if he hadn't.

BOWIE: *(with a twinkle)* Yeah, Jaimie . . . how *did* you ever manage to locate the Hawk?

The look in Bowie's eyes tells Jaimie that Jim is a bit sharper than the others.

JAIMIE: I'd heard that he had been seen near Stone Creek—so I went to that area and was fortunate enough to find him.

BOWIE: *(nodding; with a faint smile)* Yep . . . pure luck, I guess.

JAIMIE: *(as he shakes Jim's hand)* Godspeed in New Orleans, Mr. Bowie.

BOWIE: Thanks. I'll be drifting back this way one of these days soon. *(a beat; he smiles)* Maybe I'll even run into the Hawk again.

JAIMIE: *(returning the smile)* Maybe.

Susannah kisses Bowie on the cheek, then hugs her brother in a tight embrace.

SUSANNAH: *(eyes glistening)* I'll miss you dreadfully, Jonathan!

JONATHAN: I know, sis—but if I stay here, Portilla will hunt me down. *(a beat; as he mounts up)* Are you sure it's safe for you to stay on at the ranch?

SUSANNAH: *(clinging to his hand; looking up at him)* I was never a prisoner . . . with you gone, the Governor has no reason to arrest me.

JAIMIE: Take care of yourselves, both of you.

He and the girl wave the two off, as Bowie and Jonathan ride out of sight among the trees.

ON JAIMIE AND SUSANNAH
They walk together back to their horses, mount and start out of the woods, CAMERA FOLLOWING.

SUSANNAH: *(in a troubled voice)* Is it wrong to love a bandit?

JAIMIE: *(pretending confusion)* What do you mean?

SUSANNAH: He's the bravest man I know! He saved Jonathan . . . freed the men in prison . . . gave back the tax money. . . . *(a beat)* Is it wrong to love the Nighthawk?

JAIMIE: Not *wrong*, perhaps . . . but I'd say foolish. A man given to swords and pistol play and wild rides through the night . . . A hawk must fly, Susannah. He'll never settle in one place long enough for *any* woman to love him.

SUSANNAH: But I *do!* Whether he wants my love or not . . . whether anyone approves . . . or understands . . . *(fiercely)* I love him!

JAIMIE: I'm sure he'd be happy to hear it!

SUSANNAH: *(embarrassed at the thought)* He'd laugh . . . think me a witless, foolish girl!

JAIMIE: He'd be flattered.

SUSANNAH: Oh, well . . . *(shrugging)* It doesn't make any difference *how* I feel about him. *(a beat)* He'll never know.

JAIMIE: No . . . I suppose he never will.

And he looks at her, an amused glint in his eyes. They continue through the lush, sun-spangled woods, as CAMERA PULLS BACK into FREEZE FRAME.

FADE OUT.

The Bandit

BY LOREN D. ESTLEMAN

Loren Estleman writes Westerns and crime novels, most of the latter about a private eye named Amos Walker, a sort of eighties' Marlowe. The crime novels are good, but I think Loren is at his best as a Western writer. So did the 1981 Spur committee when they awarded him with a Spur for Aces and Eights, *his version of the life of Wild Bill Hickok.*

Of his work he says, "My goal in writing Westerns has always been to try and present the West that really was—not the mythical, romanticized version we usually get."

He does just that. But his writing here is so lyrical, his characters so realistic and simultaneously bigger than life, he also manages to create myth.

The following story is of the traditional school, but hackneyed it isn't. In Estleman's hands it's magic.

They cut him loose a day early.

It worried him a little, and when the night captain on his block brought him a suit of clothes and a cardboard suitcase containing a toothbrush and a change of shirts, he considered bringing it up, but in that moment he suddenly couldn't stand it there another hour. So he put on the suit and accompanied the guard to the administration building, where the assistant warden made a speech, grasped his hand, and presented him with a check for $1,508. At the gate he shook hands with the guard, although the man was new to his section and he didn't know him, then stepped out into the gray autumn late afternoon. Not counting incarceration time before and during his trial, he had been behind bars twenty-eight years, eleven months, and twenty-nine days.

While he was standing there, blinking rapidly in diffused sunlight that was surely brighter than that on the other side of the wall, a leather-bonneted assembly of steel and inflated rubber came ticking past on the street with a goggled and dustered operator at the controls. He watched it go by towing a plume of dust and blue smoke and said, "Oldsmobile."

He had always been first in line when magazines donated by the DAR came into the library, and while his fellow inmates were busy snatching up the new catalogs and finding the pages containing pictures of women in corsets and camisoles torn out, he was paging through the proliferating motoring journals, admiring the photographs and studying the technical illustrations of motors and transmissions. Gadgets had enchanted him since he saw his first steam engine aboard a Missouri River launch at age ten, and he had a fair idea of how automobiles worked. However, aside from one heart-thudding glimpse of the warden's new Locomobile parked inside the gates before the prison board decided its presence stirred unhealthy ambitions among the general population, this was his first exposure to the belching, clattering reality. He felt like a wolf whelp looking on the harsh glitter of the big world outside its parents' den for the first time.

After the machine had gone, he put down the suitcase to collect his bearings. In the gone days he had enjoyed an instinct for directions, but it had been replaced by other, more immediate survival mechanisms inside. Also, an overgrown village that had stood only two stories high on dirt streets as wide as pastures when he first came to it had broken out in brick towers and macadam and climbed the hills across the river, where an electrified trolley raced through a former cornfield clanging its bell like a mad mother cow. He wasn't sure if the train station would be where he left it in 1878.

He considered banging on the gate and asking the guard, but the thought of turning around now made him pick up his suitcase and start across the street at double-quick step, the mess-hall march. "The wrong way beats no way," Micah used to put it.

It was only a fifteen-minute walk, but for an old man who had stopped pacing his cell in 1881 and stretched his legs for only five of the twenty minutes allotted daily in the exercise yard, it was a hike. He had never liked walking anyway, had reached his majority breaking mixed-blood stallions that had run wild from December to March on the old Box W, and had done some of his best thinking and fighting with a horse under him. So when at last he reached the station, dodging more motorcars—the novelty of that wore off the first time—and trying not to look to passersby like a convict in his tight suit swinging a dollar suitcase, he was sweating and blowing like a wind-broke mare.

The station had a water closet—a closet indeed, with a gravity toilet and a mirror in need of resilvering over a white enamel basin, but a distinct improvement over the stinking bucket he had had to carry down three tiers of cells and dump into the cistern every morning for twenty-nine years. He placed the suitcase on the toilet seat, hung up his hat and soaked coat, unhooked his spectacles, turned back his cuffs, ran cold water into the basin, and splashed his face. Mopping himself dry on a comparatively clean section of roller towel, he looked at an old man's unfamiliar reflection, then put on his glasses to study it closer. But for the mirror in the warden's office it was the first one he'd seen since his trial; mirrors were made of glass, and glass was good for cutting wrists and throats. What hair remained on his scalp had gone dirty-gray. The flesh of his face was sagging, pulling away from the bone, and so pale he took a moment locating the bullet-crease on his forehead from Liberty. His beard was yellowed white, like stove grime. (All the men inside wore beards. It was easier than trying to shave without mirrors.) It was his grandfather's face.

Emerging from the water closet, he read the train schedule on the blackboard next to the ticket booth and checked it against his coin-battered old turnip watch, wound and set for the first time in half his lifetime. A train to Huntsford was pulling out in forty minutes.

He was alone at his end of the station with the ticket agent and a lanky young man in a baggy checked suit slouched on one of the varnished benches with his long legs canted out in front of him and his hands in his pockets. Conscious that the young man was watching him, but accustomed to being watched, he walked up to the booth and set down the suitcase. "Train to Huntsford on schedule?"

"Was last wire." Perched on a stool behind the window, the agent looked at him over the top of his *Overland Monthly* without seeing him. He had bright predatory eyes in a narrow face that had foiled an attempt to square it off with thick burnsides.

"How much to Huntsford?"

"Four dollars."

He unfolded the check for $1,508 and smoothed it out on the ledge under the glass.

"I can't cash that," said the agent. "You'll have to go to the bank."

"Where's the bank?"

"Well, there's one on Treelawn and another on Cross. But they're closed till Monday."

"I ain't got cash on me."

"Well, the railroad don't offer credit."

While the agent resumed reading, he unclipped the big watch from its steel chain and placed it on top of the check. "How much you allow me on that?"

The agent glanced at it, then returned to his magazine. "This is a railroad station, not a jeweler's. I got a watch."

He popped open the lid and pointed out the engraving. "See that J.B.H.? That stands for James Butler Hickok. Wild Bill himself gave it to me when he was sheriff in Hays."

"Mister, I got a scar on my behind I can say I got from Calamity Jane, but I'd still need four dollars to ride to Huntsford. Not that I'd want to."

"Problem, Ike?"

The drawled question startled old eardrums thickened to approaching footsteps. The young man in the checked suit was at his side, a head taller and smelling faintly of lilac water.

"Just another convict looking to wrestle himself a free ride off the C. H. & H.," the agent said. "Nothing I don't handle twice a month."

"What's the fare?"

The agent told him. The man in the checked suit produced a bent brown wallet off his right hip and counted four bills onto the window ledge.

"Hold up there. I never took a thing free off nobody that wasn't my idea to start."

"Well, give me the watch."

"This watch is worth sixty dollars."

"You were willing to trade it for a railroad ticket."

"I was not. I asked him what he'd give me on it."

"Sixty dollars for a gunmetal watch that looks like it's been through a thresher?"

"It keeps good time. You see that J.B.H.?"

"Wild Bill. I heard." The man in the checked suit counted the bills remaining in his wallet. "I've got just ten on me."

He closed the watch and held it out. "I'll give you my sister's address in Huntsford. You send me the rest there."

"You're trusting me? How long did you serve?"

"He's got a check drawn on the state bank for fifteen hundred," said the agent, separating a ticket from the perforated sheet.

The man in the checked suit pursed his lips. "Mister, you must've gone in there with some valuables. Last I knew, prison wages still came to a dollar a week."

"They ain't changed since I went in."

Both the ticket agent and the man in the checked suit were staring at him now. "Mister, you keep your watch. You've earned that break."

"It ain't broke, just dented some. Anyway, I said before I don't take charity."

"Let's let the four dollars ride for now. Your train's not due for a half hour. If I'm not satisfied with our talk at the end of that time, you give me it to hold and I'll send it on later, as a deposit against the four dollars."

"Folks paying for talking now?"

"They do when they've met someone who's been in prison since Hayes was President and all they've had to talk to today is a retiring conductor and a miner's daughter on her way to a finishing school in Chicago." The man in the checked suit offered his hand. "Arthur Brundage. I write for the *New Democrat*. It's a newspaper, since your time."

"I saw it inside." He grasped the hand tentatively, plainly surprising its owner with his grip. "I got to tell you, son, I ain't much for talking to the papers. Less people know your name, the less hold they got on you, Micah always said."

"Micah?"

He hesitated. "Hell, he's been dead better than twenty-five years, I don't reckon I can hurt him. Micah Hale. Maybe the name don't mean nothing now."

"These old cons, they'll tell you they knew John Wilkes Booth and Henry the Eighth if you don't shut them up." The ticket agent skidded the ticket across the ledge.

But Brundage was peering into his face now, a man trying to make out the details in a portrait fogged and darkened with years.

"You're Jubal Steadman."

"I was when I went in. I been called Dad so long I don't rightly answer to nothing else."

"Jubal Steadman." It was an incantation. "If I didn't fall in sheep dip and come up dripping double eagles. Let's go find a bench." Brundage seized the suitcase before its owner could get his hands on it and put a palm on his back, steering him toward the seat he himself had just vacated.

"The Hale-Steadman Gang," he said, when they were seated. "Floyd and Micah Hale and the Steadman brothers and Kid Stone. When I was ten, my mother found a copy of the *New York Detective Monthly* under my bed. It had Floyd Hale on the cover, blazing away from horseback with a six-shooter in each hand at a posse chasing him. I had to stay indoors for a week and memorize a different Bible verse every day."

Jubal smiled. His teeth were only a year old and he was just a few months past grinning like an ape all the time. "Them dime writers made out like Floyd ran the match, but that was just because the Pinkertons found out his name first and told the papers. We all called him Doc on account of he was always full of no-good clabber and he claimed to study eye doctoring back

East for a year, when everyone knew he was in the Detroit House of Corrections for stealing a mail sack off a railroad hook. He told me I'd never need glasses." He took his off to polish them with a coarse handkerchief.

Brundage had a long notepad open on his knee. He stopped writing. "I guess I should have accepted that watch when you offered it."

"It ain't worth no sixty dollars. I got it off a fireman on the *Katy Flyer* when we hit it outside Choctaw in '73."

"You mean that was a story about Wild Bill?"

"Never met him. I had them initials put in it and made up the rest. It pulled me through some skinny times. Folks appreciated a good lie then, not like now."

"Readers of the *New Democrat* are interested in the truth."

He put his spectacles back on and peered at the journalist over the rims. But Brundage was writing again and missed it.

"Anyway, if there was someone we all looked to when things went sore, it was Doc's brother Micah. I reckon he was the smartest man I ever knew or ever will. That's why they took him alive and Doc let himself get shot in the back of the head by Kid Stone."

"I always wondered if he really did that just for the reward."

"I reckon. He was always spending his cut on yellow silk vests and gold hatbands. I was in prison two years when it happened so I can't say was that it. That blood money busted up all the good bunches. The Pinks spent years trying to undercut us with the hill folk, but it was the rewards done it in the end."

"The Kid died of pneumonia three or four years ago in New Jersey. He put together his own moving picture outfit after they let him go. He was playing Doc Holliday when he took sick."

"Josh always said Virge was a born actor. Virgil, that was the Kid's right name."

"I forget if Joshua was your older or your younger brother."

"Older. Billy Tom Mulligan stabbed him with a busted toothbrush first year we was inside. They hung him for it. Josh played the Jew's harp. He was playing it when they jumped us after Liberty."

"What really happened in Liberty?"

Jubal pulled a face. "Doc's idea. We was to hit the ten-twelve from Kansas City when it stopped to water and take on passengers, and the bank in town at the same time. We recruited a half dozen more men for the job: Creek Eddie, Charley MacDonald, Bart and Barney Dee, and two fellows named Bob and Bill, I never got their last names and couldn't tell which was which. Me and Josh and my kid brother Judah went with Micah and

Charley MacDonald on the bank run and the rest took the train. Bart and Barney was to ride it in from Kansas City and sit on the conductor and porters while Doc and them threw down on the engineer and fireman and blew open the express car with powder. Doc said they wouldn't be expecting us to try it in town. He was dead-right there. No one thought we was that stupid."

"What made Micah go along with it?"

"Fambly bliss. Doc was threatening to take Kid Stone and start his own bunch because no one ever listened to them good plans he was coming up with all the time, like kidnapping the Governor of Missouri and holding him for ransom. Creek Eddie learned his trade in the Nations, so when we heard he was available, Micah figured he'd be a good influence on Doc. Meantime Creek Eddie thought the train thing was a harebrained plan but figured if Micah was saying yes to it, it must be all right." He showed his store teeth. "You see, I had twenty-nine years to work this all out, and if I knew it then—well, I wouldn't of had the twenty-nine years to work it all out.

"Micah and Charley and Josh and Judah and me, we slid through that bank like a grease fire and come out with seven thousand in greenbacks and another four or five thousand in securities. *And* the bank president and his tellers and two customers hollering for help on the wrong side of the vault door on a five-minute time lock. We never made a better or a quieter job. That was when we heard the shooting down at the station."

"A railroad employee fired the first shot, if I remember my reading."

"It don't matter who fired it. Bart and Barney Dee missed the train in Kansas City, and the conductor and a porter or two was armed and free when Doc and the rest walked in thinking the opposite. Creek Eddie got it in the back of the neck and hit the ground dead. Then everybody opened up, and by the time we showed with the horses, the smoke was all mixed up with steam from the boiler. Well, you could see your hand in front of your face, but not to shoot at. That didn't stop us, though.

"Reason was, right about then that time lock let loose of them folks we left in the bank, and when they hit the street yammering like bitch dogs, that whole town turned vigilante in a hot St. Louis minute. They opened up the gun shop and filled their pockets with cartridges and it was like Independence Day. I think as many of them fell in their own crossfire as what we shot.

"Even so, only six men was killed in that spree. If you was there trying to hold down your mount with one hand and twisting back and forth like a steam governor to fire on both sides of its neck and dodging all that lead clanging off the engine, you'd swear it was a hundred. I seen Charley take a spill and get dragged by his paint for twenty feet before he cleared his boot of the stirrup, and Judah got his jaw took off by a bullet, though he lived another eight or nine hours. Engineer was killed, and one rubbernecker standing around waiting to board the train, and two of them damn-fool townies playing Kit Carson on the street. I don't know how many of them was wounded; likely not as many as are still walking around showing off their old gall-bladder scars as bullet-creases. I still got a ball in my back that tells me when it's fixing to rain, but that didn't give me as much trouble at the time as this here cut that kept dumping blood into my eyes." He pointed out the white mark where his hairline used to be. "Micah took one through the meat on his upper arm, and my brother Josh got it in the hip and lost a finger, and they shot the Kid and took him prisoner and arrested Charley, who broke his ankle getting loose of that stirrup. Doc was the only one of us that come away clean.

"Judah, his jaw was just hanging on by a piece of gristle. I tied it up with his bandanna, and Josh and me got him over one of the horses and we got mounted and took off one way while Doc and Micah and that Bill and Bob went the other. We met up at this empty farmhouse six miles north of town that we lit on before the job in case we got separated, all but that Bill and Bob. Them two just kept riding. We buried Judah that night."

"The posse caught up with you at the farmhouse?" asked Brundage, after a judicious pause.

"No, they surprised Josh and me in camp two nights later. We'd split with the Hales before then. Micah wasn't as bad wounded as Josh and we was slowing them down, Doc said. Josh could play that Jew's harp of his, though. Posse come on afoot, using the sound of it for a mark. They threw down on us. We gave in without a shot."

"That was the end of the Hale-Steadman Gang?"

A hoarse stridency shivered the air. In its echo, Jubal consulted his watch. "Trains still run on time. Nice to know some things stay the same. Yeah, the Pinks picked up Micah posing as a cattle-buyer in Denver a few months later. I heard he died of scarlatina inside. Charley MacDonald got himself shot to pieces escaping with Kid Stone and some others, but the Kid got clear and him and Doc put together a bunch and robbed a train or two and some banks until the Kid shot him. I reckon I'm what's left."

"I guess you can tell readers of the *New Democrat* there's no profit in crime."

"Well, there's profit and profit." He stood up, working the stiffness out of his joints, and lifted the suitcase.

Brundage hesitated in the midst of closing his notebook. "Twenty-nine years of your life a fair trade for a few months of excitement?"

"I don't reckon there's much in life you'd trade half of it to have. But in them days a man either broke his back and his heart plowing rocks under in some field or shook his brains loose putting some red-eyed horse to leather or rotted behind some counter in some town. I don't reckon I'm any older now than I would of been if I done any of them things to live. And I wouldn't have no youngster like you hanging on my every word neither. Them things become important when you get up around my age."

"I won't get that past my editor. He'll want a moral lesson."

"Put one in, then. It don't . . ." His voice trailed off.

The journalist looked up. The train was sliding to a stop inside the vaulted station, black and oily and leaking steam out of a hundred joints. But the old man was looking at the pair of men coming in the station entrance. One, sandy-haired and approaching middle age in a suit too heavy for Indian summer, his cherry face glistening, was the assistant warden at the prison. His companion was a city police officer in uniform. At sight of Jubal, relief blossomed over the assistant warden's features.

"Steadman, I was afraid you'd left."

Jubal said, "I knew it."

As the officer stepped to the old man's side, the assistant warden said, "I'm very sorry. There's been a clerical error. You'll have to come back with us."

"I was starting to think you was going to let me have that extra day after all."

"Day?" The assistant warden was mopping his face with a lawn handkerchief. "I was getting set to close your file. I don't know how I overlooked that other charge."

Jubal felt a clammy fist clench inside his chest. "Other charge?"

"For the train robbery. In Liberty. The twenty-nine years was for robbing the bank and for your part in the killings afterward. You were convicted also of accessory in the raid on the train. You have seventeen years to serve on that conviction, Steadman. I'm sorry."

He took the suitcase while the officer manacled one of the old man's wrists. Brundage left the bench.

"Jubal—"

He shook his head. "My sister's coming in on the morning train from Huntsford tomorrow. Meet it, will you? Tell her."

"This isn't the end of it. My paper has a circulation of thirty thousand. When our readers learn of this injustice—"

"They'll howl and stomp and write letters to their congressmen, just like in '78."

The journalist turned to the man in uniform. "He's sixty years old. Do you have to chain him like a maniac?"

"Regulations." He clamped the other manacle around his own wrist.

Jubal held out his free hand. "I got to go home now. Thanks for keeping an old man company for an hour."

After a moment Brundage took it. Then the officer touched the old man's arm and he blinked behind his spectacles and turned and left the station with the officer on one side and the assistant warden on the other. The door swung shut behind them.

As the train pulled out without Jubal, Brundage timed it absently against the dented watch in his hand.